GIBSONBURG

Bob Mahaffey

First Xcelerate Media Productions, LLC Edition, June 2012

Copyright© 2012

Although this story is inspired and based on a high school baseball team that went to the State Championship game in 2005, this is a work of fiction. Names, characters, places, and incidents either are a product of the author's imagination or are used fictitiously. Any resemblance to actual persons, living or dead, events, or locales is entirely coincidental.

ISBN: 978-0-9855363-0-5

Cover design by Brian McManamon

Interior design by Kyle Price

Photography used in book design by Casey Smith

Printed in the United States of America

The author would like to express his appreciation to the 2005 Gibsonburg Golden Bears Boy's High School Baseball Team. The Bears ended the regular season with a record of 6 wins and 17 losses, before capping the season with an improbable run that took them to the Ohio State Championship game. I don't think we will ever see another team—in any sport, in any state—ever win a State Championship with a 35 percent win ratio during the regular season. Head Coach, Kyle Rase, his assistants, and the entire team should be very proud of this accomplishment as it will most likely never be repeated.

From the Author

It was 2010. I was having Thanksgiving dinner at my sister's house in Wayne, Ohio. After the Thursday afternoon feast we were sitting around watching the Detroit Lions get their usual holiday beating. I was making small talk with my relatives when I struck up a conversation with Curt Billow. Curt was married to my sister's daughter. Honestly, I didn't really know him that well.

Curt was telling me he was from Gibsonburg, Ohio. I didn't know the details, but I was aware that their baseball team won the State Championship a few years back. At the time, I wasn't all that interested in what Curt had to say. But to "be polite," I asked him about the 2005 baseball team.

My casual conversation with Curt started out with me casually listening while I watched the football game on television. The conversation ended with me on the edge of my seat.

Curt explained how the team had an uninspiring regular-season record of 6 wins and 17 losses. That was only part of the story. He then went on to tell me that they lost 13 games in a row and were mercy ruled 7 times! The icing on the cake was that they lost the last game of their season by a score of 17-0. Curt explained that everyone on the team was about 5 feet, 8 inches tall, weighed 140 pounds, and not one of them went on to play college baseball.

Under first year Coach, Kyle Rase, the 2005 Gibsonburg Boy's Baseball Team went on to win 8 games in a row to play in the State Championship. On their journey, they beat four pitchers with Division I scholarships. And they seemed to win games by odd breaks that nobody would ever believe. When he explained them, I actually questioned their validity. I just couldn't believe it!

When the conversation was finished, I sat in the La-Z-Boy recliner mesmerized. I said to myself, "Man, that would make a great book or movie."

I remember thinking that everyone loves an underdog. And who doesn't love a story that is real, as opposed to a bunch of bull? The story of the 2005 Gibsonburg Boy's Baseball Team seemed to have it all. I couldn't wait to get started.

The next week, I contacted the administration at Gibsonburg and set up a meeting to discuss the possibility of writing a book or making a movie about the 2005 team. In my conversations, one of the administrators asked me a very legitimate question. He said, "Bob, if you have never produced a movie before, how are you going to make a film about Gibsonburg?" With a stoic look on my face I asked the administrator, "How did you win a State Championship with a 6 and 17 regular season record?"

Everyone in the room chuckled. However, when I left that meeting, I actually asked myself, "How AM I going to do it?"

So, I had numerous meetings with Kyle Rase, the coach of the 2005 team. (As of the writing of the book, Kyle is still the current Head Baseball Coach at Gibsonburg.) We spent hours together and went over every pitch, of every game, in their eight game run. Kyle is a great person and we established a wonderful friendship. I can honestly say that the events of 2005 couldn't have happened to a better guy.

I also enjoyed talking to the members of the 2005 team to collect their insights on the events of that season. What a great group of young men!

Once I had the facts, I wrote this book. I then adapted the book into a screenplay, and produced a film based on the 2005 team. The book was completed in the spring of 2011. The movie was shot that summer, and it was then edited and completed on March 1, 2012.

We ignorantly submitted the film to one of the best film festivals in the country, Dances with Films. They get 1,500 submissions per year, and Gibsonburg was selected as one of the 21 feature films shown at the festival. This World Premiere took place on June 5, 2012, at 2:45 pm.

If you like stories about underdogs who blindly follow their dreams no matter how far-fetched they may be, then I think you will like *GIBSONBURG*.

Enjoy!

GIBSONBURG

1

A Country Ride

The '68 forest green Pontiac Firebird screamed down the country road in the cool morning air, the throaty engine begging for more with each passing second.

Andy Gruner quickly glanced at the speedometer as it approached 50 miles per hour. He then deftly shifted his attention back to the road. Beside him, Alex Black sat in the passenger seat, hitting the dashboard with both fists as he hollered with excitement. In the back seat, Wes Milleson hit Andy on the shoulder, pleading for more speed with reckless abandon. Wyatt Kiser, the quiet one in the group, sat with both hands gripping the passenger seat, his eyes focused intently on the road ahead.

Wes calmed down and asked, "Hey, did anyone do the extra credit project for the English Lit Final? We were supposed to read that *I am Legend* book."

Andy smirked. "Seriously?"

"Not me," Wyatt said.

"Well, I read it," Alex said, slightly embarrassed. "It was actually pretty good! I heard they are making it into a big Hollywood movie. Will Smith is going to be in it, right?"

"You know what sucks about that book?" Wes looked intently at everyone in the car.

"The dude was doing awesome. He was safe, had a great dog, nobody was there to bug him, and as soon as a woman shows up, he dies within 24 hours."

"Typical thing a girl would do," Wyatt blurted.

"And you know what the worst part is?" Wes continued. "The bitch ate his bacon. I mean, who does that?"

Andy frowned and pressed the gas pedal, forcing the Firebird to gain speed. From the corner of his eye he spotted a soaring hawk floating lazily on the breeze. From the hawk's vantage point, the Firebird looked like a shiny green jewel gliding through a sea of freshly planted corn, bean, and wheat fields lined along the narrow country road.

With a puzzled and curious look, Andy asked his friends, "What are you talking about?"

"In the book, everyone in the world is either dead or a vampire, or something" Wes explained. "The scientist is somehow immune, and he is working on an antidote. He is saving this pound of bacon for a special occasion, like when he saves the world or whatever. The next thing you know, this mop squeezer shows up while he is not at home, fries it up, and eats the bacon he was saving."

"Totally inexcusable," Wyatt said.

"That bitch," Wes muttered.

Andy glanced at Alex and was not surprised to find him already smirking. Riling up the guys was Alex's best gift. A very amusing gift, at that.

Wyatt leaned forward. "I can see her showing up right?" he said. "Maybe even just hanging out and being a general pain in the ass. Hell, it is almost excusable that she gets him killed. But man, eating his bacon? That is just wrong."

Wes shook his head. "Really! Eating his bacon? That just crosses a line that should never be crossed."

Andy glanced in the rear view mirror and finished the conversation. "You guys are idiots!"

Wes and Wyatt both chuckled, and then exchanged glances with one another. Wes crossed both arms nonchalantly behind his head, totally content and pleased with his personal analysis of the book.

Andy smiled at Wes before turning his eyes back on the road. The Firebird approached a baseball field that blended into the country landscape perfectly with its vibrant green grass and contrasting cookie dough colored infield. Acres of lush green open viewing area surrounded the field, nestling it perfectly within the beautiful Ohio farm fields. Their crops, planted only a few weeks ago, had begun peeking out of the soil.

As the Firebird barreled down the country road past the baseball field the boys were oblivious to the old man walking in the outfield, between left field and the shortstop position. He was carrying a two-gallon jug of grass-friendly, but weed-deadly spray. The old man carefully examined the left field grass and, with great precision, applied the poison on the few remaining weeds. This was the masterpiece that he had meticulously cared for all spring.

The silence of the morning air was broken by the thunder of the Firebird screaming down the country road that ran parallel to the third baseline of the baseball field. The noise approached quickly and snatched the groundskeeper's attention. With his back to the passing Firebird, he slowly turned his head to his left to see the car come into and out of sight in a matter of seconds. As the sound of the engine faded away, he casually turned his attention back to the mission of finding the few weeds still hiding in the outfield grass. Although he didn't smile, he contained a full sense of pride in the lack of weeds in the outfield grass. The old man was fully aware that his efforts were responsible for the sheer beauty of the well-cared-for field, and he was steadfastly unfazed by the fact that very few people would share his appreciation.

As the Firebird continued to rumble down the road, Wes leaned over the driver's seat. He pointed right at Andy, and excitedly yelled, "Come on, Andy! Let's see what she'll do!"

Alex beat on the dashboard and screamed out, "Henry says she'll do 140! Let's blow some carbon out and get 'er up to at least 120!"

Andy stepped on the gas, and the car began to accelerate. The speedometer steadily climbed to 70, then 80, then 90 miles per hour.

Wes was now laughing hard. He continued his encouragement by yelling, "Come on, man! Keep goin'!"

Andy looked at Wyatt and Wes through the rear view mirror and then shot Alex a look. The speedometer needle slowly climbed from 90 to 110. His palms were beginning to sweat.

As the needle hit 110 miles per hour, Wes let loose a piercing "Yeeeeeehaw!"

Andy's ears were ringing from Wes's exuberance. The back of Andy's shirt was saturated with his body sweat between his shoulder blades. Another quick glance in the mirror and he suddenly saw Wyatt's taut jawline. One mistake and they'd all surely be killed.

Wyatt's voice was terse, emphatic, and suddenly louder, far louder than the screaming engine. "Maybe take it a little easy there, Hoss. This rattly old car may fall apart if you push 'er over the limit."

Wes shouted. "You got it man! Get 'er up to 120!"

"Oh shit . . ." Alex pointed straight ahead to confirm what Andy already saw in his focused view of the road, "You got a stop sign up ahead."

The Firebird was now traveling at 175 feet per second, with 1,750 feet separating the car from the stop sign. The Firebird would be at the stop sign in 10 seconds. As the adrenaline rushed through the boys' bodies, they didn't realize that there was not a stop sign on the perpendicular road they were approaching. An old farmhouse obstructed their view to the right, so nobody in the Firebird could see that two vehicles were quickly approaching the intersection from the right. The two vehicles, a red Pontiac Grand Am, followed closely behind by a beige GMC Yukon, were on pace to hit the intersection in ten seconds as well.

Andy swallowed hard. The Firebird was only ten seconds away from the stop sign.

Wyatt switched to parent mode. "Better slow this thing down, buddy."

Oblivious, Wes sat back and said, "What a rush, though, Andy-man!"

As Andy pushed down on the brake, the pedal easily went all the way to the floor without slowing the car down at all.

Andy screamed. "No brakes!"

Wes's eyes widened. "What?"

"Oh fuck!" Alex yelled, bracing himself.

In a haze, Andy saw Wyatt in the rearview mirror staring straight ahead at the intersection. Wyatt was gripping the seat in front of him tighter and bracing for impact. Andy quickly glanced down at the speedometer to see the needle at 100 miles per hour. Four seconds until they crossed the intersection. He frantically pumped the brake pedal, as he looked straight ahead and tightened his grip on the steering wheel. "Hang on boys!"

The seconds felt like hours. Andy silently wondered if this was what free falling felt like . . .

As the Firebird passed the farmhouse to the right, only 20 feet from the intersection, Andy saw a glimpse of the approaching vehicles. Where did they come from? The horrifying intake of breath, gasping lungs, and the sound of whimpering around him told him in a split second that everyone else in the Firebird could see the other vehicles barreling towards them too.

Andy watched as the red Grand Am hit the intersection first. The front left bumper of the Firebird shot past the back left bumper of the red Grand Am, missing it by inches.

At that exact moment, Andy jerked his head to the right. He was immediately horrified to find the GMC Yukon upon him and about to crash into the side of the Firebird.

There was no escape.

Andy fixated on the fast-approaching GMC logo on the Yukon's grill. Suddenly, everything slowed down. For what seemed like an eternity, his life flashed before his eyes. A soothing calm surprisingly took over his body. The visions seemed to last forever, and were filled with a warm glow. There was no sound. Just a peaceful quiet, as the past 18 years of his life played out in slow motion. Time stood still as the fear fell away and left him with a sense that he was safe, secure, and free.

2

Wes Milleson - The Speedster
Wednesday, July 14, 2004

It was a blistering hot July day during the summer of 2004 in Bowling Green, Ohio. The two coaches-both with their ultra-bright green and white uniforms, their clipboards in hand, whistles around their necks, and stopwatches in their pockets—looked like they could have been major league baseball coaches. Coach Wellman was the head coach, and Coach Reynolds was the assistant. Both coaches were surprisingly similar in stature. They each weighed about 220 pounds, stood a solid 6 feet tall, and looked like former athletes. The main difference was that Coach Wellman had white blond hair that he wore in a flattop. Coach Reynolds had dark brown hair that was thinning a little at the top.

The coaches examined their clipboards like doctors carefully and thoroughly reviewing medical charts. On this day they were serious, all business—totally focused and ready to begin their evaluation. There was only one coveted slot remaining on the 2004 American Legion National Baseball Team.

The starting centerfielder on the USA team, Tommy Jackson, recently broke his collarbone making a diving play. Tommy's catch was the final out in the game. The win qualified the USA team for the World Baseball Championships that would take place in August.

American Legion rules allowed the team to call up players for injuries of this type. They had to find one player that could at least somewhat match Tommy Jackson's speed.

Their quest brought them to Wood County, Ohio, home of Bowling Green State University and its 15,000 students. The baseball field was at midsummer green. This particular field was considered one of the best in the state, if not the entire Midwest. Every minute detail was meticulously handled and anyone who walked the field would be hard pressed to even find a single blade of grass out of place. The groundskeepers watered and fertilized with great precision throughout the year, which over time, created one of the most perfect ball fields in the country.

When the glaciers retreated 20,000 years ago, they left a swamp in Wood County which was known as the *Great Black Swamp*. It was home to a wide variety of dark green vegetation. A few thousand years after the Ice Age, the swamp and vegetation chemically bonded when the rich plants decomposed, making the soil rich and perfect for planting crops. As such, Wood County was known as a farming community that would consistently produce the best yields per acre in the country. And it was this dark, rich soil that was a major factor in making the Bowling Green State University field one of the top in the country.

The field had a beautiful dark green bed of grass, precisely cut to three inches. The infield dirt was absent of even the tiniest pebble, and the transition between dirt and grass was seamless. The bullpens were in immaculate condition, and the dugouts were of Major League—caliber.

A brick wall was used as a border for the foul areas. It ran four feet high from the left field foul pole down to home plate and up to the right field foul pole which gave the field a feeling of strength. The home run fence was a deep forest green, and was exempt from any blemish or even the slightest tear. The Bowling Green State

University field was as perfect a field as you could find.

The two coaches stood in the centerfield grass. Two athletes from local schools were stretching their legs in the grass on the foul line between third base and the left field foul pole. Both of these athletes looked like track stars, and they were certainly dressed the part. They were decked out in top-of-the-line shoes, shorts, and shirts. The coaches teased them, letting them know that they were at a baseball tryout and not an audition for an Under Armour commercial.

As tryouts were about to get underway, the quiet morning air was broken by the increasingly loud noise of an approaching engine. The sound drew the attention of the coaches and the two athletes warming up, and they all shifted their glance to the parking lot located on the third base side of the field. It was a rusty, beat up, white Ford pickup truck that must have been at least 25 years old. It looked like the type of truck that had worked hard for years-and should have retired about ten years ago.

The screeching of the brakes sounded like fingernails on a chalkboard, and everyone within earshot cringed. As the driver shut down the engine, the old Ford continued to run for at least a minute, choking and sputtering the entire time. A final, loud backfire shut it down for good. The driver opened the creaky door, stepped out, and then slammed it hard, causing a hollow, tin sound as the door struck the rusty frame of the truck.

He was 17 years old and stood 5 feet, 10 inches tall. He looked to be 140 pounds soaking wet. He sported a green John Deere hat turned backwards, and had a mane of flaming red hair that dropped at least four inches past his collar. He was wearing beat up work boots, faded blue Wrangler jeans covered in dirt and dust, and a white T-shirt beneath a gray flannel shirt left unbuttoned.

Without a care in the world, the driver casually made his way to the back of the pickup and snatched a pair of old sneakers. The sneakers weren't anything fancy; they looked like the type that you would purchase at a Wal-Mart sales rack. They would never be confused with something *new*, and looked worse than most sneakers others would simply throw away. He slung the sneakers over his shoulder, brushed the dust off of his jeans, and began to make his way to the baseball field. He was completely oblivious to the audience observing his every move.

Coach Wellman turned his attention back to Coach Reynolds, confirming the objective for the day. "We have one spot to fill on the team," he said.

"And it's between these three?" Reynolds asked.

Wellman stared at his clipboard. "Yup," he said finally. "We need to add some speed to the team."

Reynolds looked at him. "So, who do we have?"

Wellman glanced at the two boys stretching. "Well, we have Forman Trey, two-time state champion in the 100 meter dash. Then, we have Lee Chilcote, who played on the Division I state champion basketball team this past winter. Both are real good athletes. Third up is the fella that just pulled up. He's an old farm boy from Gibsonburg, Wes Milleson."

Once inside the brick wall that surrounded the baseball field, Wes stopped between the dugout and third base and took in his surroundings. He took off his flannel shirt and work boots and tossed them in a pile on the ground. He sat on the grass and put on the old tennis shoes. When he stood, it was plain that his tryout uniform was the same old jeans and T-shirt he was already wearing—quite a contrast to the other two athletes trying out.

Coach Wellman kept his eyes on the boy. "The coach from Pemberville, Chopper Schmeltz, spoke highly of Milleson. Chopper told me he is *sneaky fast*."

Reynolds ignored the comment. He looked up from his clipboard, blew the whistle, and alerted the players to get ready. "Okay fellas, let's line it up on the foul line. We are going to check your times in the 60-yard dash."

All three athletes walked up to where Coach Wellman was standing; along the left field foul line, at a spot halfway between third base and the left field foul pole. Sixty yards out near centerfield, stopwatch and clipboard in hand, Coach Reynolds stood next to the finish line, which consisted of two orange cones spread ten yards apart.

The coaches overheard the chatter between the athletes as they made their way to the starting point.

Lee looked at Wes and spoke in a voice loud enough for Milleson to hear, "Check out this country hick."

Forman snickered. "Hey farm boy, nice ride! Get ready to eat a little dust."

Lee raised his voice. "I hear you farm boys like to suck on that hind teat!"

"Also heard you're great at cleaning up shit," Forman added.

Forman and Lee high fived each other, not even bothering to conceal their laughter.

Coach Wellman jumped in and yelled, "All right, that's enough! Line up and go on my whistle."

The three boys stood perpendicular to the foul line. Wes was in the third position, closest to third base. Lee was in the middle, and Forman was in the first position, closest to the left field fence. Coach Wellman stood about 20 feet in front of Forman, straddling the left field line. Each athlete waited with knees bent and left foot on the line, ready to spring into action.

Coach Wellman brought the whistle to his mouth. "Ready! Set!"

He blew the whistle sharply and watched the boys take off.

Sixty yards away, Coach Reynolds kept his eyes on them. He clocked Forman as he crossed the finish line first, Lee a close second, and Wes at least four strides behind, dead last.

Coach Wellman yelled for all the boys to line it up again.

After the boys lined up again, Coach Wellman blew the whistle. Again, Forman came in an easy first, Lee second, and Wes panting hard far behind. As the three boys jogged back to the starting line to line up again, Coach Reynolds followed.

As they prepared to run a third time, Coach Reynolds held up his hand. "Okay fellas. In baseball it's all about 90 feet."

Reynolds pointed to Coach Wellman walking directly out from the foul line to the pitcher's mound. "Lee, you're on first base." Reynolds said as he placed the cones 90 feet out. It was clear that Coach Wellman was on the imaginary pitcher's mound, the boys were on first base, and the cones represented second base.

Coach Reynolds turned to the runners. "I want you to watch Coach Wellman as he goes into his pitching motion from the stretch. As soon as you see him commit to the imaginary batter, take off from the foul line and run to the 90-foot marker where I will be standing."

All three boys checked their left foot. After ensuring their left foot was on the foul line, each boy focused his attention on Coach Wellman. As Lee waited on Coach Wellman to pitch, he spoke to Wes without turning his head. "Hey, didn't I see you on a *Green Acres* re-run?"

Forman busted out laughing.

"You gonna need some goggles to keep my dirt from gettin' in your eyes, farm boy," Lee said, his voice grim.

Coach Wellman overheard the ribbing and shouted, "All right, I said that's enough! Let's get ready to go! Now listen up, I am going to go through the entire motion like I have a runner on first base. The three of you each represent that runner. Take off for second base when I commit to the batter. But be careful, I could try to pick you off!"

Coach Wellman got set once he got the sign from the imaginary catcher. He moved his head slightly to the left. From the corner of his left eye, he studied the runners on first base. They were all focused on him while Reynolds stood 90 feet away at second base.

Forman and Lee kept their eyes trained on Coach Wellman's body.

Wes lowered his gaze away from the coach's body, and instead stared intently at his right heel.

Wes had worked on his family's farm since the day he could walk. Chores were plentiful, and Wes never shirked a duty. Working on the farm involved *throwing things.* God knows how many times he'd picked up manure with a pitchfork and threw it; tossed bales of hay from the field onto a wagon; threw bales of hay from the wagon into a stack in the barn; threw water from a bucket into the trough; threw seed onto the back of a truck, then hauled it into the barn and threw it again into a neat pile. Yep. Throwing things—heavy things—was a part of farm life that Wes knew a whole lot about.

He was plenty familiar with the natural reverse shift that took place when you threw anything with force. Wes learned that whenever you threw anything, you needed momentum. Before you moved anything forward, you needed to first rock forward, then move backwards. Only then could you build momentum to get the object where it needed to be.

When it came to watching pitchers, Wes was able to take what he learned on the farm and use it to his advantage when stealing bases. Most baserunners looked at the pitcher's front left leg. When the pitcher's left leg came up and started to move towards home plate, that was when they took off. Wes, however, had learned that when a pitcher was going to throw home rather than first to pick off the runner, you could see the pitcher's right heel move up slightly. The pitcher needed reverse momentum to throw the ball hard to the hitter.

So while Lee and Forman focused on the pitcher's body, Wes zeroed in on his right heel.

Then it happened. Almost in slow motion, Wes noticed Coach Wellman's right heel moved ever so slightly. To the shock of Lee and Forman, Wes took off, gaining a three-step jump on both of them.

When they crossed the finish line, Wes was easily first, Forman second, and Lee a far third. Coach Reynolds and Coach Wellman were both shocked at what they saw.

Coach Wellman shouted out, "All right, let's line up again!"

Wes easily won the second race. And the third.

By the end of the third race, the Coaches knew they had found their speedster.

Frustrated, Forman turned on Wes. "You're a cheatin' bastard!"

Coach Reynolds stepped between them. "Hold up there, Forman. He's definitely not cheating. He's got a God-given gift to get a jump on the pitcher."

Forman reached around the coach and gave Wes a hard shove before storming off the field. Lee followed.

Wes watched their backs for a moment as they left the field, then turned to smile at the coaches.

Wellman winked. "Nice work, son!"

Centerfielder. Wes Milleson.

3

Wyatt Kiser - The Blood and Guts Competitor
Friday, October 29, 2004

It was football Friday night in Gibsonburg, Ohio. The crisp cool air was charged with energy that bounced off the players and reverberated throughout the crowd. Along the far end of the field the line of trees had already started to color, the leaves a burnt orange and deep golden glow glittering among the hot lights. It was no doubt another one of those stunning autumn evenings in Ohio – the kind that made you thrilled to breathe in the air just to know you were alive. Gibsonburg was playing Oak Harbor for the Suburban Lakes League Football Championship for the 2004 season.

Gibsonburg, with its nine and one regular season record, was the clear underdog against undefeated Oak Harbor and their All-State running back, Bo Smith.

Everyone in the county knew about Bo Smith. Bo stood a solid 6 feet 2 inches tall, weighed 205 pounds, had 6 percent body fat, and ran a 4.5 second 40-yard dash. He held the school record in the bench press by putting up 375 pounds. He was also the league champ in the high jump, clearing 6 feet, 5 inches the previous spring. The athletic director let Bo play baseball and run track.

He was a unanimous first-team selection in the league, county, and state for football and baseball as a junior. Most likely, he would do the same his senior year. The fact that he had already rushed for 1,800 yards his senior year made him a solid choice to win the "Mr. Football" award as the best football player in the state of Ohio. That honor had previously been won by players such as Robert Smith and Eddie George who both went on to star at the Ohio State University and then the National Football League. Many compared Bo's natural running style to that of the great Eddie George.

Bo was always considered a man amongst boys and excelled in all sports, just like his father, his grandfather, and his great-grand-father.

There had never been a better athlete to ever come out of San-dusky County than Bo Smith. He had all the elements to succeed at football or baseball at just about any Division I school. And if he could control his temper, many thought he could play in the NFL someday.

Everyone in the county knew Bo Smith and his family, and they did what they could to keep their distance. Nobody was immune to the abuse they had been serving out to county residents for as long as anyone could remember.

Bo was a bully, as was his father, grandfather, and great-grandfa-ther. But Bo was not your *typical bully*, either. He had a mean side to him that was more intense and frightening than any other Smith to come before him. What set Bo apart from the rest of his family, though, was his uncontrollable, hair-triggered temper.

If somebody looked at Bo the wrong way, a fight soon began, and Bo never lost. His goal was to inflict as much physical pain as pos-sible and to never stop.

Nobody was off limits to Bo Smith. He picked on boys, girls, chil-dren, the elderly, the handicapped, and anyone else that set him off.

One of the more famous stories about Bo involved him get-ting called out on strikes during a baseball game as a junior in high school. When he argued with the umpire, the umpire threw him out of the game. As Bo walked back to the dugout he told the umpire he was going to beat his ass after the game. As promised, Bo waited and beat the umpire to a pulp. He then warned him that there would be more if he told anyone or tried to press charges. The umpire quietly resigned from his part-time profession and, even against the urging of many of those close to him, he never pressed charges.

Bo came about his disdain for officials honestly enough. The entire Smith clan, mother included, had a reputation for getting tossed out of sporting events for yelling at officials. Although nobody dared to say anything to their faces, they all shook their heads and chuckled to themselves as the Smith clan would scream and yell at football games, basketball games, and baseball games. There was always a one-in-three chance that the official would toss a family member out of each game. When one of them did get tossed, they never left quietly either. The cursing and yelling would continue during the entire drawn-out exit. Nobody ever chuckled because he or she thought it was funny. They just chuckled because they could not understand how anybody, let alone an entire family, could act in such a ridiculous manner. They were the joke of the county. They earned their reputation well.

One time, Bo's father and grandfather were thrown out of a girl's softball tournament for yelling at the 14-year-old umpire. When Bo found out, he raced to the tournament, confronted the umpire in the parking lot, and knocked four of his teeth out. All 205 pounds of Bo beating on the 130 pound umpire. When the umpire's mother and father approached, Bo pushed down the mother and chased after the father. It took four men and an off-duty sheriff's deputy to hold off Bo.

That misstep cost the Smith's thousands of dollars in legal bills. And the court put Bo on probation.

Although Bo Smith had plenty of talent, he didn't have plenty of fans, but did he care? Hell no!

Back to the championship game: The fourth quarter was winding down. Oak Harbor had the ball and was winning 28 to 7 with only four minutes left in the game.

The quarterback tossed a short two-yard hitch to their wide receiver who was quickly tackled by safety, Wes Milleson. Gibsonburg linebacker, Wyatt Kiser, was running at full speed toward the play. When the whistle blew, he began to jog and slow down.

Wyatt Kiser was known as just a good ole farm boy. He was the fifth generation to work the family farm, where they grew corn and soybeans. He and his 14-year-old sister, Courtney, worked alongside his parents, Tim and Sue, on the 1,100 acres that had been in the family for more than 80 years. Wyatt was very quiet, strong as an ox, and had a reputation as being a good kid. He stood 5 feet 11 inches tall, weighed 170 pounds, and had a mop of sandy brown hair that he combed to the side.

Wyatt was the type of kid that the girls adored: muscular, good looking, quiet, and just the right amount of shyness. The girls were always after him, but he was too shy to get into a relationship. This made him even more in demand amongst the female population in Gibsonburg. He was known for giving a helping hand, and looking out for others. It didn't matter if it was assisting an elderly person with their groceries or stopping a bully from picking on a kid at the bus stop. He was quick to lend a hand and was willing to take on the toughest and hardest task. Everyone joked that they had never seen Wyatt get upset. They would play pranks on him to try to get him riled, but it never worked. He would shrug it off, smile, and get back to whatever it was he was doing. They didn't come much stronger, straighter, or as easy going as Wyatt Kiser.

Which made him a perfect target for Bo Smith.

Even though the whistle blew, Bo Smith did not slow down at all. He had his sights set on blocking Wyatt, and as Wyatt slowed down, Bo accelerated and hit him blindly from the left side, driving him hard into the ground. Nobody saw the cheap shot except Bo's father who was sitting in the stands, and Wes Milleson, who was getting up from his tackle. Bo pointed at his father, who gave a head nod of approval. Bo's mother proudly looked at her husband to declare, "That's our boy! Nine hits like that one this year! Could be a Smith family record."

The hit knocked the wind out of Wyatt. Disoriented, he got up slowly and felt a sudden, sharp pain in his left forearm. He held his forearm with his right hand and jogged to the sideline where he was met by Wes.

Wes glanced at Wyatt's left forearm, shocked by what he saw. "Wyatt! Holy shit, are you okay?"

Wyatt looked down to see that his disfigured left forearm was clearly broken. The bone looked like it might even pop through the skin.

"I'll be all right. That cheap-shot prick," winced Wyatt in pain.

Wes started to jog away toward the huddle forming on the field. He turned back to his good friend Wyatt and said with a smile, "I'm going to go make amends." Wyatt got a confused look on his face and sat down on the bench away from the rest of his teammates. Nobody else really took notice of what took place.

Wes put his helmet on and ran into the huddle on the field and addressed his teammates. "Okay fellas," he said sternly. "That cheap-shot bastard Smith did some serious damage to our boy Wyatt. This is what we do: When Smith gets the ball, we tackle him. All eleven of us! Don't listen to the whistle, just tackle him. Once we get him down, start pinching as hard as you can all over his body. Get his arms, legs, ass, neck, whatever. Pinch him every-where!"

Cornerback Cody Fisher nervously cleared his throat. "But Wes. What if, um, what if . . .,"

Wes stopped Cody in mid-sentence by pinching him as hard as he could on the side of his neck. "Just fuckin' do it! Ready, break!"

On the next play, Bo Smith had the ball and came around the right end on an option play. Bo got about five yards before Wes tripped him. In a flash, eleven Gibsonburg Golden Bears piled on top of Bo Smith and started pinching him as hard as they could.

Completely immobile with 1,500 pounds on top of him and 22 hands pinching every part of his body, his neck, inside his thighs, and even his balls—Bo screamed in rage and agony.

The officials blew their whistles, charged the gang pile and re-moved the players one by one. And it was no easy task. Each player was pulled off slowly and stubbornly, like an old piece of sticky gum from the bottom of a shoe. The last player grabbed by a referee was Wes Milleson, who managed to deliver one last, extra hard, final pinch to Bo's side, right above his beltline.

Free at last, Bo popped up like a jack-in-the-box, swinging his right arm with all his might at Wes's head. Wes ducked and just missed getting hit by the punch.

The official immediately pointed toward the Oak Harbor bench and ejected Bo from the game. "You're outta here!"

Bo jumped in the official's face. "That's bullshit! You chickenshit weasel; they were pinching me all over!"

Bo's teammates tried to restrain him while the official screamed at him again. "You're gone!"

Bo took off his helmet, slammed it to the ground, and marched off to the bench while he continued his screaming tirade at the of-ficial.

Wes smiled and jogged to the bench where Wyatt sat.

"Wyatt, what are you doing man?" Wes approached his team-mate and watched in amazement as Wyatt had placed a shin guard over the broken bone and was just about finished wrapping his entire forearm with white athletic tape.

"I'm going back in dude," Wyatt said simply.

"Wyatt, we're down three touchdowns with three minutes left. There is no way we can win."

Wyatt walked on the field, holding his helmet in his right hand. He turned around to face Wes, putting his helmet on with his uninjured arm. "Sometimes it's not about winning. It's about finishing. C'mon. Let's go bang some heads!" Wyatt turned and jogged out to the huddle.

Wes stared at his friend, stunned. He shook his head and slowly clasped his helmet back into place, then followed Wyatt back on the field.

Left Fielder. Wyatt Kiser.

4

Alex Black - The Athlete
Friday, February 18, 2005

I t was a cold evening in February 2005. Alex Black was sitting at the kitchen table doing his homework while his mother was cleaning up the supper dishes. His sister, Bridget, sat beside him doing her geometry homework.

Alex's mother, Sara, stood at the sink quietly washing dishes. "Alex," she said. "I don't see why you feel the need to get up at 4 am every morning, before chores, to do your silly little work out—especially, on the days when you have basketball games."

Alex smiled to himself but didn't answer. He finished his homework and gave his mother a quick peck on the cheek before going up to bed.

As he headed upstairs, Bridget called out behind him. "Alex, I'll help you with the chores if you want so you can keep workin' out. I don't mind."

Alex smiled at his sister and continued upstairs. He knew he was lucky to have a sister like her: So loving, kind, and generous with her time. She was like a little puppy, always hanging around, waiting for his attention. There wasn't a bratty bone in her body and he was glad for it. There was plenty of work to do on the dairy farm—never any breaks—and anything she did to help was definitely appreciated.

The Black family raised Ayrshire dairy cattle. With 50 head of cattle, they were considered a medium-sized dairy farm. The dairy cattle needed to be milked twice daily at dawn and dusk. Milking wasn't as hard of a task as it was in the old days, but it still took time. The Black farm used milking equipment that was automated, but certainly not new. The milking process involved herding cows in the chutes and connecting the hoses from the milking machines to the udders. When the cow was out of milk, the four suction hoses disconnected themselves. The cow would then be moved out of the chute, and the next cow ushered in.

With eight milking machines, it took five minutes to get three to five gallons of milk out of each cow. With 50 head of dairy cattle, it took 60 to 90 minutes to get through all of them. Milking 50 cows twice a day yields about 400 gallons of milk that would fetch about $500 dollars. In a good year, the farm would gross $180,000 to $200,000. When you backed out expenses, the farm was lucky to make over $30,000 per year.

Alex's grandfather started the dairy farm in 1962. In 1980, the year Alex's father, Jack, graduated from high school, his grandfather suffered a heart attack and died while removing an old fence row on the farm. Rather than pursue the basketball scholarship he was offered at Kent State, Alex's father took over the dairy farm for the family. Jack embraced his destiny. He was never bitter and enjoyed everything about the work on the dairy farm. Jack took great pride in how efficiently he ran the operation, just like his own father had.

Despite his workload on the dairy farm, Alex was one of the best natural athletes to ever come out of Gibsonburg. He excelled in football, basketball, and baseball. With his head of ruffled blond-ish hair and baby blue eyes, Alex looked like a California surfer. He stood 6 feet, 3 inches tall and weighed 190 pounds, but his most distinguishing feature was his smile. He could brighten up any conversation with his amazing, bright white, Hollywood-ready smile.

Given his height and weight, Alex Black had somewhat of a lanky build, yet he was much stronger and faster than he looked. In every sport he played, the opponents were always a little surprised at what a fierce competitor he was. And when it came to defense, they quickly discovered that when Alex Black guarded you, you didn't have too much of a chance. He had good range with his long limbs, and he couldn't stand losing.

Off the field, he was very different. He was fun-loving, easy-going, and never took life too seriously. In fact, his friends had to work hard to keep Alex from getting into trouble. He had a mischievous streak, which often came close to crossing the line and getting into real trouble.

Alex awoke the next morning, after a deep, dreamless sleep. He was so used to his morning routine that he didn't require the aid of an alarm clock. When the screen door to the back porch slammed shut, the old clock on the kitchen wall read 4 am. Just like every other morning, Alex started to run when he crossed in front of the weather-beaten sign in the front yard that read:

Black's Dairy Farm
est. 1962

And just like every other morning, Alex was off on his standard five-mile run down the rolling country roads outside of Gibsonburg in the pitch-black darkness that preceded dawn.

A little over 35 minutes later, Alex crossed in front of the weather-beaten sign again. This time, it was his finish line. He looked down at his watch. "Damn, I was hoping to get better than seven minute miles" he muttered.

Alex entered the barn, peeled off his sweatshirt, and got ready to start the next part of his work out. Wearing a gray muscle shirt and black shorts, he knew it was important to keep moving, and not slow down at all.

Alex ran up the stairs to the hay loft. He then jumped up and did 50 pull-ups while hanging on the rafter that was ten feet off of the ground. When he counted off the fiftieth pull-up, he popped down on the ground and cranked out 50 push-ups. He repeated the process four more times.

He ran back down the stairs to an old rope hanging in the middle of the cattle pen. As dawn had not yet arrived, the cattle were still out to pasture. With unbridled energy, Alex grabbed the rope and began an all hands climb to the top of the rope which was tied to a rafter, which was one of 40 rafters that supported the barn roof. When Alex had climbed 50 feet to the top, he carefully let go of the rope with one hand and grabbed the rafter with the free hand. He then grabbed the rafter with his other hand and hung for a second or two. He twisted upside down, brought his feet through the inside of his arms and curled his legs around the eight by two inch wooden rafter. He slowly let go of his hands and hung upside down like a bat. The only thing that kept him from falling 50 feet were his legs tightly curled around the eight-by-two inch piece of wood. For the first time in 45 minutes, he rested for about 30 seconds.

After taking a few deep breaths, he crossed his arms on his chest and slowly brought his right shoulder up to his left knee. He went all the way back down and immediately went back up and touched his left shoulder to his right knee. He repeated the process 98 more times, clearly struggling on the 100th rep. He grabbed the rafter with his hands, uncurled his legs, and hung for a few seconds. He reached for the rope and using only his hands, made his 50-foot descent to the ground.

Alex looked outside and could tell by the color of the sky that in 30 minutes it would be about 5:30 am. The sun would rise, and he would have to start milking. Thirty minutes left to work out, he thought.

He went to the corner of the pen and pulled out the weathered and beaten up throwing target his dad gave him for his birthday when he was 12. It was a blue piece of canvas hanging from a bar that was supported by two upside down "T" legs. The entire piece of canvas was about eight feet tall by four feet wide. There was a crude batter with a sad face painted on the canvas. In the strike zone area, there was a hole that was as wide as home plate and stretched from the knees of the sad-faced batter to his chest line. There was a flap over the hole that deadened the thrown balls, which were neatly collected in a heavy-duty burlap bag that was sewn to the back of the hole.

Alex positioned the target, grabbed his five gallon bucket full of old baseballs, and carefully walked off 20 paces and one foot for 60 feet six inches—the precise distance from the pitchers mound to home plate. Alex continued on with his daily throwing workout. He began with 30 warm-up throws and then 80 pitches, all fast-balls, to the target. In a well-thought-out and methodical manner, he worked the strike zone hard, never throwing to the middle. Like following the hands of a clock he began with high outside, high inside, low inside, and then low outside. He went around the clock 20 times for a total of 80 pitches.

After the eightieth pitch, he collected the 22 balls that missed the target and emptied the burlap bag of balls into the five gallon bucket. He put away the target and looked outside. The sun was just rising. It was 5:30 am and time to get to work.

Alex took the next 90 minutes to complete his chores. He worked with his father to milk the cows, feed the chickens, and muck out the stalls for their four quarter horses.

Around 7:00 am Alex grabbed a tin pail and headed towards Jessie, his favorite Ayrshire that he helped deliver when he was ten years old. Just like they did in the old days, he grabbed a teat and squirted a quarter of a gallon of fresh milk into the pail. He proceeded to the chicken coop and grabbed four fresh eggs from the hens, cracked each egg, and dumped their contents into the bucket of milk. He lifted the bucket to his lips and drank it all down. As he swallowed the warm mixture, he wondered if anyone would consider it odd that he preferred warm milk and fresh eggs instead of refrigerated milk and cooked eggs. A tiny trail of the white liquid ran down the corner of his mouth and he wiped it away with the back of his hand. He washed the pail out using the spigot just inside the barn door, and he walked toward the house to get ready for school. As soon as he walked out, the odor from the dairy cattle faded away and another stronger odor caught his attention. An odor that put a smile on his face.

As Alex walked toward the house, he heard the screen door slam shut and noticed his mother, Sara, heading towards him, carrying a plate covered with a red and white checkered cloth. They met halfway between the house and barn. She lifted and revealed six freshly-baked buttermilk biscuit and bacon sandwiches.

"I made up some breakfast sandwiches for you and your father."

Alex responded, "Nice. I'm starving!"

"How was your workout, honey?" His mother asked.

"Terrific." Alex grabbed three of the biscuits, shoved one in his mouth, and headed toward the house.

"Who do you play in your basketball game tonight?" his mother called out after him.

"We play at Elmwood," he shouted and walked inside.

Pitcher. Alex Black.

5

Andy Gruner - The Leader
Monday, March 7, 2005

The silence of the bedroom was shattered by the alarm clock. The annoying beep, beep, beep clawed at Andy's ears until he couldn't take it anymore. Blindly, Andy Gruner reached over to shut off his alarm. He then picked up the clock to check the time. The red digital display showed 4:30 am.

Andy turned over on his back, rubbed his eyes and looked straight up at the ceiling. Six days a week, Andy would wake up at this time so he could get to the Ideal Bakery by 5 am and open for business. Andy turned his head to look out the window. It was black outside. Just like it was every morning.

Andy Gruner was senior class president and would be captain of the Gibsonburg baseball team his senior year. Andy was a natural born leader. He never asked to be a leader, nor did he really enjoy being a leader. However, ever since he was young, everyone always seemed to follow Andy. He had a very level head, really didn't say much unless he had something to say, and had a knack for making good decisions. Andy's best quality, though, dealt with his strong will. Andy had never quit anything in his life, and he had a strong track record for sticking with things, no matter what the circumstances, and never quitting.

When Andy was 13, he was asked to play on Woodmore's 14-year-old travel baseball team for their fall league, as they needed to fill the roster in case anyone got hurt. Because Gibsonburg did not have a fall baseball team, Andy jumped at the opportunity. The fall baseball league only had games on Sunday afternoons, which worked well for Andy because that was the only day of the week he didn't work at the bakery. Andy was considered a good player but not really a great player. He always played with a lot of heart, though, and the coach on the Woodmore team knew this.

On this particular team, there were four older boys who, for no good reason, liked to pick on Andy. They would chase Andy down after practices and games and shove him around, grab his hat to play *keep away*, and when Andy resisted, they would get rough with him. On many occasions, Andy would come home with a bloody nose, a few bruises, and sometimes, a black eye. Each of the boys were bigger than Andy, and because there were four of them, he never had too much of a chance at fighting back.

At 13, you couldn't find too many boys that would put up with this type of abuse for two months. They would quit! Andy Gruner never thought of quitting. He never complained. He never thought about telling his parents. He just stayed on the team and did his best. While all this was going on, the catcher on the team, Bill Warner, started to observe what was going on with the boys picking on Andy. Bill began to pay a little more attention.

Now, on the fall baseball team, Bill Warner was almost 15 years old, but he looked like he was 18. He stood a solid 5 feet, 11 inches tall, weighed 185 pounds, was very fast, and had the physique of a body builder. Bill was the best player on the team, but his favorite sport was football. He was one of the best linebackers around and, as a freshman, got to see some varsity action on Woodmore's High School football team on Friday nights. Bill was such a good athlete that the coach of Woodmore's fall baseball team made an exception and let Bill play in the Sunday games, even though he could not practice during the week due to football.

It was a 12 game season, and after seven games, Andy had yet to play an inning. And then, in the eighth game of the season, Woodmore was getting beat by seven runs. So, the coach put Andy into right field. Bryce Baxter, the starting right fielder and ringleader of the group that picked on Andy, tripped Andy as he walked through the dugout gate and onto the field.

Bryce laughed. "Walk much?"

Andy quickly got up and ran to right field. As Bill Warner walked to his catcher's position behind home plate, he observed as Andy enthusiastically ran to right field with a smile on his face. Bill could not help but notice that Andy was the only one on the team that seemed to really care about winning the game, even though they were down by seven runs.

Andy was nervous but excited to get some playing time. As he got in position for the first batter, the pitcher on Andy's team delivered a hard fastball that the left-handed hitter smacked down the right field line. Andy saw the line drive and sprinted toward the foul line. The first base coach told the batter as he approached first base that he should go for a triple. As the ball was in flight Andy was in a dead sprint and had an angle that would put him ten feet shy of the ball just as the ball would hit the ground. It looked as though the line drive would hit the ground about 40 feet from the outfield fence when Andy dove with all his might to the approximate point where the ball would hit the ground. Andy and his glove hit the ground hard at the same time as the ball. The ball came down inside the webbing of Andy's outstretched glove. Andy popped up to display that he caught the ball. The umpire shouted, "Batter's out!"

On the bench, Bryce Baxter mumbled, "Lucky catch."

Their catcher, Bill Warner, looked at the joy on Andy's face and smiled. He pulled his catcher's mask down to get ready for the next batter.

Adrenaline pumping, Andy sprinted back to position to get ready. Andy noticed that it was another left-handed batter, so he turned around and checked his distance from the right field fence. He took about four steps back toward the fence to accommodate for the fact that a left-handed batter would hit a deeper ball to right field.

The pitcher wound up and delivered another fastball. The batter hit a deep fly ball to the right center gap. The centerfielder and Andy sprinted to right center as the first base coach yelled at the batter, who was halfway to first base, to *go two*, which meant keep running to second base. The ball hit the ground, bounced once, and hit the fence. Andy got to the ball first and with all his might threw the ball to second base, above the cut-off man's head. The ball Andy threw had a low trajectory, bounced once, and went cleanly into the waiting glove of the shortstop at second base at about the same time the runner was sliding into second. The ball went into the shortstop's glove just a hair before the runner's right foot hit the glove. The umpire yelled, "OUT"!

Andy jumped for joy and yelled, "Yeah!" Bill Warner smiled again. On the bench, Bryce Baxter was still seated. He said to himself, "Big deal. We're still going to lose."

The next batter struck out to make the third out, and Andy sprinted for the dugout. The coach met Andy and congratulated him on two great plays.

Andy's team still lost the game. Andy sat on the bench feeling sore from his diving catch but with a good feeling in his heart. He took off and admired the Puma baseball cleats that his mother had just given him for his birthday two weeks ago. He tied the shoelaces of his two cleats together and slung them over his shoulder. He slowly put on his tennis shoes, reflected on the game, and smiled.

After a little more reflective thought, Andy looked around and realized he was the last person to leave the bench.

As Andy walked along the backside of the dugout, he felt a very violent "pop" in the middle of his back. His head jerked back sharply while the rest of his body was thrust forward. He slammed to the ground, turned around on his back, and saw Bryce Baxter.

Bryce stood over Andy and pointed at him. "What's the big idea trying to steal my position, scrub? I'm gonna beat your ass!"

Andy got up and started to brush himself off, but Bryce charged him. Unbeknownst to Andy, another one of the bullies was on his hands and knees behind Andy's legs. When Bryce pushed Andy, Andy fell over the boy's body and onto the ground. When he got back on his feet, Bryce and all three of his buddies surrounded Andy in a tight circle. The four boys began pushing Andy hard to each other, like a pinball in a pinball machine. With each push, the intensity increased. On one of the pushes, Andy's baseball cleats dropped to the ground.

Bryce picked up the cleats, which were tied together by their shoelaces. After examining the cleats, he said, "Nice," and smiled.

He tossed the cleats up toward an electrical wire that was 20 feet in the air. The shoelaces caught the wire about halfway between the light pole and the concession stand and then wrapped around the wire twice. The cleats hung in the air swaying back and forth, and the four bullies all looked at each other, and burst into laughter. Andy looked at the cleats hanging from the wire and knew they would be about impossible to get down.

Bryce stopped laughing long enough to push Andy hard with his hands, knocking him back several feet. "Whaddya gonna do now, scrub?"

Andy staggered for a moment, straightened, and then walked towards Bryce until they were nose-to-nose. With an open hand, Bryce whacked the left side of Andy's head. Andy just smiled, took his left hand and gently pushed Bryce in the chest. As Bryce looked down at Andy's left hand, with great force, Andy popped Bryce in the nose with his right fist. Bryce stumbled back, bent over, and then stood up with his hand covering his nose. There was blood all over Bryce's hand and blood was coming out of his nose. Bryce charged Andy. Andy bent over and flipped Bryce over his body.

One of Bryce's friends ran up to Andy and blind-sided him hard with his body and knocked him to the ground. Bryce jumped on top of him and began delivering blows to his face while the others encouraged him on.

Andy feebly tried to block the blows, but there was no escaping them. Bryce reared back with his right arm to deliver another hit to Andy's face. When his arm was cocked back as far as it would go, Bryce tried to move his arm forward, but it didn't move. He turned around to see Bill Warner's left hand gripping his wrist right below his clenched fist.

Bill jerked Bryce's arm back and threw him back at least ten feet. Bryce got up, charged Bill, and Bill hit Bryce with one controlled punch that was of such force, it knocked him out. Bill walked up to two of the boys that were standing close together. He got very close to them and was looking at the fear in their eyes. Bill put his left hand on the neck of the boy on his left. He then put his right hand on the neck of the boy on his right. He looked at each of the boys, moved both of his hands up to the boys' ears, and in one solid and fierce motion, knocked their heads together, and they both fell to the ground. As the two boys lay on the ground holding their heads in pain, Bill just looked at the fourth boy. The fourth boy cautiously took four steps back and then turned around and sprinted away.

Bill went up to Andy, helped him up, and examined his face. His left eye was bloody, and he had a few other cuts but no missing teeth.

Bill smiled. "I think it's an improvement."

They both laughed. Andy winced a little and rubbed his chin.

Bill looked up to see Andy's baseball cleats hanging on the wire. "My dad is a tree trimmer," he said. We can get his extension pole and get those down in about two seconds." Andy smiled gratefully.

Andy started in right field for the next two games, while Bryce sat on the bench. After those two games, Bryce quit the team and Andy started each of the remaining games.

Andy's experience on Woodmore's fall baseball team was just one of many events that shaped Andy's character. Andy would never quit. Andy would never give up. Andy Gruner would never give up on anything for the rest of his life!

When Andy was 13 and on the Woodmore fall baseball team, he was 5 feet 2 inches tall, weighed 130 pounds, had braces, and a few facial blemishes. From the age of 13 to 17 he grew to a height of 6 feet and weighed 170 pounds. He had straight white teeth, a mop of brown tussled hair, and a strong lean build that was a result of working so hard at the bakery and participation year round in his favorite sport, baseball. He came out of adolescence as a fine young man that any parent would want their daughter to date. The girls at Gibsonburg secretly and informally voted Andy as the cutest boy in school. Andy went on dates, but he never had a serious relationship with anyone. In his heart, he had one true love that he could never stop thinking about.

It was 4:33 am. Andy popped out of bed, took a quick shower, and drove to the Ideal Bakery, his family's business.

Andy unlocked the front door, turned on the neon *Open* sign, and got busy with his duties. He put bread in the oven, made coffee, put icing on the doughnuts, and prepared three special orders that would be picked up by 7 am.

The Ideal Bakery had been in the Gruner family for a long time. Andy's great-grandfather and his two brothers bought the three-story, all brick building and opened the bakery on the first floor in

1927. In 1933, two separate tragedies struck the Gruner family, leaving Andy's great-grandfather as the sole proprietor. Andy's grandfather took over the business in 1962. And in 1984, after Andy's grandfather retired, Andy's father, Ron, took over the business.

The bakery was as famous a landmark as you could find in Sandusky County. It was full of charm, and the Gruners did everything they could to maintain the same atmosphere that you would have found in the 1930's. The display case was always full of fresh baked goods. Their specialty was éclairs, and people would drive from miles around to get them.

The bakery was located in the middle of downtown Gibsonburg at the intersection of Route 600 (which ran east to west) and Route 300 (which ran north to south). The building was rectangular with the long east wall of the bakery parallel to the north/south running Route 300. There was a large plate glass window on the north end of the building that looked out toward Kirwen's Market on the other side of the street. Customers entered the bakery from the angled door located on the northeast side of the building. Walking in the bakery felt like stepping back in time . The charm and aroma of the bakery was overwhelming. The bakery had two large display cases containing all kinds of freshly baked breads, doughnuts, cookies, and numerous specialty pastries.

An "L"-shaped counter with a blue Formica top had room for six people on the long side and three on the short side. Nine stools were bolted to the floor, each with shiny blue upholstery on the seat. There wasn't a kid in town, or an adult for that matter, that had not spent time spinning around on those bar stools. Between the long part of the counter and the wall that ran on the east side of the building, there were two tables. Each table had a blue Formica top and sat four people on matching chairs, each with the same shiny upholstery as the bar stools. Behind the display case and the counter, it looked like a snapshot you would see from a 1930's diner. Coffee pots, cups, plates, signs displaying the specials, and an old-time soda fountain were all neatly organized in front of a large mirror that ran the full length of the counter.

At the opposite corner of the room from the customer entrance, there was a swinging door with a glass porthole at eye level, providing a peek into the room where all the prep-work and baking took place. As the door swung both ways, the porthole window was a necessity to keep you from slamming the door into anyone entering from the other side.

Andy would open the bakery at 5 am, and by 5:10 am, you could count at least six regulars helping themselves to their own coffee behind the counter. In no time, Andy would promptly deliver each customer their "usual" order.

At the Ideal Bakery, conversations and opinions were as plentiful as the baked goods. There wasn't a topic that was off limits within its four hallowed walls. Politics, religion, and most certainly the weather were constantly discussed. But the most popular topic, by far, involved the sport that was being played at that particular time of year at Gibsonburg High School.

Vince Lombardi? Bobby Knight? Sparky Anderson? They all paled in comparison to the collective knowledge and understanding of sports that was maintained in the minds of the locals that visited the Ideal Bakery each morning. These homegrown experts had all the right answers, knew all the right moves, and never made a poor decision. The only real problem was that all decisions were made in hindsight after the events had taken place.

It was an amusing place to eavesdrop. And in an odd sort of way, even the locals themselves had a notion of how ridiculous they were in the critiques. The trouble was, they would never admit it.

Six days a week, Andy would go to the bakery and get things running for his parents. He would do prep-work until 7:45 am, then leave for school.

On the morning of March 7, 2005, at about 7 am, Andy was putting icing on doughnuts in the prep room. His mother, Jennie, walked in. "Andy, where's your father?"

Andy noticed his mother looked worried.

"He's in the cake room," replied Andy.

She patted Andy on the shoulder, smiled warmly, and went off to find him.

Curious, Andy moved closer to the cake room door.

Straining, he could barely hear the conversation.

"I can't believe this bakery has been in our family for over 80 years and we're going to lose it now," Ron said.

Jennie sighed. "Well, we held the creditors off as much as we could. But we are still $89,000 short. I told them that we would plan on shutting things down by the end of May so they can put everything up in a sheriff's sale."

"When are we going to tell Andy?" Ron asked.

"Let's wait as long as we can. With school and everything he has enough pressure."

Andy quickly went back to the work table to put icing on the doughnuts. As he was working, he felt someone tap him on his right shoulder. He turned around, and nobody was there. When Andy looked back over his left shoulder, he saw his father smiling, disguising his worry. Andy hesitantly smiled back with the news he just heard still processing in his mind.

Ron examined the doughnuts Andy had been icing. For one of the first times, he realized that in a couple of months, there would not be any more bakery work to be done. But he had always been good at masking his sadness and this time was no different.

"Well, you're all set for the morning rush," Andy said.

"Nice work." He looked at his son with a deep sense of pride. In his heart, Ron knew with an unshakeable certainty that his son was destined for greatness.

Andy glanced at his dad. "Well, I better get going to school."

"I love you son," Ron said, patting his shoulder.

Andy drove down Route 300 south to the high school located outside of town. He glanced at his mobile phone. It was 7:58 am and he was still five minutes away. This would be the fourth time he would be late in the past two weeks which meant he would get a detention. He had a presentation he was supposed to give to the freshman class at 8:10, and he figured he would be at least ten minutes late. Andy sighed deeply and began to play back in his mind what he just heard in the bakery.

"This bakery has been in our family for over 80 years!"

"We owe over $89,000 dollars!"

"We have been holding the creditors off for eight months!"

"We have no choice but to sell at the end of May!"

He couldn't get the last line out of his head.

"We have no choice but to sell at the end of May!"

"We have no choice but to sell at the end of May!"

As he replayed the line for the third time, he caught a glimpse of something to his right with his peripheral vision. He jerked his head to his right and nearly jumped out of his seat as the deafening sound of a train whistle screamed through the air. Instinctively, he hit his brakes just as the train swept three feet in front of the bumper of his red Toyota pickup.

Stunned, Andy stared at the 45-car train rumbling past the front of his truck and realized how close he came to getting hit. The thundering sound of the train on the tracks was deafening. He looked down in his lap, thought for a few seconds, and ran his fingers through his thick brown hair.

What if I don't get into college? What if I flunk calculus? I still have to pay off fixing the bakery truck I wrecked! My savings are gone! Why can't I have a girlfriend? I can't believe we are losing the family bakery! I just about got killed!

The rush of thoughts overwhelmed him. His eyes welled up.

Andy left the school office, detention slip in hand, and ran down the hall to the school auditorium. As he rushed down the hall, a student caught up from behind.

"Andy, we have a 10 am meeting to discuss the high cost and low quality of our school lunches. As the President of the Senior Class, it would be great to have you there." The kid had to run to keep up with him.

"Okay, I'll try to make it," Andy replied.

Andy spotted another student coming at him. He groaned inwardly.

"Andy, we could use your help to stop senior skip day this year. The principal thinks the rest of the students will listen to you," the girl said.

"I don't think they listen to me as much as you think," he muttered.

At the end of the hall, the Athletic Director, Jeff Stewart, stopped him. "Andy, when you get a minute can we talk about the plans we have for the new baseball coach?"

Andy knew he couldn't side-step the Athletic Director. "Sure, can we talk right after lunch? I'm 15 minutes late for a meeting."

The Athletic Director gave him a quick nod as to say, "We'll talk later."

Andy turned down another hall and passed a flipchart on an easel as he headed into the auditorium. He glanced at the chart and laughed to himself. *Right.*

2005 Senior Class President
Andy Gruner
9 AM Student Address
TOPIC: How to juggle your commitments

It was a typical March Monday at Gibsonburg High School. When the bell rang for the final period at 2:30 pm, all the students swarmed out of the school.

Andy Gruner got in his beat-up old truck and headed home. He was planning on getting a little something to eat, go for a run, and then playing a little catch with friends to get his arm ready for baseball season.

Bobby Graff

On his way home, Andy decided to take a short-cut down Baxter Street, which was lined with residential homes built in the 1960s. Something to his left caught his attention. He noticed another student on the sidewalk he didn't recognize. The boy had all kinds of stuff in his arms. He wore a backpack that looked as though it was bursting at the seams. His arms were filled with notebooks, textbooks, and all kinds of school supplies that were dropping to the ground.

Andy slowed down and shouted out the window toward the boy. "Hey there! Looks like you'll be doing some serious studying over the weekend."

The boy barely glanced at him and kept walking.

Andy shouted again to the boy. "Hey, want a ride, man? I don't know how far you have to walk, but this town isn't that big. I'd be happy to take you wherever you need to go."

The boy hesitated and dropped a book and a few other supplies on the ground. He bent over to pick up the book only to have more stuff fall from his arms.

Andy shifted into park and got out to help the boy. After helping him gather the school book and remaining supplies, he stood and introduced himself.

"Name's Andy Gruner! You're the kid that just moved here in the fall, right?"

The boy nodded.

"Listen, let me give you a stinking ride. It might not look like much, but it's paid for. And it's pretty safe. If it breaks down, I could use some help giving it a push."

The boy laughed.

"Well?" Andy waited.

"Okay," he said finally.

Andy led him to the truck. There wasn't much room so the books were put in the back of the pickup. As Andy put the truck into gear, the boy said, "I live on Front Street."

As the truck began to roll, Andy asked, "Ya gotta name? Ya gotta have a name."

"I'm Bobby. Bobby Graff."

"Where did you move here from?" asked Andy.

"Bloomington, Indiana" Bobby replied.

"Cool. How do you like it here so far?"

Bobby shrugged but said nothing.

"I get it," Andy said. "Must be rough moving to a new town. What year are you?"

"Senior."

Andy looked back at him in surprise. "Man, you must keep a low profile. I thought I knew all the seniors. Well, Gibsonburg isn't so bad. The principal is a real idiot. But we have good folks. Hard-working folks. Not much to do but we do like our sports. You play any sports in Indiana?"

"A little baseball when I was younger."

"Baseball?" Andy grinned. "That's awesome. We have a high school team. We're not too good but we have a fun time. Practice starts on Friday. You should try out. Anyone that tries out gets on the team. Just one of the advantages of living in a small town."

Bobby shook his head. "Nah. Thanks for the offer though. I

haven't played since my freshman year."

Andy shrugged. "You do whatever works for you. Might be nice to get involved with something. And hey, I'll even introduce you to some of the guys."

Bobby was silent for a moment. "My last experience wasn't too good," he said finally. "I made a vow to not play anymore. Hey, this is my house up here on the left."

Andy stopped the truck. "Nice to meet you Bobby. No pressure at all, but please reconsider joining the baseball team. Our first practice is at 2:45 on Friday, 15 minutes after school lets out. We're startin' late in the year 'cause we had to wait until basketball season ended. You just need a glove and cleats."

Bobby collected his backpack and books. "Thanks for the lift."

Andy put the truck in gear and drove away.

Smiling, Bobby watched him drive away. He turned towards the house, hoisted his load into a better grip, and allowed the smile to fade as he headed up to the porch steps.

Shortstop. Andy Gruner.

6

End of Basketball Season
Tuesday, March 8, 2005

"And that's another three pointer by Alex Black," cried the announcer, his voice bursting with enthusiasm. The visiting crowd cheered every time the announcer called out Alex's name. "And another three pointer by Alex Black!"

"And Gibsonburg is coming from behind to challenge this talented Patrick-Henry in what has turned out to be a great semi-final game!"

As the Gibsonburg basketball team headed to the locker room, the announcer on the PA system continued. "Ladies and gentlemen, your final score is Patrick-Henry, 59, visiting Gibsonburg, 58. Your leading scorer is Alex Black from Gibsonburg with 36 points."

Gibsonburg made it all the way to the regional semi-finals for basketball. After a valiant effort by the entire team, and a great game by Alex Black, they lost the game. Just like that the 2004-2005 basketball season was over.

Afterwards, the entire team hit the showers and left the locker room to catch the bus back to Gibsonburg. As Wyatt and Alex walked down the long hallway to the bus they heard a locker slam. When they reached the next hallway, two older boys had a smaller, younger boy pinned against the lockers. One of the boys was about 6 feet tall, very muscular, and about 180 pounds. The other boy was about 5 feet, 10 inches tall, a little chubby, and about 200 pounds.

"What's goin' on?" Alex asked as he and Wyatt approached the three boys.

Wyatt assumed that both of the older boys were from Elmwood High School. The kid pinned against the lockers appeared to be around 15 years old, roughly 135 pounds and pretty scared. He recalled seeing him in the lunch room at Gibsonburg.

"Hey, aren't you a freshman at Gibsonburg," Wyatt asked the frightened boy.

The taller of the two bullies let go of the boy, stuck his chest out, and faced Alex. "Mind your own business farm boy."

Wyatt stepped between Alex and the taller boy. "You like pickin' on freshman? Does that make you feel tough?"

The other boy stepped toward Wyatt.

"You want some, hillbilly?" he growled.

The first bully took a step toward Wyatt. "Get lost, hicks."

Alex glanced at Wyatt and saw a strange new intensity he'd never seen before. His palms began to sweat. Alex was almost scared of Wyatt.

Wyatt stepped toward the taller boy and grabbed him by the neck. "He's only a kid," Wyatt said, his voice quietly menacing.

"But he was mouthin' . . ."

Wyatt squeezed his fingers harder.

The bully tried to pull away, but Wyatt held his vice-like grip and dug his fingers deeper.

"I said he's just a kid."

Again, the bully tried to talk, but Wyatt pushed him hard against the lockers. Suddenly, he let go.

The taller bully grabbed his throat and rubbed it.

"This ain't finished," he said angrily.

At that moment, Coach Noggle, Gibsonburg's basketball coach, stepped around the corner and saw five students standing together. "What's goin' on, fellas?"

"Nothin' much coach," said Alex. "Just getting ready to head to the bus."

Coach Noggle eyed the boys for a few seconds. "All right then, let's get goin'. And Alex? Great game tonight."

"Thanks coach." Alex and Wyatt glared at the bullies one last time before heading back to the bus.

7

The Town Of Gibsonburg
Friday, March 11, 2005 – 7:00 am

It was a typical spring morning in the town of Gibsonburg. The sky was blue, there was a gentle breeze, flowers were beginning to bloom, birds were chirping, and the thermometer displayed an unseasonably warm temperature of 66 degrees for early March. Like many small Midwestern towns, folks in Gibsonburg got up early to get after whatever they needed to be doing, making this small town come to life with the busy movement of the locals.

Gibsonburg, Ohio. Population 2,000. Located between Toledo and Fremont, Ohio. Gibsonburg was full of good, down-to-earth, hard-working folks. If you lived outside of town, you were most likely a farmer or raised livestock. If you lived in town, chances are you worked at the Brush-Wellman plant in Elmore or the limestone plant in Woodville. Not much to do around Gibsonburg but work, watch high school sports, critique high school sports, and question every miniscule coaching decision. Oh, and the best hangout in town was the infamous Ideal Bakery. It has been around for over 80 years, and it's famous in these parts for the best sweets in the world-according to anyone that has ever been there, that is.

Gibsonburg Economy

The tough economic times struck with great force in the town of Gibsonburg, but you really wouldn't know it to look around. People kept their heads up high. The town didn't have too much to hope for. It didn't have too much to believe in either. But all that changed in the early summer of 2005.

All communities within a ten-mile radius of Gibsonburg funneled their children to Gibsonburg for their education. As with many school districts in this region of Ohio, 50 percent of the children came from households in the rural areas around Gibsonburg. These families made their living from some sort of agricultural means such as farming or raising livestock. Throughout the Midwest, the proliferation of factory farms set off a major price reduction in commodities such as corn, wheat, and soybeans. These three types of crops were the primary crops planted in Sandusky County. When the price per bushel began to slide, already-struggling families had no choice but to sell their farms. In 2004, nearly 20 percent of the farms in Sandusky County were put up for foreclosure.

About 40 percent of the households had family members who worked for, or previously worked for, one of the two largest employers in area: Brush-Wellman or the Limestone Plant.

Brush-Wellman manufactured products made from beryllium and their largest customer was the United States government. Beryllium is a highly toxic metal. Many of the products manufactured at the plant were used in products related to aviation related products. Brush-Wellman was also a major supplier to NASA's space shuttle program. The light weight and high strength of products made from beryllium were ideal for building components used in the aviation industry. When the space shuttle program was all but eliminated, Brush-Wellman's workforce was too, leaving many residents of Gibsonburg unemployed.

The Limestone Plant was another major employer in the area. Limestone has many uses, but it is primarily used in building materials. Consequently, when building slowed in 2002, most of the orders for limestone did too. This again, left many residents in Gibsonburg unemployed.

So, 50 percent worked in the agricultural field, 40 percent worked in the factories, and the remaining 10 percent of households were involved in some sort of profession that either supported the agricultural businesses or catered to the needs of the households that were supported by the factories. Small grocers, gas stations, restaurants, and the like made up the remaining workforce in and around Gibsonburg. As you would guess, when all major parts of your economic engine suffer, everything else in the community suffers too as there is no money to be spent.

Hope

In 2005, the Gibsonburg boy's high school baseball team seemed to change the attitude of the entire town. This type of seismic change in thinking doesn't happen too many times in too many places in the world. For certain, though, it happened in Gibsonburg in 2005.

8

The People Of Gibsonburg

The Locals
Friday, March 11, 2005 – 7:30 am

It was 7:30 am in the Ideal Bakery. Gary Kathrens and Tim Mallett were sitting down to their morning coffee, just like they did every morning at this time. Like most of the regulars at the Ideal Bakery, the two men took their coffee black in an old white porcelain coffee mug.

Tim put down his cup and turned towards Gary. "I hear the boy's baseball team is getting ready to start practicin'."

The paper hid Gary's face. "That's what I hear, too."

"Maybe they'll go .500 this year," Tim said.

Gary pulled the paper down from his face and stared at Tim like he was delusional.

Henry

If you walked out of the front door of the Ideal Bakery and looked to the left down Route 600 one block, you'd see an old time car repair shop with two 12-foot high garage doors. The building used to be an old gas station and was made out of concrete, which was a common practice in the 1950's. The exterior of the garage had not been painted in at least 20 years. Now, it was a dingy and dirty white, with a black border, three-feet-wide, painted around the exterior top and running around the entire building. The garage had an indestructible look to it, like it could weather a head-on collision with a tornado. The garage doors always seemed to be open, and there was constant but not hurried activity taking place from 7 am to 8 pm every day from the lone mechanic in the garage.

There was a tired and faded wooden sign hung in the front center of the building right above the two garage doors. It read:

Henry's Car Repair
est. 1977

Henry Tillman was not only the local mechanic, but he was the town's premier high school sports fanatic. Henry graduated from Gibsonburg High School in 1976 and he actually played college baseball at Alabama. At Alabama, Henry once pitched against Eric Davis, who went on to star for the Cincinnati Reds. On the very first pitch, Henry challenged Davis with a fastball down the center of the plate. Davis promptly launched the ball 450 feet over the center-field fence.

When a small town boy goes to a big college, the transition is not always smooth. In the case of Henry Tillman, the transition was as bad as it could be. Henry actually held his own on the baseball field, but all of the other elements that go along with college did not suit him very well. A big issue was the school. Henry had the smarts to make it through, but he didn't have the passion or drive. The social aspects of a big college were actually harder for Henry to handle than the school. He didn't like parties. He never drank or smoked. He missed Gibsonburg. He missed the only place he had ever known and returned for good after his freshman year.

In terms of ethics and integrity, there wasn't a better man than Henry Tillman. For the line of work he was in, this was a characteristic that was hard to find in locations outside of Gibsonburg. It was as if his business was a little secret that everyone around town wanted to keep to themselves.

Just about every person in town would go to Henry to get work done on their vehicles, for Henry was great with cars. However, he was not the best with people. He was a man of few words. For those who did not know him, you would almost think he was rude. He had trouble making eye contact and was not very tactful at explaining things. He was very blunt and abrupt when working with customers. He had a way of making you feel bad because your car needed repairs. In an indirect way, he would scold you and make you feel as if it were your fault! There wasn't a car owner in Gibsonburg, though, that didn't mind paying the mental price of dealing with Henry to get their vehicle fixed properly and at a fair price.

Henry stood a solid 6 feet 2 inches tall and weighed 210 pounds. He stood rail straight, had a very muscular build, and was very fit. He had dark brown hair that he usually kept hidden under an old baseball cap. Henry's hairline was as solid as his build without even the slightest hint of male-pattern baldness creeping in. There was a little bit of gray just beginning to appear on his temples. Absent the gray, it looked as though Henry could still play for Alabama.

Henry was not married to any woman, but many joked that he was married to sports. Most small towns have a die-hard fan who attends everything, and in Gibsonburg, that fan was Henry Tillman.

On a normal day, Henry would work from 7 am until 8 pm. However, if there was a football game, basketball game, or baseball game, he would always close up in time to make it to them. Henry rarely missed a kick-off, tip-off, or a first pitch. Win or lose, close game or blow-out, Henry never left until the game was completely over.

If you ever needed to locate Henry Tillman, it was easy. You would either go to his garage or a Gibsonburg High School sporting event.

Kathy Colaner
Friday, March 11, 2005 – 1:30 pm

Gibsonburg was your typical high school in the Midwest. Just about every boy was wearing blue jeans, a T-shirt, and either work boots or tennis shoes. Baseball caps were common, but not allowed in school. The girls didn't wear the same things as the boys, for sure, but they were usually dressed in a similar manner if you compared them. Even though they were from a small town, they somehow got the money to dress in what they could get on their trips to the malls in nearby Toledo. Walking the halls, the girls were dressed remarkably similar in the clothes they bought on sale at Abercrombie or Aeropostale.

On this afternoon, there was much activity taking place at Gibsonburg High School.

Kathy Colaner sat in the lunchroom and looked at the number that appeared on her cell phone. It was Steve, her boyfriend. He was a freshman at the Ohio State University. With only ten minutes before the fifth period bell would ring, she stepped out to the sidewalk in front of the school to take the phone call.

Kathy answered her phone.

Steve's voice was loud. "Hey babe! What's up?"

"Why did you have to go so far away to college?"

"Hey, Ohio State isn't that far," he said.

"Yes, it is!" she wailed. "It's almost two hours away!"

"Don't worry, babe. I'll be home at Easter. Maybe I'll let you do a few of my English assignments to keep me close to your heart. Hey, gotta run. Later."

Abruptly the phone went dead. Kathy looked at her phone, surprised. He didn't even give her the chance to say good-bye!

Kathy Colaner grew up on a small horse farm just outside of Gibsonburg. She was 5 feet, 5 inches tall, weighed 105 pounds, had shoulder-length, sandy-blonde hair, and beautiful blue eyes. Growing up on a horse farm, she learned about the importance of hard work. In the third grade, Kathy was riding the bus to school when she lost the 20 dollars her mother had given her for school pictures. As the other students filed off of the bus, Kathy frantically looked for the money and started to get upset. After looking in and around her seat, the efforts to find the 20 dollars were unsuccessful. Her eyes welled up and she began to cry.

The last student on the bus was walking down the aisle and noticed that Kathy was upset. He asked what was wrong, and she told him about losing the picture money. Kathy recognized the boy from school. She thought he was in the other third grade class. The boy helped Kathy look for the money. But after a few minutes, they still could not find it.

The bus driver glared at her from the rearview mirror. "C'mon!" she yelled. "I gotta get goin' on my next route."

"Two more minutes," Kathy pleaded.

Bertha, the driver, snapped at her. "The meters tickin', girly."

She looked at the boy, afraid she'd never find the money.

"Retrace your steps," the boy said quickly.

"Well, on my way out of the house, my mother held the 20 dollars up to my face and told me it was for class pictures. She told me to be careful and to not lose it. She then took the money, folded it up tightly, and she stuffed it in my right front pocket. Right here."

Kathy patted the right front pocket that her mother put the money in.

The boy replied, "Check your pockets again."

Kathy frantically put her hands deep into every pocket she had.

The bus driver yelled out, "All right, that's it! Let's go!"

Kathy started to cry, looked at the ground and said to herself, "My mom's gonna kill me!"

The young boy pursed his lips. He looked on the floor to his left and right. He looked behind Kathy's seat, and he looked in front of Kathy's seat. He saw nothing. He looked around a little more when he spotted something on Kathy's jeans. He noticed a little sub-pocket, that was located *within* the pocket of Kathy's right jeans pocket. It was a decorative pocket that was so small that it didn't have much use at all.

The boy whispered to himself quietly, "Maybe?"

The boy looked at Kathy, looked at her pocket, looked back at Kathy and said, "May I?"

Still crying, Kathy nodded her head, "yes." He reached into the small pocket. At first, he felt nothing, but then, he slowly began to smile. He cautiously pulled out the 20 dollar bill, which was folded up into a half-inch square.

"I think your mother put it in that pocket because she thought it would be safer."

Kathy yelped. "Thank you!" She threw her arms around his neck and gave him a big hug. He blushed.

The bus driver snapped, "You two get off of my bus now, or I'm callin' the principal! And then you'll both be sorry!"

The two children, still smiling, looked at her, and then looked at each other. Kathy put her hand out and introduced herself. "I'm Kathy Colaner."

The boy shook Kathy's hand. "Nice to meet you Kathy. I'm Andy Gruner. You know, you should do what I do with anything of value. Stuff it deep into your back left pocket, and it will be safe there for sure."

Kathy nodded and then firmly placed the twenty dollars deep into the back left pocket of her jeans. "We better get off to school!"

As Kathy walked off of the bus, Andy stared at her. Even in the third grade, she was beautiful. Andy felt something in his heart that day, but he was not sure what it was exactly. All that mattered was that their encounter was the start of a beautiful friendship. They would go fishing and swimming at the White Star Quarry just outside of town. Andy would ride his bike out to Kathy's house, and they would ride ATV's all around her parent's 80 acres. Kathy would continually tease Andy about teaching him how to ride horses. Andy was always hesitant and Kathy kept after him. She told him one day she was going to teach him how to ride. Many times, Kathy would go up to the Ideal Bakery and just hang out while Andy worked.

As the years went by, their favorite past time was talking while he worked at the bakery. Nothing was off limits. Andy would usually take a break in his duties, and they would sit at their favorite table. Andy would serve Kathy her favorite treat—an Ideal Bakery éclair. Sometimes they'd talk for hours about school, parents, sports, friends, dreams, future plans, relationships, and old memories.

From the time they first met, Andy had a big crush on Kathy, but he never showed it, for fear of losing her friendship. He was too scared, too shy, or just did not know how to be more with Kathy. At least she was something to look forward to each and everyday.

Kathy, on the other hand, looked at Andy as a good friend and nothing more. Unbeknownst to Kathy, it bothered Andy when Kathy would talk with him about different boys she had crushes on. Although it bothered him, he never showed it.

Andy would always consult with Kathy and offer advice. In the back of his mind, he developed quite an inferiority complex. When Kathy used their friendship to discuss other guys, it simply confirmed what Andy thought: that Kathy's only interest in Andy was as a dear friend. Over time, Andy accepted this as a fact and he tried to be the best friend he could be to Kathy.

The Coach
Friday, March 11, 2005 – 2:00 pm

It was a Friday afternoon in the Ideal Bakery. Tim Mallett and Gary Kathrens were taking their afternoon coffee and reading the afternoon newspaper, which was just delivered.

Tim scanned the paper and stopped at something he saw at the bottom of the sports page. He looked at Gary, then back down at the paper. "Says here they hired a new baseball coach. Some guy named Rase."

Gary continued to look at his section of the paper, disinterested. "Uh huh."

Tim read the paper to Gary. "Young fella. Only 24 years old. Says he has never been a head coach before."

"Looks like we will be a lock to win state for the first time ever this year," Gary said sarcastically.

Tim raised an eyebrow. "Ya never know."

Gary dropped his paper down from his face and looked at Tim as though he was an idiot.

The sign outside of the office at the high school read:

Athletic Director
Jeff Stewart

Jeff Stewart had been the Athletic Director at Gibsonburg High School for three years. In 2004, he was also the boys' basketball and baseball coach. Basketball was Jeff's passion and Gibsonburg consistently turned out good basketball teams. As a favorite, basketball got preferential treatment—although unofficially, when it came to funds, resources, and equipment. In the Athletic Director's mind, baseball at Gibsonburg was something that was used to kill time until summer vacation started.

At the end of the 2004 season, Jeff decided to step down as the head baseball coach for Gibsonburg. He didn't see any baseball talent headed in his direction and didn't feel like coaching a losing team for the next several years.

When he decided to step down, he was conscious to bring in a new coach that would lose more games than Jeff would have lost. If a new coach would come in and do the unthinkable, like win half of their games, then it would make Jeff look like he was a bad coach.

Since Gibsonburg was usually subpar in baseball, it was easy for him to convince the school board to bring in a new coach with no experience. It would save money, and as Jeff explained to the school board, even if they did spend money on a great coach, the coach would still not win many games because of the current and future pool of baseball talent.

Jeff Stewart was preoccupied as Kyle Rase sat across from him in the chair on the other side of his desk. Jeff was putting in his votes for league basketball coach of the year. His strategy was to select coaches who nobody else was voting for. This would then increase his actual odds of winning the award.

"I know today is your first practice," Jeff said. "I just wanted to say we are real happy to have ya on board as the new head coach of the baseball team, Kyle."

"I'm excited as well," Kyle responded eagerly.

Jeff sighed. "Kyle, just so ya know, we don't expect much so don't put too much pressure on yourself. We are more of a basketball town. We've never done anything in baseball, and we would be happy just to win a few games."

"I'll do my best Mr. Stewart," Kyle replied.

For the first time, Jeff put his ballot down. He took off his reading glasses and looked across his desk at Kyle. He looked very bored and unsympathetic when he finally said, "I'm sure you will. Good luck."

Kyle Rase was born in Convoy, Ohio. He attended Crestview High School where he played football, basketball and baseball. During his junior and senior years, he started and excelled in basketball and baseball. During his senior year, his baseball team got beat in the regional semi-finals by Kalida and their legendary Coach McBride.

After high school graduation, he attended Bowling Green State University. He graduated on May 4, 2003 with a degree in elementary education. After graduation, he got a job teaching eighth grade science for Gibsonburg.

Although he played baseball his entire life, he had never done any real coaching, other than to help buddies with Little League.

Kyle Rase had a very athletic build. He was a fitness buff that liked to take good care of himself. He kept his brown hair cut short and was blessed with a youthful look which made him look much younger than what he really was.

It was hard to find much bad to say about Kyle Rase. Growing up in Convoy, Ohio, his parents did an exceptional job of raising a young man that was polite, courteous, truthful, and hard-working.

In the spring of 2005, at the age of 24, Kyle Rase was offered the opportunity to be the head boy's baseball coach for Gibsonburg High School. He wasn't seeking the job and was surprised when the Athletic Director called him to his office to offer him the position. Kyle loved baseball. He loved playing it while growing up. He loved watching baseball on television, and he knew he would enjoy coaching baseball. However, with not much of a coaching background, he felt that he might be in over his head coaching a high school team.

Jeff Stewart explained that they just needed someone to fill the role. As a former player, he gave Kyle confidence that he could do a job that would meet the expectations of the Gibsonburg community. Kyle said he needed a little time. Jeff countered with he needed an answer right away, or he had no choice but to go to the next guy.

After much pressure from Jeff, Kyle Rase took the job, feeling a little uneasy and full of self-doubt.

9

The First Practice
Friday, March 11, 2005 – 2:45 pm

The date was March 11, 2005, the first day of baseball practice for Gibsonburg. In normal conditions, practices would have started two weeks ago. However, practices were put off until March 11th because the basketball team had a great year and made it all the way to the regional semi-final game. Their last game was three days ago, and because many of the players were on the basketball team, the Athletic Director prohibited baseball from starting until basketball season was over.

On this particular day, the sky was a clear blue, the wind minimal, and the temperature was a gorgeous 72 degrees. In the open field surrounding the ball field, farmers were busy getting their acres of land ready for the planting .

As most of the players were warming up their arms in left field, a young student, glove in hand, hat on head, by the name of Derek Eddings walked up to examine the practice. He approached a young man observing the players warming up.

Eddings stood there for a moment. "You must be the new kid."

He watched the practice for a moment or two more, began to chuckle and said, "I heard this new coach is a real tool. What have you heard?"

"Not much."

He turned to him and extended his hand. "I'm Derek Eddings! What's your name?"

"Coach Rase!"

Shocked, Derek quickly looked at the ground. "Oh Shit," he muttered.

Coach Rase smiled because he wasn't offended at all. He patted Derek on the back. "Don't worry about it. Go out there and get your arm warmed up."

The coach observed as the players warmed up their arms. Beside him, his two assistant coaches, Jackson and Reiter, also stood and watched as the players threw to one another.

An unknown player approached the practicing players from the left field foul fence and peered over at the team playing catch. He stood there a moment, watching. The young man hopped the fence and began to walk toward the warm-up area in left field.

Andy Gruner immediately recognized the boy and jogged up to him. It was Bobby Graff.

"Hey Bobby! Decided to come out after all, huh?" Andy smiled.

"I thought I would give it a try."

Andy tapped him on the shoulder. "C'mon, I'll warm up with you."

Coach Rase blew his whistle and shouted out to the players. "All right fellas, everybody on me! At the dugout!"

All the players jogged over to the dugout and sat on the ground in front of the coaches. Behind the coaches the word GIBSONBURG was painted onto the backside of the white, orange, and black dugout. For an uncomfortable period of time, Coach Rase, practice fungo bat in hand, examined his team.

Finally, for the first time, Coach Rase addressed the players. "I'm your head coach, Kyle Rase. I like coaching baseball, and you're gonna like playing for me."

Derek Hetrick leaned to the player beside him, Derek Eddings and said, "He looks more like a player than coach."

Derek Eddings eyed the coach. "Tell me about it."

Coach Rase continued talking. "I have two rules. Rule number 1. You never give up. Ever. No matter what the circumstances. Rule number 2. Believe. You gotta believe. You gotta believe in yourself, and those around you at all times."

After some further examination of the team, Coach Rase released them. "All right, that's it. Let's go take some batting practice. Let's go! Hustle!"

As Coach Reiter threw batting practice, Coach Rase and Coach Jackson stood in front of the third base dugout and observed. Amazingly, the team looked even worse than what Jeff Stewart described. Many of the players couldn't even make solid contact with the lobbed balls thrown by Coach Reiter. When the players did make contact, the players in the field couldn't catch a ball or make a decent throw.

Cody Fisher, a freshman, came up to the plate while senior scrub, Jeff Feasel, warmed up in front of the first base dugout. For a freshman, Cody Fisher hit the ball well.

While Cody continued with his swings at the plate, Coach Rase asked Coach Jackson, "Well, you know the players better than me. How do you think we'll do this season?"

Right after Coach Rase asked Coach Jackson the question, Cody Fisher swung and pulled a hard line drive foul that drilled Jeff Feasel, right in the balls. The impact sent Jeff right to the ground like a sack of potatoes. Jeff squirmed around on the ground in pain.

Coach Jackson repeated Coach Rase's question back to him, "How will we do this season?"

Coach Jackson turned to look at Coach Rase and said, "You a religious man, Coach?"

Coach Rase responded, "A little bit, why?"

As Coach Jackson started to jog and assist Jeff Feasel he turned around and said, "Well . . . I'd pray."

Upon hearing his comment, Coach Reiter, on the pitchers mound, started to laugh. Upon looking at Coach Reiter, Coach Rase began to chuckle too.

10

The Rest Of The Team
Friday Afternoon, March 25, 2005

Cody Fisher and Bobby Graff

Cody Fisher and Bobby Graff were both smart kids. Cody grew up in Gibsonburg his whole life. Bobby moved to Gibsonburg in the fall from Indiana, and he was really struggling with the whole transition.

After completing the practice ACT exam, Bobby and Cody headed down the school hallway, relieved it was over.

"Bobby," Cody began. "You got a 35 on the ACT, why practice and take it again? I took the practice exam and got a 30. If I got that for real, I would never put myself through that torture again."

Bobby shrugged. "I don't know. I just thought I could do a little better."

Third baseman. Cody Fisher.

Second baseman. Bobby Graff.

Derek Hetrick and Derek Eddings
Friday Evening - March 25, 2005

Derek Hetrick and Derek Eddings were both good kids, but just a little mischievous. They were often referred to as "D squared" because they hung out together so much (and because their first names were the same, of course).

It was a crisp spring evening with a temperature of 46 degrees. Hetrick and Eddings were driving Hetrick's old Chevy Impala westward, down Wooster Street in Bowling Green. Bowling Green was about 14 miles to the west of Gibsonburg and it was a place to visit when you wanted a break from the small town. To their right was a 12-foot-wide sidewalk that ran the entire length of Wooster Street until you got downtown. This sidewalk was the main thoroughfare that the college students used to walk to and from the bars on campus.

Hetrick watched the throng of students on the crowded sidewalk. "Awesome. B.G.S.U. on a Friday night."

"Each babe has at least a mile to walk to their dorm room after they leave the bars," Eddings replied.

On this particular Friday evening the sidewalk was busier than normal. This was the first warm day in a while, which prompted more students than normal to head out to the bars.

Hetrick laughed. "Yup. We need to work on our outfield arms, and the ladies need to get rid of that stinky bar smell."

Eddings slowed the car to a stop next to three girls who were clearly drunk, and stumbling as they walked down the sidewalk. Hetrick stuck his head out the passenger side window and shouted, "Would you ladies like a lift back to your dorm?"

One of the girls who was holding up her drunk friend, shot them a glance. "That would be great."

The third girl sighed with relief. "Oh yeah! You are our heroes!

We have to walk another mile yet."

As they stumbled toward the passenger door at the rear of the car, Hetrick and Eddings got out and placed a cardboard box on the ground between themselves and the girls. The girls, surprised, stopped in their tracks.

"What are you doing?" one of them said.

Eddings and Hetrick grinned, then reached into the box, and began pelting them with water balloons. They went through two dozen in a matter of seconds.

The stunned girls began screaming. The screams continued even after the last water balloon was thrown and the boys jumped in their car and sped off.

They laughed hysterically as they continued to drive, taking great pleasure as they recounted the sheer disbelief that registered on each girl's face. Eddings was laughing so hard that Hetrick had to reach over and grab the wheel so they didn't wreck. As he straightened out the car, he noticed a lone drunk girl stumbling along with a little flower.

Hetrick glanced at the floorboard. He whooped out loud when he spotted one remaining water balloon rolling around.

The girl was peeling petals off the flower one at a time. As she tossed each petal aside, she chanted the same two questions over and over: "Should I dump his worthless ass? Should I abuse him some more? Should I dump his worthless ass? Should I abuse him some more? Should I dump his worthless ass? Should I . . ."

Hetrick picked up the water balloon from the floorboard. "Bimbo at 2 o'clock," he said, his voice now sounding like a radio announcer. "Line shot hit to Hetrick in right field. The runner on third is tagging. He is going for home. Hetrick throws to home plate..."

The girl never saw them coming as she continued to mumble to herself. "dump his worthless . . ."

Eddings swerved toward the curb by the sidewalk where the lone girl was walking.

Hetrick threw the water balloon and struck the girl right in the top third of her forehead soaking her entire head. She screamed. Frantic, she looked around and spotted Eddings and Hetrick in the car laughing like hyenas. As the car took off, she heard them laughing as one of them yelled, "OUT! OUT at home! What an arm by Hetrick!

She glared at them. "I will abuse him some more!" She slammed the remains of the flower on the ground and stomped away in disgust.

Third baseman. Derek Eddings.

Right fielder. Derek Hetrick.

Thom Brinker
Friday Evening – March 25, 2005

Thom Brinker was a farm boy whose family had raised hogs in the area for more than 60 years.

Thom pulled open a rickety gate and hurried into the hog barn. Immune to the smell of pig manure, he raced to the very back corner of the hog pen as the 70 pigs in the pen grunted. Together, the rich baritones sounded as if they had an audience and were belting out a concert to the other livestock on the farm.

When Thom got to the corner of the pen he found a large sow, Kristen, on her side and ready to give birth. As the sow sent out low deliberate grunts, Thom knelt down at the business end of Kristen and examined the situation. To his surprise, a mucus covered nose appeared, and with one push, a tiny piglet popped right out. Thom caught the piglet with both hands and gently placed it on the ground to his right. Another piglet popped out and Thom repeated the procedure.

Thom looked like a catcher during the home run derby at the Major League All-Star game. The catchers in the home run derby discard the pitches the hitters do not want, and throw them to the right side of the plate. After eight piglets were caught and gently placed in a heap, he cleaned them up and put them on Kristen's teat to get their first meal in the real world. Thom looked at the cute little piglets chowing down as the mother watched over them. Thom Brinker said a silent prayer to God, thanking him for all that he had. A dirty sow pen, covered in mud, and the beauty of new life.

Catcher. Thom Brinker.

The Scrubs (Also Known As Scrub Nation): Josh Sanchez, Jeff Feasel, Trent Snowden, Greg Reynolds Friday Evening – March 25, 2005

Four nerdy looking kids were playing video games in Josh Sanchez's basement. They were yelling at each other and rubbing it in when they got the best of their opponent. Pretty much all of the four scrubs went out for the baseball team for one reason. Their parents told them they would take away their video games if they didn't get outside and join some sort of activity.

The scrubs affectionately named themselves *Scrub Nation*.

Sitting out: Josh Sanchez, Jeff Feasel, Trent Snowden, and Greg Reynolds.

11

A Party At Wes Milleson's Place
Late Friday Evening / Early Saturday Morning,
March 25, 2005

In 2005, Wes Milleson had the best party house of anyone around. His family had a modest ranch-style home with a two-car garage. The ranch sat on Cloverdale Road and faced west. The other three sides of Milleson's three acres were surrounded by farmland that stretched far out into the horizon.

Behind the house, he had a large yard that was always nicely mowed. There were plenty of mature maple trees, fir trees, and even a half-acre sized clean and crystal clear pond that had a 40-foot dock. The dock was the focal point of the pond. It was used for sunbathing and was generally the jumping off point whenever a quick cool down was needed during the hot Ohio summer months. In fact, the pond was well-used in the summertime. Along with the dock, the area surrounding the pond was equipped with a firepit, multiple picnic tables, and a grassy area where many of Wes's friends lounged away the summer. They swam, played Frisbee, played football, drove four wheelers, and made memories that would last a lifetime.

At the back southeast corner of the property stood a large yellow barn. It housed all of the tractors and equipment his family used to farm their 2,000 acres.

A big pole barn straddled the northeast corner. It was 50 feet by 25 feet long, and was formally used to house mowers, ATVs, and a small fishing boat before their larger barn was built on the southeast corner of the property. The room had 20-foot ceilings, and on the west side, or front of the building, there were two ways to enter. There was a regular door and a 15-foot by 12-foot garage door. When the Milleson's used to store riding mowers, the boat, and ATV's, they would drive them right into the building through the open garage door.

When the big barn was completed, Wes's dad gave him the go ahead to do whatever he wanted to do with the inside. When Wes was finished, it contained a foosball table, ping-pong table (which also worked great as a beer pong table), two old-school pinball machines, and poker table. His father even helped him put in a small kitchen and bathroom. The floor was covered with a miss-matched group of carpet pieces that he got for free at Veh & Sons Furniture on Madison Street in downtown Gibsonburg. The walls were covered with all kinds of things that any high school kid would have loved to have in their own rooms. There were pictures, beer signs, school pennants, posters, and an eclectic number of fixtures that Wes had found lying around the farm. Things like riding spurs, wagon wheels, an old saddle, and a stuffed deer head from a deer he had killed and mounted when he was 14.

In nice weather, Wes would open that garage door to the open air. At dusk, you could be in the room, look out the garage door, and watch some of the most beautiful sunsets you have ever seen over the open fields. Everyone had fond memories of the many sunsets they viewed while attending the parties at Wes's.

After hanging out all day at the pond, standard protocol was to proceed to the barn at dusk to cook out, eat, talk, play games, sit by the firepit, and yes, sometimes illegally drink beer and alcohol that somebody would sneak over. Although there was sometimes alcohol, it was never excessive and there were never really any problems. Most of the kids were cool, and if they weren't, well, they usually didn't get invited back.

If you were a teenager around Gibsonburg in 2005, Wes Milleson's place was Utopia.

On more than one occasion, at the firepit after a few hours of drinking and contemplating life, some of the self-proclaimed philosophers would talk about what happens after you die. Many times they would discuss that if heaven was like Wes Milleson's place, that would be pretty cool.

Although Andy, Alex, Wyatt and Wes enjoyed the parties more than anyone, they really didn't drink alcohol. They were kids at heart and liked to have fun and screw around. This was especially hard for everyone to believe because of Wes's antics. He was truly the crazy one in the group. His friends would ask him, "Dude, what are you *on* to make you do the things you do?"

Wes's response was always the same, "I'm just high on life, man."

It was approaching midnight on Friday evening and the team had a baseball game scheduled for the next day at 1 pm. The Milleson place was hopping with activity. The light splashed out of the open garage door to the dark outside while much activity was taking place inside.

The four players that never played—Josh Sanchez, Jeff Feasel, Trent Snowden, and Greg Reynolds—were well-liked and affectionately referred to as *Scrub Nation*. They were all playing a friendly game of foosball. A few other kids were playing beer pong, some boys were playing pinball, and a bunch of girls were checking out some of the facebook pages of boys they thought were cute. In the grassy area between the pond and the barn Andy, Alex, Wes, Wyatt, and Thom were hanging around a picnic table talking.

"What's this new coach all about?" Wyatt asked no one in particular.

"Dunno," Wes said. "But we have to break him in right, though."

"That's right!" Alex added. "This is his first head coaching job. Probably the best talent they could get for us."

Andy snickered. "As Vince Vaughn says, *If you don't set high goals, you will never be too disappointed.* That should be our motto this year."

Wes nodded in agreement. "Hey, let's at least have some fun then, right?"

Wyatt grinned and said to Wes, "Sounds good *biggs*."

He continued to the rest of the group, "Who's up for a nice game of cards?"

Andy took the challenge. He hopped toward the barn, did a front flip and stumbled upright on his feet like a gymnast before turning around to smile smugly at them. "I'll take your money. Let's get after it."

They laughed and followed him into the barn.

They walked in like they all owned the place. Weaving through the crowd, Andy spotted Kathy Colaner texting. He waved at her. "Hey Kathy."

She looked up, waved, and smiled as he passed. The boys continued their trek to the back corner of the room to settle in at the poker table.

Kathy texted her boyfriend. "miss u. wish you were here – luv Kathy <3"

Steve texted back, "Lonely and missing u – luv Steve"

Kathy smiled as she read Steve's text and thought, "How sad that he is all by himself."

Steve's Dorm Room – The Ohio State University

Steve snickered as he texted back his girlfriend. "What a ditzy girl," he thought. What she didn't know was that while Steve was texting, he was on top of another girl in a dorm room at Ohio State. While on top of the girl, his elbows were resting on either side of her head as he was texting and smiling like a sly fox.

As Steve chuckled at his deceptive text, the girl that was with him snapped at him "Hey, what about me?"

He looked down at her, as she was underneath him and told her to, "shut up," then took his time to re-adjust and get back to business.

Steve Dunn was Kathy's boyfriend. He was 5 feet, 8 inches tall, weighed 170 pounds, had a stocky build, and wore his dirty blond hair short. Steve graduated from Gibsonburg a year earlier, in 2004, and was now a freshman at *the* Ohio State University in Columbus, Ohio.

At Gibsonburg, he was not a bad athlete, but got kicked off of both the football team and basketball team because he got caught sneaking alcohol onto the team bus—twice. It was probably just as well. He needed time to bring up his 1.70 grade point average. There wasn't a person that knew the two of them that could make sense of what Kathy saw in Steve. For some reason, nobody could ascertain why they had been dating for a year. Kathy was pretty, sweet, hard-working, courteous, smart, and had a heart of gold. Steve was a jerk in everyone's opinion. He was loud, lazy, cocky, and obnoxious.

Steve's parents owned a car dealership in Maumee, Ohio. He was never without a new car that was given to him by his parents and never worked, which left him much free time to get into trouble.

In four years at Gibsonburg, Steve had quite the resume. He was caught spray painting *Steve Rules* on the Gibsonburg water tower. He was banned from Kirwen's grocery store after he was caught shoplifting for the third time, and he was the only person ever banned from the Ideal Bakery. He spray painted obscene pictures on the brick wall outside of the bakery, with the caption, "You'll love our cream filled sticks." In his senior year, he had wrecked two of his dad's brand new cars. Now, most kids do a few things that they shouldn't when growing up. Steve did a lot of bad things, and for some reason, he seemed to get caught most of the time!

Everybody in Gibsonburg was surprised when Steve got into Ohio State in the first place. Some felt that his dad's gift of cars to the university had something to do with it, although there was never any real proof.

Steve took Kathy, who was a junior at the time, to his senior prom and tried to spike the punch. After many unsuccessful attempts, he went to the bathroom and chugged the 16-ounce flask of cheap Vodka. He told Kathy he wasn't feeling well and they left the prom early. In the car, Steve threw up all over Kathy's new prom dress, and her dad's car. They had to take Kathy's car because Steve had wrecked his car the day prior. Kathy fell for his story about getting food poisoning at the prom.

A Poker Game

Andy pulled his attention away from Kathy, sat down, and began shuffling the cards. He looked up at Wes "Did you invite Bobby and Cody?"

"Sure did," Wes replied. "Said they both had to study though."

Andy smiled. "Shoot, we'll probably all be working for them someday."

His mobile phone vibrated. He pulled it out of his pocket and laughed when he saw the picture text he'd received. "Hey, check this out. I just got a picture from *D squared*." He showed it Wes.

Thom Brinker looked at Wes, puzzled. *"D Squared*?"

"Yeah *D squared*," Wes explained. That's Derek and Derek." Wes passed the phone to Thom.

Thom looked at the picture and grimaced. "That's not too cool in my book."

Andy nodded. "They just toilet papered the new coach's house . What a couple of morons."

Wes got up out of his chair and climbed to the top of the refrigerator, which was easy to do with the 20-foot high ceiling. Most attendees had seen this before and they knew the routine. They started chanting, "Parcor! Parcor! Parcor!"

Wes Milleson jumped off of the refrigerator, did a forward flip while his long flaming red hair followed the flow of his body like the tail on Haley's Comet. His back came crushing down on the top center of the food table breaking the eight-foot folding table in half. His landing was like an explosion, which sent chips, pretzels, and crackers all over the room. He popped up, unhurt, while everyone at the party started to go crazy. He then screamed, "PARCOR!"

Wes sat down, breathing hard and Wyatt told him, "Nice parcor, dude," and gave Wes a high-five. This move turned the get-together into a full-blown lather and transformed the party into another dimension, from party to memorable event and Wes knew it.

Thom Brinker stared at him. "Parcor?"

Wyatt chuckled. "You need to stop workin' so much and get out more Brink. Yeah, parcor! Parcor is an incredible move, usually from a high place, where you break something."

Thom nodded. "Nice."

Andy began shuffling the cards when Thom got up, stood on his chair, and *parcored* a cheap coffee table nearby into smithereens, sending all of the contents on the coffee table throughout the room.

The crowd stared at Thom when he got up, and all was quiet.

Thom looked at everyone and said, "Like that?" and the entire room broke out into frenzy.

In unison, everyone at the party screamed, "PARCOR!" Thom took his place back at the poker table while Andy, Alex, Wyatt, and Wes continued to laugh.

After thoroughly shuffling the cards, Andy passed the deck to Alex Black to deal a hand of five-card draw.

Alex told the four poker players, "Ante up boys, a dollar each." All the boys threw a dollar into the middle of the table.

"You know what bugs me?" Alex asked the group as he dealt out the cards. "We have so much pressure and nobody gets it. This guy comes in the bakery. He's got an unbelievable FUPA. It's like he's gonna have a baby any minute. You know, the type you could rest a cup of coffee on."

Wes laughed hard and replied, "Yeah, I know the type, my man."

Andy picked up the cards Alex was dealing and continued, "He looks at me and says. Man, you're young. You're strong. You have a great future ahead of you. Enjoy this while you can. You shouldn't have anything to complain or worry about."

As Alex finished dealing the fifth and final card to each player for the five card draw game, while still looking down at the table, he said, "He doesn't get it does he?"

Andy looked at Alex, looked at his cards, and then interrupted Alex's comment to say, "By the way, I bet one dollar."

Alex announced, "Call."

Wes announced, "Call."

Wyatt announced, "Call."

Thom announced, "Too rich for me. I'm out."

Andy looked to Alex and asked, "What's that you were sayin' Alex?"

Alex responded, "The man. FUPA man. He doesn't get it does he?"

Andy goes on, "Nope. Adults these days have no idea of what we go through. Some kid commits suicide, and they say, *How could they?* They had their whole life in front of them."

Alex responded, "I know! Being in high school these days is a bitch. How many cards, boys?"

The players tossed their discards to Alex. Alex then began to deal out their replacement cards by saying, "Wes takes three, Wyatt takes one, Gruner takes two. And three for the stud," as Alex dealt three cards to himself.

As the boys continued with the card game, the party rolled on like a wildfire out of control. Wes continued to look around, but at this point it looked like a bunch of harmless fun. The beer pong game was in full swing as the others played foosball, pinball, and watched TV. Two boys entered the party with two cases of Natty Light, and a dozen of the kids were outside at the firepit talking.

Def Leppard's "Pour Some Sugar On Me" was blaring out of the speakers when all of a sudden, the music went silent. Thom Brinker stood up, looked around, and then focused on scrub Jeff Feasel. Jeff had accidentally jerked the cord out of the wall with his foot as he stumbled by. Thom screamed, "Turn that back on!" Everyone at the party stared at Jeff. He plugged the power cord back in, and the music resumed, Thom smiled and pointed at Jeff. In turn, Jeff pointed back at Thom and smiled back.

Jeff, kind of drunk, yelled at Tom, "Yeah, baby!"

Jeff started dancing around to the music while Thom laughed.

Andy continued on with his story, "Ya know, and another thing. If I don't get an 85 percent on my Calc final, I go to summer school. I owe my dad $1,200, which will take me seven months to get, for sideswiping a car with the delivery truck. My ACT score sucks, so it looks like I have no chance at getting into Ohio State. And then, this class president stuff has everyone, teachers and students, thinking I am the man on the mountain with the answers to everything."

After venting to his friends, Andy was clearly upset. He just shook his head, looked up at the ceiling and then looked back down to examine his cards. After looking at his poker hand, he got a surprised look on his face, smiled and said, "By the way, I bet five bucks, the max bet."

All of the other players folded, when Alex asked him, "Whaddya have top gun?"

Andy laid his cards down and announced, "Royal Flush!" He started to rake the chips in with both of his hands and said, "Come to papa."

Wes, chuckling, teased Andy for letting on that he had such a good hand by saying, "Nice nine dollar pot Andy." Wes knew Andy could have gotten a lot more money if he disguised his hand a little better.

Wyatt followed, "You sure seem to get the lucky breaks, Andy-man."

Alex, sitting to Andy's left, slid his body over to Andy. He gestured his shoulder in Kathy Colaner's direction and kind of whispered, "You're on a roll buddy, might be time to ask Kathy out." Alex nodded to Kathy, who was 30 feet away.

Kathy was standing by herself trying to text Steve who wouldn't respond. She said to herself, "Why won't he answer my texts?"

Unbeknownst to Kathy, Steve picked up his phone every time Kathy texted him and chuckled at her messages. He was still in bed with the girl he was with earlier.

Andy responded to Alex, "She's got a boyfriend."

Alex snapped back, "You kiddin' me? Steve? He's such a douche-bag."

At Alex's comment, many thoughts hit Andy at once. He thought about how he and Kathy would never be together. He worried about college, money, about graduating, and the thought that bothered him the most, however, was the conversation he overhead about losing the Ideal Bakery.

In contrast to the festive and loud party, Andy got a solemn look on his face. He forced a little smile, and quietly announced, "Hey, I gotta get up early tomorrow. I'm outta' here. See you guys at the game."

As Andy walked from the barn to his truck he found himself all alone. He stopped and looked up at the sky. It was a clear night and the sky was filled with stars. As he looked up at dark star-sprinkled sky, he replayed the words Coach Rase told them after the first practice, "You gotta believe. You gotta believe in yourself and those around you at all times."

While still gazing upward, Andy said to himself, "Easy for you to say, coach."

He walked to his truck, opened the door and sat down in the driver's seat. Andy was staring straight ahead contemplating his life and trying to search for something positive. Deep in thought, he was startled and jumped a little as someone knocked on his passenger side window. He looked over and saw Alex Black with that big white smile on his face, looking in the window. Andy couldn't help but smile when he saw Alex. Alex hopped in the truck.

"Leavin' a little early, chief," said Alex.

Andy looked straight ahead, clearly bothered. There was a pause.

He finally responded, "Just a lot on my mind."

"Lay it on me bro'. I can tell you haven't been yourself lately," replied Alex continuing to smile in an effort to cheer up his friend.

Andy told Alex, "Don't worry man, I'm fine."

Alex pressed, "C'mon Andyman. What's up?"

Andy responded to Alex's full court press by saying, "It's a lot of things. All the stuff I was talking about at the poker table and then . . ."

Andy stopped himself in mid-sentence and looked forward into space with a worried look on his face.

Alex, acting very concerned about his friend, continued to push him, "What Andy? What is it?"

Andy almost began to tell Alex what was bothering him. He then stopped himself and said, "Aw. Just . . . Just forget it."

Alex responded, "Andy, I'm your boy. Maybe I can help!"

Andy stared straight ahead and was deep in thought. He waited several seconds and then explained, "Please don't tell anyone, 'cause it's kind of embarrassing. Well, I was listening to my mom and dad and you know the bakery. It has been in our family for like over 80 years."

Alex was at full attention and said, "Keep goin'."

Andy continued, "Even after paying $100,000 in back taxes and debt, we owe creditors and the IRS over $89,000. It's money we don't have and mom and dad have been fighting them off for over eight months."

Alex raised his eyebrows. After listening to the story about the bakery, he got very serious and told his friend, "Man, I had no idea."

Andy looked at Alex and told him, "Keep it hush, hush for now, but we are closing up at the end of May. We will have to sell our house and move in with my mom's sister."

Alex shook his head. "Shit!" he whispered.

In a quiet tone, Andy told Alex, "Owning your own family business one day to living with your aunt's family and being unemployed the next. How's that for depressing?"

Andy looked down at the steering wheel and clenched his jaw. "Hey, keep this quiet."

Alex punched him lightly in the arm. "Hey, you don't have to worry about me. It's the people I tell you gotta worry about."

They both laughed at Alex's little joke.

Andy changed the subject. "Hey, remember when we were little kids, and we would all pile into my dad's '71 red Chevelle? We would just scream down those country roads."

Alex smiled, remembering. "Yeah, that was a blast. We didn't have too many worries back then. But didn't your dad just sell that Chevelle to the mechanic that works in town?"

Andy's smile disappeared. "Yeah. Henry Tillman. Now I know why dad sold it."

"Yeah, I see what you mean, said Alex, searching for the right words to say. "But cheer up buddy. Things always have a way of workin' out. I don't know how, but they will. If nothing else, it'll put a smile on your face when I give a pitching clinic at the game tomorrow."

Andy forced a small grin. "Thanks, man."

"Hey, I gotta run. Still a little money left for me to take at the poker table," Alex told Andy, as they bumped fists.

Alex touched the door handle. "Later, man. See you at the game tomorrow." He opened the passenger side door of the truck and left.

12

The 6 And 17 Season
March 17 thru April 22, 2005

The Gibsonburg boy's high school baseball team started the 2005 regular season by winning their first three games. On the bus after the third win, Coach Rase stood up to address the team. "All right fellas. We are 3 and 0 after today's win."

Everyone on the bus applauded.

Coach Rase turned to the bus driver. "Jim, let's stop by the McDonalds up the road to celebrate."

This announcement led to shouting and vigorous applause.

What Coach Rase could not have guessed was that those few minutes on the bus after their third game would be the only highlight of their 2005 regular season.

As the season progressed, they were regularly thumped by every team they played. Their pitchers could not find the strike zone, their hitters could not hit much more than a foul ball, and they led the league in errors. It was almost like they were allergic to catching a baseball. Gibsonburg led the league in strikeouts, and they had the lowest team batting average as well.

Throughout the dismal season, Coach Rase was adamant about only playing the same nine guys in every game. When someone other than Alex Black pitched, he just moved Alex Black to that position. The four scrubs on the bench were much worse than the other nine players and Coach Rase was a winner. He wanted to do everything he could to give his team a chance to win in every game. Getting the scrubs better would not translate into wins. He had to get his starters to perform better.

Josh Sanchez

With eight games left in the regular season, the team was taking time for batting practice in the cage out by the field. Andy Gruner and Wes Milleson observed as Josh Sanchez practiced his swing inside the cage.

Wes Milleson shot Andy a look. "Man, I feel bad for Sanchez. Eight games left and he hasn't played an inning all year."

Andy kept his eye on Sanchez. "Yeah, but he still keeps working hard."

Josh was a frail-looking boy with a thick mop of dark hair. He was something of a computer geek.

Josh considered his video game collection and his ability to beat every competitor at Casualties of War as one of greatest accomplishments. A straight "A" student with a quirky sense of humor, Josh was a favorite among teachers. He claimed that drinking water gave him a headache and he lived on sugar and fast food. It was hard to find him without a candy bar or some other sort of sugary treat in his hand. He was a night owl and would play his video games until 3 or 4 in the morning, every night of the week. It was common for his parents to march in his room and physically jerk him out of bed to get to school.

He had a sweet mother, but when Josh needed a fire lit under his butt, she wasn't above threatening him to get him moving. However, she usually wouldn't follow through on her threats to get Josh motivated. It was sometimes hard for her to punish Josh because for all the time he spent on video games, as he was still able to perform extremely well in school.

Similar to the rest of the scrubs, Josh's parents gave him an ultimatum. He had to go out for a school activity or get a job. They were tired of him sitting in the basement all day, every day, on the computer or playing video games. Josh wasn't a huge sports fan, but he thought baseball would be the way to go. With his build he would get killed on the football field. He didn't like to exercise much, and he thought basketball and track would involve too much running. He also had a strategy. He thought his parents might forget about making him participate in a school activity, and he could finish his junior year without participating because baseball was one of the last activities of the school year. He knew the team was terrible and would have a short post season anyway.

After trying out for the team, Josh discovered that his parents were right. It was nice to get outside during the spring after a long winter. He made some close friends with the other players on the team and kind of liked how everyone referred to the four scrubs as *Scrub Nation.*

Fremont St. Joe

During the regular season Gibsonburg had to play Fremont St. Joe twice. Fremont St. Joe and their star pitcher, Tyler Pinkus, had a reputation as Gibsonburg's longtime nemesis.

Tyler Pinkus was a man among boys. He was first team All-State as a sophomore, junior, and most likely would be as senior. He was as dominating a pitcher as there ever was in Ohio high school baseball. He created nightmares for every member of the Gibsonburg team since T-ball. He threw very hard, was somewhat wild, and had easily beaten Gibsonburg every single time he faced them. Prior to the season beginning, Tyler Pinkus signed a letter of intent to pitch for Division I Eastern Michigan.

As much as everyone feared Tyler Pinkus, it was his mother that caused real problems for Gibsonburg and every other team they faced. She did not discriminate. She yelled at umpires, opposing players, opposing coaches, her own son's coach, parents of Tyler's teammates, and her own family.

Tyler Pinkus' mother stood 5 feet, 2 inches tall, weighed 120 pounds, had flaming red hair, and had two levels of talking: loud and louder. She never missed attending her son's games and she looked liked the ultimate St. Joe fan decked out in crimson, white and gray. Every piece of jewelry had St. Joe insignia on it, and she was never without her throne, a decked out crimson fold up chair. Her throne was complete with baseball trinkets, crimson ribbons, and picture buttons of Tyler from three years old to his senior year.

At each game she sat in the exact same spot. She claimed the area close to the fence right by the on deck circle on the first base side of the field.

A typical game day for Tyler Pinkus' mother would include:

Pre-Game: Bragging to anyone that would listen about the greatness of her son.

1st Inning: Yelling at the St. Joe Coach for not batting Tyler in the proper place in the lineup.

2nd Inning: Confronting the parents of other St. Joe players about the poor play of their children, which in her mind made Tyler look bad.

3rd Inning: Yelling at the pitcher on the other team for intentionally walking, and not pitching to Tyler, when he was up to bat.

4th Inning: Berating the umpires, even if they did not deserve it.

5th Inning: Accusing the opposing team of cheating.

6th Inning: Yelling at Tyler to hit the batter on the other team.

7th Inning: Screaming at her husband for not putting enough mustard on her hot dog.

Post Game: Pointing her finger at Tyler and criticizing him if failed to get more than 12 strike outs in a game.

Tyler Pinkus' mother had quite a reputation at the baseball diamonds in and around Sandusky County. Frankly, it was well deserved. You never had to see her. As long as you were within 200 yards, you could hear her.

During the 2005 regular season, St. Joe beat Gibsonburg by a score of 10-0, and by 16-4. Both games ended after the 5th inning because Gibsonburg was losing by more than ten runs. They called this the *mercy rule*.

Bo Smith Returns

Alex and Andy were in the field during a home game against Oak Harbor. And wouldn't you know it? Their old friend Bo Smith was up to bat. Bo hit a high foul ball that went out of the field of play and landed in the parking lot about a foot from Andy's truck and bounced about ten feet in the air.

Alex walked from the pitcher's mound to Andy at shortstop and asked him, "Whoa, was that your truck Bo almost hit?"

Andy glanced at the parking lot. "Yep."

Alex smiled. "Andy, you sure get some good breaks."

As Alex headed back to the pitcher's mound Andy spit on the field. "You have no idea how wrong you are," he muttered to himself.

Only Nine Guys

After the thirteen losses in a row, Coach Jackson approached Coach Rase on the bus ride home. "Coach Rase, we have lost 13 games in a row! You still think we should keep playing the same nine guys?"

Coach Rase gave him a withering look and he knew never to ask that question again.

Who Cares?

During the 22nd game of the season, Oak Harbor beat Gibsonburg by 14 runs and the team was dejectedly riding the bus home. Two of the scrubs who had yet to see any play all year, Jeff Feasel and Trent Snowden, were sitting in the last seat of the bus playing their handheld video games. As the rest of the team looked as though they were in a funeral procession, Greg and Trent were all smiles. They never played and really didn't care if they won or lost. Greg playfully nudged Trent in the ribs, which caused Trent to look at him. Greg mouthed the word, "McDonalds," and they both started laughing as quietly as they could. Their trip to McDonalds after game three was the only time of the 2005 season they would see the golden arches.

As they rumbled down Route 6 back to the high school, a carload of college-aged girls, were following behind the bus and getting ready to pass. Trent looked back, nudged Greg and said, "Let's do it. Get Feasel and Sanchez too."

Greg and Trent both looked to make sure nobody in the front of the bus was looking toward the back. The four scrubs positioned themselves in the last four seats of the bus on the driver's side. When the carload of girls started to pass the bus, all four of the scrubs pulled their baseball pants, jocks and everything else down, and pushed their bare bottoms against the glass windows of the bus. As the carload of girls passed they looked up and to their right to see four windows, each filled with a naked behind. Each bottom that was pushed against the glass looked just like a pressed ham. The entire carload of girls started laughing.

Wes Milleson nudged Andy Gruner and they both looked back to see what was going on. Pretty soon, the rest of the team was watching and just before Coach Rase turned around, the boys took their bare bottoms off the glass and pulled their pants up, leaving a sweaty imprint on each bus window.

The carload of girls continued to pass the Gibsonburg bus, honking their horn, laughing, yelling out the window, and swerving all over the road after it got by the bus. Coach Rase, with a puzzled look on his face looked at the carload of girls passing the bus, and looked back at the bus to see all four of the scrubs laughing and giving each other high fives.

As the bus continued to roll down Route 6, all four scrubs were now in a punchy type of mood. Jeff Feasel took his cleats off, looked at them and said, "These things suck, I'm gonna get new ones." He then threw both shoes out the open bus window."

The other three scrubs looked at each other, looked at Jeff, and all four of the scrubs broke out into laughter. Greg looked at Jeff and said, "You're an idiot!" and for some reason, this made all four of the boys laugh harder.

Coach Rase, still upset about the season and losing to Oak Harbor, heard the commotion. He looked back and got ready to stand up and tell the *Scrub Nation* to settle down. However, weeks of losing had taken their toll on him. The tired coach turned back around in his seat, dejected. He mumbled to himself, "Who cares? Who really cares?"

The Last Game Of The Season
Friday, April 22, 2005

Gibsonburg lost the last game of the season by a score of 17-0 to Woodmore on April 22, 2005. Coach Rase actually had to bench Alex Black in the last game for a bad attitude. Jeff Feasel got to start in his place. It was the only time Jeff played all year.

Behind the home dugout, Coach Rase scowled at the team. "We frickin' just lost 17 to 0. I'll tell you what, no more practices between now and our first tournament game. We're all just a little spent. Bus leaves at 3 pm on Friday for our first sectional game against Bettsville. Don't be late."

Coach Rase walked away from the rest of the team. Everyone else sat on the grass and didn't say much. And why would they? Everyone knew it was one of the worst baseball seasons in Gibsonburg history.

During the regular season the 2005 team went on a losing streak where they lost 13 games in a row. They were mercy ruled seven times. This meant that because they were losing by more than ten runs in the 5th inning, they stopped the game. They show mercy to the losing team. Fremont St. Joe beat them by a score of 10 to 0 in their first encounter and by a score of 16 to 4 in their second meeting. They lost the last game of the season by a score of 17 to nothing.

In the state of Ohio, all high schools with baseball programs get the opportunity to play in the single elimination State Tournament. Each team plays until they lose one game. You start with two sectional games, move on to two district games, and continue with two regional games. There are four regions in Ohio so the champion in each of the four regions gets to advance to the state play-offs in Columbus at Huntington Park. The two semi-final winners play in the State Championship. The bottom line is you need to win eight games in a row to win the State Championship!

Given the fact that they only won six games all season, the odds were certainly not in Gibsonburg's favor.

A Little Extra Preparation

Alex, Wyatt, and Wes were walking to the parking lot after the Woodmore massacre.

Alex stopped. "You guys hear that?"

Wyatt and Wes both responded, "Yeah." They listened and heard a faint ping, about every five seconds.

It was about 30 minutes from getting dark and the three boys walked back to the baseball field. Andy Gruner was in the batting cage next to the fence along the left field line. He was taking batting practice as the pitching machine delivered 70 mile-per-hour fastballs every five seconds.

Amused, Alex walked up to the outside of the batting cage. "Are you serious? What are you doing?"

Andy continued to hit the fastballs. "Got Bettsville on Friday, man. Our first sectional game."

Alex and Wes both laughed. Wyatt did not laugh at all.

Alex told Andy, "Keep swingin' away Andyman. We'll see ya later."

Wes turned away. "Later Andy."

Sixty minutes later, with the lights from the parking lots supplying a warm dim glow to the baseball field and batting cage, the ping of Andy's bat continued to sound off every five seconds.

13

A Dilemma
Saturday Morning, April 23, 2005

It was a Saturday morning in the Ideal Bakery, typically the busiest day of the week. Andy was in the back room washing dishes, struggling to keep up with the steady flow of customers when his mother approached him.

"Andy, I need to speak with you." It looked as though she was going to cry and Andy knew what was coming. "I'm afraid I have bad news. There are some real financial issues with the bakery. Your father and I have been working real hard to resolve them but . . ."

"But what?"

She looked in Andy's eyes and gently said, "At the end of May, we have to close down."

Andy looked away, but his mother continued. "It will be up to the creditors from there. Your father is looking for another job, and we will be living with your aunt for a little bit in Pemberville."

Seeing his mother so upset made his throat ache. "Isn't there anything I can do?"

After a long silence, she sighed. "I wish there was Andy."

She composed herself, wiped her tears, and said, "Here, let's take these clean dishes up front." She grabbed a handful of clean plates and cups and carried them to the dining area, and Andy followed.

As they were putting the clean dishes away Kathy walked in.

Andy's mother smiled at the sight of her. "Hi there, Kathy. How are you, and how are your folks?"

"Fine Mrs. Gruner. I'll tell them you said *hello*."

Mrs. Gruner looked at Andy. "We'll talk a little later honey."

"Okay, mom. Hey, don't worry. We never give up, right?"

Andy's mom just smiled at Andy, and then walked through the swinging door with the porthole to the prep area of the bakery.

14

Peer Pressure
Saturday Morning, April 23, 2005

Kathy came up to the counter where Andy was working. "What's up, buddy?"

He grinned at her. "Not much, want an éclair?"

She grinned back. "Sure do. These are the best éclairs ever."

She watched him as he took out a delectable éclair and placed it on a plate for her. He concentrated on the pastry, his brow creased. "Something wrong, Andy?"

He glanced up quickly and realized she'd seen the worry on his face. The last thing he wanted to do was bring down his good friend Kathy. He forced a smile. "No, nothing at all."

She shrugged. He'd talk when he was ready. "Well then, mind if I vent a little?

"No, not at all. Let's sit down and talk."

Just like they had done many times before, Andy joined Kathy at their favorite table.

Kathy didn't waste any time. She began talking fast, her pitch going up and down, clearly frustrated. "Well, I hate high school. I'm just so tired of everyone that keeps telling me these are the best times of my life. Well, they aren't! These times suck!"

Andy smirked amusingly at Kathy's comment.

Kathy continued. "And I hate Fridays and Mondays. On Friday, everyone talks about the parties they are going to go to all weekend. On Mondays, they talk about all the parties that they went to over the weekend and all the crazy stuff that happened."

Andy shrugged. "Personally, I've never been into that wild party scene too much."

"You should be happy for that," she replied.

Kathy began to tear up and Andy was not sure what to do. "Aw, c'mon. It's not that bad, is it?"

She seemed to be losing it a bit. "Steve is at college, and I miss him so much. I'm hanging out with the twins, and it is so tough. They are blond, blue-eyed, and get all the attention. I'm always like a third wheel. Last night . . ."

Kathy stopped abruptly.

"What? What about last night."

Kathy took a deep breath and explained. "Last night, we were at this party at the Austin's. Their parents flew to Branson for the weekend. Liz is upstairs with Tommy and I am downstairs with Jen and Brin shows up. Brin pulls out a bottle of vodka and this water bottle with stuff in it. It looked like cotton balls. There is a little hole in the side with a big straw in it.

"What the heck was it?" Andy asked.

"Don't really know," she replied.

Andy gave a concerned, "Hmmmm."

Kathy continued. "So Brin says, *Let's go have some fun.* They all start to head to the basement, but I don't go. They all start teasing me and calling me a priss. They really put the pressure on me. So, I finally give in and go with them. First time I go out in a month and the whole night is nothing but pressure."

Andy shook his head. "Aw man! You should have just left."

She nodded. "I know. But Jen and Liz are both good friends. I really don't have any other good friends. It's awful! And with Steve gone, I just don't have anything to do. I should have just stayed home. Just like every other weekend . . ."

Andy leaned toward Kathy and scolded her "You should have called me!"

Realizing she made a mistake by staying at the party, she sighed. "I will next time. So, you know what the worst part is Andy?"

"What's that?"

"I think Jen and Liz are actually pretty good. They have their own faults, but there is just so much stupid peer pressure at our school. When you look at the other girls, they are doing stuff that is much worse. Liz and Jen are actually really good when you compare them to everyone else. I mean, at our lunch table, I am the only one actually eating food and I get stared at because of it. Isn't that stupid? No one else eats because they are too worried about gaining weight."

Andy laughed. "Can you imagine Alex not eating?"

"I know it doesn't happen with you. Everyone knows you. You will do what's right. Plus, you just do what you want to do no matter what. You are special that way. You don't let the pressure get to you at all."

Andy urged her to continue her story. "So, then what happened?"

"Well, they light this thing up and start passing it around and smoking from it. Then, they pull out the big bottle of vodka. Everyone starts taking hits off this water bottle thing and taking swigs of the vodka.

Andy exhaled and sat back in his chair. "Wow!"

Kathy looked at him and continued. "They push the thing to me and I tell them no thanks. They keep pushing and teasing and laughing so finally, I take a hit. It tasted like butt. It was awful. I started coughing, and they just all laughed at me."

"Man, how could you try something if you have no idea what it is?"

Kathy shook her head. "I know, pretty stupid." Then, Brin said, *Watch this.* She downed half of the bottle of Vodka and then took a big hit off the water bottle. She was fine for a few minutes.

Then she said, *Let's see how many boys I can kiss tonight.* You could tell she was really drunk and started going up to every boy she saw and grabbed them and kissed them. It started out pretty innocent and everyone was laughing."

Andy chuckled a little bit.

Kathy continued, "And then wham, she started falling all over the place and knocking stuff over. Almost like a switch went off. She was totally out of it and could hardly talk. We all kind of thought she was acting."

"Holy crap," he muttered.

"So, we got her outside and started to walk her home. None of us had a ride. She fell completely down and we started to drag her. I had one arm and Liz has the other arm. Then, Reed Murray drove by and saw what was going on. He asked if we needed help. We got her in Reed's car . . ."

"The new Mustang his rich folks just bought him?" he interrupted.

She laughed a little. "Yep. After Brin threw up all over the dash Reed threw us all out."

"Whoa."

"So," she continued. "We dragged her to Liz and Jen's house. Liz distracted her parents while me and Jen dragged Brin up to Liz's bedroom. We texted Brin's parents from Brin's phone to tell them she was staying all night at Liz and Jen's. I stayed for a little bit to make sure she was okay and then went home around 1 am. I bet she threw up eight times. Until she had the dry heaves. At 4 am, Liz texted me that they got scared because Brin was unresponsive! So, her parents took her to the Flower Hospital Emergency Room."

Andy felt exhausted just listening to the story. He exclaimed, "Unbelievable story!"

"I guess they pumped her stomach, gave her an IV and she is going to be okay. But, how scary? I'm sure all of us will get in big trouble once they put the pieces of the puzzle together."

"What a night," he said, shaking his head.

"I just can't wait till school is done, and I am out of here. I am tired of all the work from the teachers. They are so unfair. I hate the *not knowing* about getting into college. That is about killing me, and I just hate not having any good friends."

Kathy's big blue eyes started to well up again.

Andy put his hand on top of Kathy's hand. "Hey! I'll always be your buddy."

She looked up at him and smiled. "You are so sweet. Always have been."

Kathy regained her composure. "Hey, I'm so sorry just talking about me. How's everything for you?"

The bakery foreclosure instantly came to mind but he forced it down. "Me? Awww . . . I'm all good."

15

The Ohio High School Athletic Association

O HSAA stands for the Ohio High School Athletic Association. It is commonly pronounced *Ohhshaw* by the communities in Ohio that follow high school sports. They are located on Roselea Place in Columbus, Ohio. They are the governing body for all high school sports in the state of Ohio.

In 2005 OHSAA was still lagging when it came to technology, not because they couldn't change but because they really did not want to change. Baseball was such a national institution that they tried to hang on to the old way of doing things as long as they could. Each team entering the state boy's baseball tournament had their high school name written with a marker on a 4-inch by 8-inch piece of white cardboard.

The tournament administrator took each team and organized them by the various sectional tournaments in Ohio on a long 50-foot wall with a corkboard backing in the OHSAA boardroom. As the tournament progressed, the administrator would then organize by district, by region, and then he would take the final four teams and organize these teams for the state semi-finals and championship game.

Pudge Lowery was the tournament administrator and he was an

interesting character. He was 5 feet, 2 inches tall, 200 pounds, and usually could be found chomping an unlit stub of a cigar in the corner of his mouth. At work, Pudge would wear the same outfit every day: blue-jean bibbed overalls, a red handkerchief hanging out the back pocket, a white T-shirt, work boots, and a green John Deere hat. As this was the first day of the State Tournament, Pudge had hundreds of high school names pinned up on the wall, organized by their individual sectional tournaments. When the winning coach would call in results, he would refine the tournament brackets and then document the results twice. He would put the data in the computer system and in writing on a special bracket form, which he then filed.

2005 was Pudge's fortieth year of managing the tournament. Nothing had ever changed in his process.

16

Game #1 - Gibsonburg vs. Bettsville
Friday, April 29, 2005

On April 29, 2005 at 2 pm, out of all the teams on the wall, for some reason Pudge stared at two teams. Bettsville (11–13) vs. Gibsonburg (6-17).

Jim the bus driver took a left out of the school parking lot and headed north on Route 300. He hit the red traffic light at the four corners of Gibsonburg, waited for it to turn green, and turned right onto Route 600. He was taking Gibsonburg to their first game in the tournament to play Bettsville at Bettsville.

When Jim arrived at Bettsville, he was not surprised that the crowd was fairly thin. After all, it was 2 pm on a Friday and most parents were working.

Despite the small crowd, Henry Tillman, Gibsonburg's main mechanic, was already in the stands when the bus arrived. He attended every game, home and away, and was never late.

Jimmy Yarnell, a Gibsonburg student, was calling the game to get practice for his broadcasting class. A radio affiliate in Fostoria, *720AM*, agreed to pick up the game's broadcast. They had an arrangement that they would continue to use one announcer for a team and keep using that announcer until the team lost. In 2005, they started with the Gibsonburg-Bettsville game. At the end of the tournament, a Broadcasting Achievement Award for the best game called would be awarded.

At 5 feet, 5 inches tall and a mere 120 pounds, Jimmy did not play sports. He had somewhat of a large head covered by a bushel of curly blonde hair. He usually wore his orange Gibsonburg Golden Bears T-shirt, blue jeans, and black Chuck Taylor basketball shoes. He oozed with school spirit, and there wasn't a bigger sports nut at Gibsonburg High School. Jimmy followed all the sports with great enthusiasm and passion. He planned on attacking the opportunity to call the games with gusto, especially since he figured he would only be calling one game.

When it was time to begin, Jimmy took a deep breath and leaned into the microphone. "Well sports fans, here we go, the start of the 2005 Ohio State Boys' High School Baseball Tournament. We begin with 267 teams, and only four will make it to the state finals at Huntington Park in Columbus on June 3rd and 4th.

"Today, we have Gibsonburg and their 6 and 17 record versus Bettsville with an 11 and 13 record." His voice boomed out over the radio to the listeners at home.

In the dugout, Coach Rase glanced at his team. "All right, fellas. Here we are."

He turned his attention back to the field without a hint of excitement or energy, and the team's mood matched his lack of enthusiasm. In a blasé manner he told his players, "Not much more to say. Let's have a good game. Gruner, bring 'em in."

The team got in a tight circle around Andy Gruner. "All right!" Andy shouted. "Go Bears' on three. One. Two. Three. GO BEARS!"

The responding cheer was half-hearted at best.

Even though the game was at Bettsville because it was a tournament game Gibsonburg was selected as the home team. This meant they would take the field first. All nine players lazily jogged out to their positions.

Up in the box, Jimmy continued to call the game. "All right. We have top of one and Alex Black for Gibsonburg struck out the first two batters he faced, but he is now struggling."

"The number three batter, Rothenbuhler, walked on four straight pitches. And then the number four batter, Hoiles, was hit by an Alex Black pitch."

Scrub Nation member Jeff Feasel looked at Josh Sanchez. "Well, looks like our calendar will get wide open after today."

Josh Sanchez nodded his head like it was no big surprise.

Jimmy deepened his voice for the listeners at home. "We have men on first and second with two outs and a full-count on the fifth batter, Crawford, for Bettsville. There's the windup, and the pitch! Crawford hits a line shot to left field. Base hit."

"If that ball would not have been a line shot then Rothenbuhler probably would have scored from second as all runners were moving on the pitch with two outs and a full count. We now have the top of one. Two outs. Bases loaded with Max Davis up to bat."

Coach Rase yelled out to Alex Black. "Black, get this guy! C'mon!"

Alex glared at Coach Rase. Rase stared right back at him and you could feel the tension in the air. Alex hadn't forgotten about being benched during the last game of the regular season. There was still tension between them.

Alex wound up and delivered the pitch to the batter. The batter dribbled a slow grounder right back to him. He fielded the grounder lazily. Although he could make an easy out at first base, he casually jogged to home plate, touched it, and got the force out barely in time. It was the third out of the inning. He made the play at home just to get under Coach Rase's skin.

Coach Rase ran out to Alex and stood in front of him, toe-to-toe. Rase was beet red with anger. "Alex! You need to go to first on an easy play like that with two outs!"

Alex sidestepped his coach, unfazed. "I like controlling my own destiny coach."

Frustrated, Coach Rase grabbed him by the arm, looked him in the eye and sternly said, "You need to either believe in your teammates or not. If you are not going to trust them, then leave right now."

Alex started to step away but stopped.

Coach Rase stared hard. "If you walk away now, don't bother coming back, son."

Alex looked down at the ground, then his teammates. Awe, shit, he thought and headed for the bench. He slammed himself down on the bench, crossed his arms, spit, looked at the ground, and didn't say anything.

Josh Sanchez and the rest of the team had watched the exchange between Coach Rase and Alex. This game was going to be no different than any other game, they thought.

In the stands, Ron Gruner turned to his wife Jennie. "Well, I thought we could win at least one game."

Jennie shrugged. "They just don't have much talent. They'd struggle against a middle school team."

The next several innings were uneventful. The two teams seemed to be matched up pretty well, and after six and a half innings, it was a scoreless game. Unless there was a tie, only one inning remained.

At the bottom of the seventh inning, Cody Fisher struck out to give Gibsonburg one out. The next batter was Wes Milleson. He drew a walk to give the team a baserunner.

Jimmy continued to call the game. "Okay. Wes Milleson just walked on a 3-2 count. We have no score, bottom of seven, one out. We've got Milleson on first, and Andy Gruner at the plate.

The pitcher, Coe, deals . . . And there goes Milleson, he is stealing second! Gruner swings and the ball is bobbled by the catcher,

Overton, and Milleson gets to second standing up."

Jimmy spoke into the microphone. "Milleson takes a big lead off of second base. Even with Milleson's speed, we probably won't see him steal third as the catcher, Overton, has a bazooka for an arm. The pitcher, Coe, gets his sign, checks the runner at second, and delivers to Gruner. It's a good hard fastball, and holy cow, there goes Milleson taking off for third. It's a called strike, and Overton throws to third, and it looks like he's got him. No! Safe! Milleson is safe at third base on a very close play."

Jimmy leaned forward in his seat. "Here we are at the bottom of the seventh inning. We have one out, Gruner at the plate with an 0-2 count, and Wes Milleson on third base. The pitcher, Coe, gets his sign from the catcher, Overton. He checks the runner at third, and he delivers to Gruner. Gruner swings and misses, but the catcher can't hold onto the ball. Gruner takes off for first because it's a dropped third strike. Overton has all kinds of time to throw Gruner out at first. Overton checks Milleson at third then throws to first to get Gruner. I don't believe it! As soon as Overton released the ball to first, Milleson took off for home. Gruner is easily out at first for the second out. The first baseman throws home. Here comes the throw. Here comes Milleson. It's gonna be close. Milleson slides headfirst. Overton catches the ball. It is a close play at the plate. Overton puts the tag on Milleson. Milleson is safe at home! Milleson is safe! Gibsonburg wins! Gibsonburg wins their first tournament game against Bettsville with a score of 1 to nothing!"

Gibsonburg ended up beating Bettsville by a score of 1 to nothing.

Gibsonburg defeated Bettsville with the speed of Wes Milleson!

Coach Rase called the game into the OHSAA headquarters and Pudge advanced Gibsonburg to their second game.

As Jim drove the team back to Gibsonburg on the bus, everyone was in a good mood and was actually a little proud of winning their first game.

On the bus ride home, the players were horsing around, while Coach Rase was on his cell phone talking to an old high school buddy.

He practically yelled into the phone. "Okay, when's the bachelor party? May 28th? That sounds awesome. So, we have one of those rooftop decks reserved to watch the Cubs play at Wrigley. And then we are heading to Division Street? This should be one to remember. Just book me on the flight with you to Chicago direct from Toledo. Good. I'm in unless, of course, we are playing in the Regional Final game to get us to state."

Coach Rase paused, pulled the phone away from his ear and stared at it quizzically because the person on the other end of the line was laughing hard. "Hey, take it easy," he said, annoyed. "There are a ton of first year coaches that take their 6-17 regular season teams to the State Championships. Later!"

Coach Rase pushed the end button on his phone, smiled and took in the country scenery as the bus rumbled back home to Gibsonburg.

Trent Snowden sat next to Sanchez at the back of the bus. When he spoke, his voice was dripping with sarcasm. "Well, we didn't see any action during the regular season. Didn't see any action today. I'll bet we get in as we continue to win though. Don't ya think Josh?"

Josh Sanchez just shrugged his shoulders.

Andy Gruner sat alone, staring out the window as the trees rushed by.

Behind him, Alex leaned forward and rested his elbows on Andy's seat. "Watcha thinkin about?"

Andy looked up at him. He wasn't ready to unload again about losing the bakery. It was all he could ever think about now. "Nothing really."

Alex smiled. "Just think, seven more wins and we are state champs!"

Andy snorted. "Yeah. I think we would have a better shot at going to Mars."

Alex chuckled, but he could see something was bothering Andy. "Somethin' wrong buddy. You okay?"

Andy just smiled, not ready to share. "Yeah, I'm good. Nice job pitching today, Alex. Twelve strikeouts. You looked good."

"I think you mean 13 strikeouts. Actually, I'm surprised to say that the whole team looked pretty good today. No errors! Alex grinned. "Hey, you goin' over to Milleson's tonight?

"Yep. We'll see you there." Andy nodded and turned back to watch the country scenery fly by. Only an hour of daylight remained.

He pulled out an old wooden bat that was painted black out of his equipment bag. He sometimes used this bat to practice his bunting. He examined the bat carefully and pulled out a beat-up pocket knife that he used to clean the mud out of his baseball cleats. He carefully carved one notch in the handle of the bat to represent their first tournament win. When he was completed he looked proudly at his crude craftsmanship. He took a little more time to perfect the notch as he figured it would be the only one he would ever carve.

Back at OHSAA headquarters, Pudge physically moved Gibsonburg in position to play Tiffin Calvert on May 6, 2005 at 2 pm. It would be the second game for both teams.

17

A Small Town Friday Night
Friday, April 29, 2005

Winning the first tournament game was as good a reason as any to have a little party. Wes Milleson's place was the only place to be that Friday night.

After the bus ride to Gibsonburg, Andy gave Bobby Graff a ride home. They were both covered with sweat and grime and couldn't wait to hit the showers and get to the party.

"Thanks for the ride." Bobby said as they left the school parking lot in Andy's truck.

Andy waved the words away. "No problemo. Just take a quick shower and I'll drop you off at Wes' before I head home to get ready."

Bobby and Bo

As the truck pulled up to the house on Front Street, Bobby cried out, "Oh, crap!" There was a white Ford pickup parked out front.

Andy glanced over. "What?"

Bobby groaned. My sister's dick boyfriend, Bo Smith, is here."

Andy smiled amusingly and said, "Bo Smith from Oak Harbor?"

"Yep."

Andy laughed.

Bobby glared at the truck. "He's such an idiot. He's always pushing me around thinking he's funny. Park in the alley by my house and wait. I'll jump in the shower, change quick, and get back here before he sees me."

As he told Andy, Bobby took a quick shower, changed, and ran down the stairs. As he turned the corner, he ran right into Bo Smith, clumsily bouncing backward.

Bo grinned. "Hey shithead. How was your bullcrap baseball game?" He didn't give Bobby any time to respond and kept talking. "Too bad I'm the only good player on our team. We got beat already today. We're already out of the tournament."

Bobby tried not to make eye contact. "What's up, Bo? Where's Suzie?"

"Gettin ready. I got paid today and am gonna splurge and take her to Sizzler."

"Are you sure you can afford it?" Bobby regretted the words before they were all out.

Bo looked at him menacingly. "Funny, cockbreath. Hey, nice shirt. Looks like it could even fit me."

Bo grabbed the front of Bobby's shirt with his right hand.

Bobby tried to pull away. "Let go Bo! Suzie got me this for Christmas."

Bo continued to stretch the shirt, and then he gave it a big yank which jerked Bobby downward and ripped the shirt badly. Bo raised an eyebrow. "Oops. Guess I don't want the piece a shit now. You can have it back loser."

Bo pushed him away.

"What is your problem?" Bobby shouted. He opened the front door of the house and ran past Bo's truck to the alley where Andy was waiting. He jumped in and slammed the door shut.

Andy eyed the ripped shirt. "What happened?"

"Never mind," Bobby muttered. "Let's go."

Andy looked at the house, then Bo Smith's truck, and then at Bobby. "Hey, what type of truck is that?"

Bobby was still upset and wasn't in the mood to talk. "I don't know. Some old piece a crap."

Andy smiled slowly. "Wait here," he said and opened his door and slid out.

Ten seconds later he heard a hood slam and Andy returned.

Bobby looked at him. "Where'd you go?"

"Just listen and enjoy."

They waited in the parked truck, in the alley just out of view but still close enough to hear them when they came out. Andy leaned back in his seat and got comfortable.

"Just sit back and relax."

Bo and Suzie finally walked out of the house.

"You have an amazing truck, Bo," Suzie said.

Bo smirked. "Like I don't know that. Get in. Oh, and whaddya doin tomorrow?"

She looked at him eagerly. "Nothing Bo, why?"

Bo smiled down at her. "I thought I'd give you the honor of washing my truck for me while I go fishing.

"You're such a jerk," she mumbled as she approached the passenger door.

Bo and Suzie climbed into the truck. Bo turned the key, but nothing happened.

Suzie could see the confused look on his face.

The truck wouldn't start. Bo kept turning the key forcing the engine to turn over multiple times. "What the hell?"

Andy and Bobby slid down in their seats and giggled like kids as they heard the engine try to start.

When it finally started, the engine ran rough, blue smoke billowed out of the exhaust, and then it backfired. The backfire was so loud that Andy and Bobby both jumped. It sounded like somebody pulling the trigger on a shotgun.

Bo sighed with relief. "There we go. It might need a little tune-up."

"It doesn't sound right," Suzie said, worried.

"Shaddup," he snapped.

The truck backfired several times, and smoke continued to billow out the exhaust. As they drove off, the truck lurched, backfired, lurched some more, and continued to backfire loudly. Each time it sounded like a shotgun blast.

Andy and Bobby were in Andy's truck laughing uncontrollably.

"What did you do?" Bobby was laughing so hard, he could barely get the words out.

Andy grinned. "One of the beautiful things about those old trucks is that it's easy to get under the hood and switch around a few spark plug wires."

Bobby leaned back in the seat and smiled gratefully at Andy. Finally, after all those years of moving around, he had a friend he could count on.

Andy Hitches A Ride

Andy dropped Bobby off at Wes's and headed home, figuring that he could drive home, take a shower, get changed, and be back at the party in 30 minutes.

He had his hat on backwards, and his dirty, sweat-stained baseball uniform was sticking to his body. From the angle of the sun, he knew that it would be dusk in about 20 minutes.

As he drove home on the scenic country road, his thoughts wandered. Their first win in the tournament. He replayed the game in his mind well aware that it was probably the last win he would experience for his senior year.

Four miles from home, the truck engine started sputtering.

He tried to determine what was wrong before he finally glanced at the gauges.

"Crap!" He said. He was out of gas. He pulled to the side of the road. Andy started to reach for his phone when he remembered that he'd left it on the kitchen table that morning.

There was nothing he could do but start walking. "It's only four miles," he said to himself.

Andy walked for about a mile and noticed that the sun would be setting soon. His thoughts were wandering when, suddenly, he was startled by the sound of hoofs beating on dry earth. He turned to see Kathy Colaner riding up to the fence along side him on a tall horse. Andy couldn't help but smile at the sight of her. "God, was she beautiful or what?" he thought.

"Hey, didn't get enough exercise in the game and decided to walk home, eh?" she teased.

Andy laughed. "Very funny. I ran out of gas. My truck is down the road a bit."

She patted her horse right behind the saddle and told Andy, "Well, for a small price, I'll give you a lift."

"On that thing? Are you kiddin'?"

"C'mon. At least she won't run out of gas."

Andy eyed the horse skeptically. He'd never been on one. "Well..."

Kathy felt his resistance and prodded him to move. "C'mon chicken. Hop on. I'm not about to hurt the team captain."

He grinned, embarrassed. "You sure you know what you're doin'?"

"Haven't killed anyone yet. Let's go. It's starting to get dark."

Andy slowly walked to the fence, and sized up the horse.

"How do I get on?" he muttered.

"Just climb up on the fence and hop on right behind the saddle," she instructed.

He climbed up on the fence, which was parallel to the horse. Andy guessed the horse was about two feet away from the fence, so he steadied himself, then jumped from the fence to the horse and completely went over the back end and hit the muddy ground.

Kathy burst out laughing.

Andy brushed off his already-dirty baseball uniform. "Now what?"

Kathy pointed down at her left foot. "Put your left foot in the stirrup, swing your right leg up and hop on."

He did as he was instructed and ended up sitting right behind Kathy.

"Hey, this isn't so bad," he said nervously. "What's her name?"

Kathy paused for a second and, with a smile, told Andy, "Tornado."

"Great," he thought. "I'm sitting on a freaking tornado."

The sun set as they rode westward. The sky was streaked with brilliant strokes of red and orange. By the time they reached the stable, it was dark. Kathy pulled the reins, and the horse stopped. They dismounted and stood there for a moment.

"You see, I got you here safe and sound," Kathy said.

"Thanks for the lift," Andy said, rubbing his behind.

"For such a little ride, my rear end is more than a little sore."

Kathy giggled. "Yeah, that happens. I'm gonna get you back here and give you a few lessons. You game?"

"Let me think about it. Hey, I hate to ask you for another favor. You goin' to Milleson's tonight?"

"I was thinking about it. Why? You need a lift?"

"Do you think you can take me home. I can clean up and then grab my dad's car."

"All right! But you owe me," she warned.

"Just put it on my tab." He brushed the dirt from his uniform. "Man, look at me. I'm a mess!"

Kathy looked up at him. The light outside the barn was dim, but she could still make out his features. She didn't notice the dirt on his uniform, his ruffled hair, or the smell of sweat on his skin. But she did notice the warm feeling that grew inside of her as she watched him try to brush away the grime. It was something she'd never felt for him before.

For the first time ever, she looked at Andy a little differently. She couldn't help but notice how cute he looked. She'd never looked at him this way before, and as she watched him brush off his uniform, she smiled warmly.

Celebrating the Bettsville Win
Friday Evening, April 29, 2005

Later that night, the Milleson party was in full swing. The music was playing, the firepit was roaring, a foosball tournament was underway, two seniors were dominating at beer pong, and there had been at least three *parcors* so far. And the night was still young.

Andy was in the kitchen area with Alex, Wyatt, and Wes. "Well fellas," he said. "One game down, seven to go."

Alex laughed. "Very funny, Andyman."

"I know," Wyatt added. "I thought the torture was over after going 6-17."

Wes shook his head. "Brutal year, man."

"If we do beat Tiffin Calvert, then we'll have to play St. Joe. We haven't beaten them since the third grade!" Wyatt exclaimed.

Alex frowned. "That bastard, Pinkus. Someone said he is throwing in the mid '90s."

Wes nodded. "I heard he got a full ride to Eastern Michigan.

As much as I hate him, he is good. Beat us 10-0 and 16-4 already this year."

Andy listened for a while, knowing that he'd never give up. "Big deal. Let's still kick his ass if we play him!"

Alex shot Andy a look. "Yeah, we may beat Pinkus, but what about his old lady?"

Wes was in the middle of taking a drink of Mountain Dew when Alex's comment made him choke with laughter. He spurted out his drink. "Seriously! She has been the biggest pain-in-the-ass parent since we were kids. I heard she tried to get his Legion coach fired over the summer because she claimed that she knew more about the pick off play than he did."

"What a tramp," Alex muttered.

Andy tried to comfort the group by saying, "Well, what comes around, goes around. She'll get hers someday."

Wes smiled and told everyone, "I'd like to be there when that happens."

Kathy and Andy

Kathy walked up to the group. "What's up gang?"

Wes smiled. "Hey Kathy. No entourage of friends tonight?"

Kathy smiled as to say she was exhausted of her wild friends and responded, "Naw, just me."

She looked at Andy. "Thanks for being such a good listener the other day, Andy."

He blushed. "No big deal."

After a few minutes, Andy touched her arm. "Hey, it's a little crowded in here. Wanna grab some fresh air?"

Kathy smiled. "Sure!"

As Andy and Kathy started to walk out of the barn to the firepit, Kathy's phone rang. She looked at the number on the screen. It was Steve. She turned to Andy. "Hey, it's Steve," she said apologetically. "Let me take this call first and then we can talk."

Andy nodded. "Sure," he said easily. "Just come over to the firepit when you're done."

She walked out of the garage door and stood outside where she could talk without being overheard. "Hey, Steve."

She could hear the roar of another college party in the background. "What's up, babe?"

"Not much, just hanging out with everyone at Wes'."

"Wes'. That's interesting."

She frowned. "What do you mean?"

With loud music blaring in the background, Steve smiled as he quickly devised a plot in his mind. He told Kathy, "Hey, tomorrow is Saturday. Why don't you drive to Columbus and see me. I miss you, babe."

She hesitated. "Exams are coming up. That might be a little tough."

"Listen, babe. Just do me this favor. Wes' parents have a pole barn at the back of their property. There is a locked closet in the bathroom. They keep all of their liquor in that closet. The key is under the tray in the silverware drawer in the kitchen area."

"How do you know this?" she asked, surprised.

Steve smiled. "Let's just say I paid it a visit or two in high school." He laughed obnoxiously.

"Steve! That isn't right!" she scolded.

"Just mosey on over there, get the key, and then head to the bathroom. Nobody will be paying attention. Grab a bottle of Jack Daniels and a bottle of Absolute. And then bring it with you tomorrow. Nobody will miss it."

Her voice became stern. "No way, Steve. I'm not gonna steal for you. Plus, I have to study tomorrow."

Steve wiped the drunken smile from his face. "You snobby little bitch!" he barked. "Thanks a lot. I'm getting a little tired of this bullshit high school stuff."

Kathy was stunned by his outburst. "Steve, why are you talking to me like this?"

Steve grunted. "Thanks for nothing!" He pulled the phone away from his ear and hit the end button with his finger as hard as he could.

Kathy shouted into the phone, "Steve? Steve?" She pulled the phone away from her ear and looked at the display. He'd hung up on her!

Back at Steve's college party, his beer-fueled mind soon helped him forget about his conversation with Kathy. He was standing in the far back yard of the frat house where the party was taking place, and it was fairly dark. He was at the spot where most guys go when they have to relieve themselves because they don't want to wait in line inside to go to the bathroom.

He looked at the house to see hordes of people hanging out on the back porch. Tiki lights splashed soft light on the college students drinking on the porch. There was a constant flow of people in and out of the back door because there were two large troughs filled with ice and cold beer at the bottom of the steps.

As the loud music rang out of the house, Steve attempted to take a drink out of his SOLO cup and realized it was empty. He stumbled a little bit and caught himself. Before he went up to get a refill, he decided to relieve himself. He unzipped his pants and got a wide smile on his drunken face as he urinated on the grass next to a large fir tree. Steve took his SOLO cup, held it down low, and filled it up with urine. His stream of urine ran dry at the same time that the cup was about full. He zipped his pants and proudly headed to the back porch with a cup of urine.

As he approached one of the troughs of beer, a very drunk girl stumbled out of the back door and down the steps to get another drink. In one fluid motion, Steve swung his arm high, then low and snatched a cold beer from the trough. He stumbled toward the girl, gave her the SOLO cup and said, "It looks like you could use a drink. Let's chug!"

He started chugging his beer, and the girl started to slam the cup of pee thinking it was beer. She started to chug the contents of her cup so hard that it was half gone before she realized that it was not beer. She was not sure what it was. She cried out, "What the hell was that?"

Steve bent over because he was laughing so hard. As he walked away he heard the girl say, "Ew, that was awful," and she attempted to spit out whatever was left in her mouth.

He walked up the steps to the house and smacked the ass of a girl standing on the steps, talking to a friend. She responded by yelling, "You jerk!" as he passed by. Steve didn't care.

There were two girls talking in the doorway to the house. Steve, put his arm around one of the girls and said, "C'mon babe, let's party," and he walked inside with his arm around the girl.

Kathy found Andy sitting by the firepit alone. She settled into the chair beside him.

"Well, am I a loser or what?" she suddenly blurted. "Don't really like the friends I have been hanging around; Steve has been acting like a real jerk lately; and then this morning, I back into my dad's car."

"I can relate to that," Andy said. It wasn't too long ago that he wrecked the delivery truck for the bakery.

Kathy sighed. "I just don't like this senior year of high school at all. And guess what?"

He stared at all the stars that seemed to fill up the night sky. "What?"

"I just got the letter that I didn't get into Northwestern."

He turned to look at her. "Aw. I'm so sorry."

He leaned toward her and took her hand into his. He touched her chin and stared at her. He wanted desperately to kiss her, but he didn't. He couldn't.

He let go of her chin and held her hand. She was Steve's girl. And until that changed, there was nothing he could do. Still, he began to get lost as he gazed into her eyes under the stars, as the light from the fire bathed the side of his face with a comforting warmth.

After a long moment of silence, Kathy finally spoke. "I better get going, Andy," she whispered.

He blinked. He wanted her to stay, but knew she couldn't. "I understand. Good luck studying tomorrow."

Still holding his hand, she stood. "Thanks for being such a good friend."

Her hand slipped out of his and she turned and walked away. Inside, he cringed. "Friend," she'd said. From inside the barn, he could hear the sounds of the party raging on in full force. Yet it was no match for the surge of emotions he felt for Kathy. Alone again, he sat down, looking into the fire. He silently cursed himself as he covered his face with his hands.

18

A Spring Saturday In Gibsonburg
Saturday, April 30, 2005 – 9:00 am

It was a sunny and unseasonably warm April morning in Gibsonburg. Birds were chirping, the flowers were in bloom, and there was a light rain before dawn, which added a fragrant spring freshness to the air. Like most Saturday mornings, the small town was buzzing with activity.

The Team
Saturday, April 30, 2005 – 9 am

Coach Rase was up early enjoying his morning coffee. He was deep in thought, studying a scouting report on their next opponent, Tiffin Calvert.

Across town, the team was busy with their daily lives. Andy was working away at the bakery. Wyatt Kiser was baling hay. You could find Wes Milleson leisurely cleaning up from the party the night before. And Alex Black was delivering a baby calf with the help of his sister, Bridget.

Thom Brinker was feeding his family's hogs, oblivious to the smell. If you drove by Cody Fisher's or Bobby Graff's house, you would have found both of them at their kitchen table studying. And then there was Josh Sanchez, still in bed, exhausted from being up all night playing HALO II.

Derek Eddings and Derek Hetrick had both camped out all night at Hetrick's grandfather's farm. They planned on getting up early and go fishing for smallmouth bass in his grandpa's quarry. After bringing in seven nice keepers, they went searching for something a bit more adventurous – the Hetrick barn.

They packed up their fishing gear and went off to attempt something they had wanted to do since they were young. They walked up to the old red barn and stopped. They gazed at the barn like a mountain climber gazes at Mount Everest before the ascent. Hetrick and Eddings weren't excited about the ascent. They were excited about the descent!

The 70-year-old barn belonged to Hetrick's grandfather and was a majestic monument on the property. The roof looked like one big slide which had two slopes: A gradual 30 degree slope for 40 feet at the top that dramatically dropped off to a steep 70 degree slope for another 40 feet. The 70 degree slope bottomed out at the top of a flat-roofed chicken coop.

To this day, they would tell you that their plan was brilliant. They would use a ladder on the inside of the barn and would gain access to the roof through a weather vane box at the top-center of the barn roof. The weather vane had louvered shutters on each side so they felt it would be easy to get out and onto the roof. They would then shimmy down the 30 degree slope part of the roof to the cliff-like drop off at the edge. They would slide down the 70 degree slope just like a child would go down a slide. For years, the boys had been planning out this feat, but the timing had never been right. Until now.

Everything went exactly as planned. They got on the roof, shimmied down the 30 degree slope and stopped when they reached the drop to the 70 degree slope part of the roof. It was much higher and steeper than they anticipated. The metal roof was also rough and covered with rust. Suddenly, it didn't seem like such a *brilliant* idea to Hetrick, but Eddings pushed on.

"You ready?" Eddings asked, eyeing the nearly vertical drop.

Hetrick glanced over the edge. "I'm not sure about this."

"We came this far, let's go on three," Eddings urged. "Don't worry, chicken: the chicken coop will stop us at the bottom."

Both of the boys glanced at the chicken coop hesitantly, but neither one was willing to call it quits.

Eddings slowly counted off. "One. Two. Three."

When they pushed off and sailed straight for the chicken coop, they suddenly realized that they had a problem: they'd severely underestimated the slope. It was drastically steeper, rustier, and slipperier than they'd imagined.

The friction of sliding on the rusty metal roof burned holes completely through their blue jeans and underwear.

They hit the top of the chicken coop with incredible force. Both boys fell and stumbled forward until they rolled and fell off of the front of the 10-foot high chicken coop.

Once they hit the dirt ground they rolled around in pain. They were actually crying like two-year old babies. They finally got up and inspected each other's bottoms. There was no cloth from their jeans or underwear at all. The friction made their clothes disintegrate faster than a magician's flash paper. Each butt cheek had a bright red, blood-colored strawberry similar to the type a baseball player gets on their hip from sliding. They proceeded to the house to locate some ointment. The abrasions were so tender that the boys couldn't even put any medicine on the wounds. It was too painful.

A Visit To Steve
Saturday, April 30, 2005 – 1 pm

Kathy was still upset about her conversation with Steve the prior night. Even though she had plenty of studying to do, she decided to drive two hours to Columbus and pay him a surprise visit, with fresh-baked cookies in tow. Kathy drove down Route 23 South to Columbus, and proceeded to the house Steve lived in with five other guys. She walked up to the beat-up old house with the cookie tin in her hands. She knocked on the door. A college student answered. He seemed extremely hung over, with pronounced bags under his eyes and ruffled, untamed hair. Still, Kathy flashed a winning smile and asked, "Is Steve around?"

The boy squinted in Kathy's direction and mumbled, "Haven't seen him in a few hours."

Kathy asked, "Okay if I go up to his room?"

The boy shrugged his shoulders like he didn't care, opened the door, and sloppily gestured for Kathy to help herself. When she walked past him, she noticed the reek of stale alcohol from the night before. She proceeded to the staircase to go up to Steve's bedroom.

Her pace slowed as she observed the first floor of the house. She couldn't believe the filth, the empty beer cans, the empty liquor bottles, and the old food strewn about. It all looked like it had been on the unwashed plates for weeks. There were trash cans overflowing with beer bottles, and the place was generally a complete wreck. When she got to the stairs, she walked up fast to get away and escape the apocalyptic scene downstairs. She made her way down the hall to Steve's room and saw the door was shut. There was a sign on the front of his door that said, "Keep out!"

Kathy knocked on the door. Immediately, she heard a gruff voice from the inside yell, "Go away!"

Ignoring the yell from inside, Kathy ventured inside. Much like downstairs, the room was incredibly messy. When Kathy looked to the right, she saw Steve's bed. She couldn't see Steve at all. Whoever or whatever was underneath was completely hidden by a dark purple bedspread.

As Steve slowly pulled the covers away from his head, Kathy greeted him with a smile. He seemed groggy as he squinted at her, his eyes adjusting to the light.

He looked at her puzzled. "Kathy?"

Her smile broadened, "What are you doing in bed at this time of day?" She paused, straightened herself and said, "Hey, I felt really bad about our conversation last night and wanted to bring a peace offering."

Steve sprung up, alert. He matched Kathy's smile. "You brought the liquor?"

He then burped in such a way that it could have easily developed into a vomiting episode. It snuck up on him, but he was able to concentrate hard, completely focused on not throwing up. Still, he knew that he probably wouldn't survive a second wave . . .

Kathy laughed, "No, silly! Me and my mom baked you some of our world-famous chocolate chip cookies."

Smiling, she continued, "I also brought you your favorite drink: A Blue Giant Slurpee from 7-Eleven. I just got it."

His smile vanished just as quickly as it had appeared. He absently waved his hand to the corner of his room and said, "Just put them on my desk."

The silence that followed was full of awkward staring. Suddenly, a cell phone ringer went off underneath Steve's covers. The ring tone was from the Brooks and Dunn song *Save a Horse, Ride a Cowboy*. While the ringer was going off, Kathy saw something move under the covers between Steve and the wall. Kathy wasn't sure what was going on. She stared at the spot that moved, glanced at Steve, and then back at the spot under the bedspread. Slowly, Kathy got on Steve's bed and shuffled to the mysterious lump on her knees. Steve didn't move. He was avoiding eye contact, looking straight down on the bed. Kathy grabbed the top of the covers and pulled them off in one fluid motion. To her shock, under the covers was a rather heavy-set girl between Steve and the wall. From what Kathy could tell, she was only wearing a T-shirt. Steve was in his underwear.

Kathy's face flushed with anger. She fought hard to hide the hurt she felt. She turned to Steve and took off the lid to the giant Slurpee. He looked at the frozen drink in her hand. Kathy held the 32-ounce Slurpee over Steve's groin area for a few seconds. When he finally looked her in the eyes, Kathy slowly dumped the entire contents of the chilled drink on him.

She flung the lid off of the cookies and dumped them on him too, for good measure. As she made a beeline for the door, she noticed his laptop on the desk. She grabbed it with both hands, looked at Steve, and threw it out his open window, like a Frisbee.

Steve yelled as the laptop flew out the two-story window. "Hey!"

Kathy looked at him in disgust. "Enjoy your cookies!"

She slammed the door and stormed off.

After she was gone, the girl under the covers sat up. "Well . . . she seemed sweet."

She noticed the cookies on the bed. "Hey, can I have a cookie?"

Steve tended to his frozen nether region. He slowly shook his head and mumbled under his breath, "I can't believe she caught me."

Steve pushed his bedmate aside and stumbled to the open window. He cringed as he watched Kathy get in her car. He saw his laptop on the ground not five feet in front of Kathy's car. With a breath of mild relief, he said, "Maybe the laptop will still work. It is shockproof."

Kathy accelerated forward hard. The two wheels on the driver's side went completely over the laptop once. For good measure, she put the car into reverse and drove backwards so the rear wheel went over the laptop again. When she felt the front wheel of her front wheel drive Honda Civic roll on top of the laptop she stopped. This made the front left of the car slightly higher than the other three corners. Looking straight ahead, she noticed a large green metal trash bin that was larger than her car about 50 feet ahead.

With a devilish smile, she put her left foot on the brake while at the same time accelerating hard with her right foot. When the RPMs were screaming, she let go of the brake, which spun the front tire of the Honda. This hurtled the laptop out from under her car like a missile! The laptop shot out hitting the large green metal dumpster, causing it to explode like a beer bottle thrown against a brick wall. There was not a chunk of laptop bigger than a candy bar to be found.

Kathy granted herself a moment to survey her handiwork, then sped off—away from campus, away from Steve, and back home.

19

Game #2 - Gibsonburg vs. Tiffin Calvert
Friday, May 6, 2005

If anyone searched for a while on Pudge's bracket wall in the OHSAA conference room, they would eventually locate Tiffin Calvert (12-12) vs. Gibsonburg (7-17). It would be the second game for both teams and they would play on Friday, May 6, 2005 at 2 pm at Old Fort High School.

Jim, the bus driver, took a left out of the school parking lot and headed north on Route 300. He hit the one red traffic light at the four corners of Gibsonburg, waited for it to turn green, and turned right on Route 600. He was taking Gibsonburg to their second game in the tournament to play Tiffin Calvert on neutral ground at Old Fort High School.

When the bus arrived, as usual, there wasn't much of a crowd. The fan base was comprised of parents of players and Henry Tillman, who was already in the stands before most parents arrived.

Gibsonburg looked strong against Tiffin Calvert and beat them 5 to 1. All of Gibsonburg's runs were scored on Tiffin Calvert errors. During the game, Derek Hetrick and Derek Eddings were able to get on first and second base on two different occasions. Each time, Coach Rase called a double steal causing both boys to sprint and slide to the next base. Neither one sat on the bench or on their bus seat during the ride home.

When the dust settled, Jimmy finished calling the game by announcing, "There you have it sports fans. Gibsonburg beat Tiffin Calvert by a score of 5 to 1. Well, THIS win surprised everyone, as Tiffin Calvert mercy ruled Gibsonburg earlier in the year 14-3. Alex Black pitched another strong game, and Gibsonburg did not have any errors."

As Jim drove the team back to Gibsonburg on the bus, Andy Gruner carved a second notch into his wooden bat handle.

Although they were happy with the win, nobody on the team was looking forward to their next tournament game. It was a matchup they were all dreading: they had to play Fremont St. Joe.

Back at OHSAA headquarters, Pudge physically moved Gibsonburg in position to play Fremont St. Joe. The date was set for Monday, May 16th. It would be the third tournament game for both teams.

20

Getting Ready For The Auction
Saturday, May 7, 2005 – 8:00 pm

Andy walked down the street making deliveries, like any other workday. He then ran into Kenny Fork, one of the many locals that followed Gibsonburg sports.

Kenny stopped Andy to say, "Great game yesterday Andy!"

Andy smiled. "Thanks!"

Kenny shook his head. "Too bad you have to play Fremont St. Joe next. Have you ever beat them?"

"We have never had too much luck against those guys," Andy said. "But we'll do our best."

Kenny nodded. "I'm sure you will. Tell your mom and dad I said *hello*."

"Will do," Andy replied and continued on with his deliveries. As he walked down the street with his arms full of boxes, his phone started buzzing. It was a text from Wes Milleson. He read the message, and immediately, got a surprised look on his face. His look of surprise slowly transformed into a contrite smile that said "What if?"

He wore that smile all the way back to the bakery.

It was just past dusk when Andy made it back, and there was not much activity inside the bakery. Andy and his mother were the only employees left for the day, and they were getting ready to close up for the evening.

Andy was busying himself by wiping down the display case. His mother slowly walked up to him and said, "Thank you for getting all of the bread deliveries taken care of, honey. You mind locking up tonight?"

"No, I'll take care of it," Andy said.

She affectionately touched him on the shoulder. "Don't worry, Andy. Things usually have a way of working themselves out."

Andy smiled warmly at his mother. Although the family was going through a tough time, he knew he was fortunate to have such great parents. In his heart he was confident that together, things would work out in the end.

"Andy, after you close up tonight, can you start getting things ready for the sheriff's sale at the end of May? Your dad wants you to bring up those old boxes of his stuff from the crawlspace in the basement. Would you mind doing that before you leave?"

"Sure, mom," he replied.

Andy's mother told him, "Okay, honey, I'm going to head home now and get things ready at the house."

She started to walk out the front door of the bakery. When she opened the door, she looked outside. In the short time of their discussion, it had started to pour down rain. There was much thunder and lightning. She pulled the hood up on her raincoat, when out of nowhere, Kathy Colaner almost ran into her as she was walking out the front door. She was running from her car and into the bakery to see Andy.

As she shook the rain off her coat, Kathy said, "Hi, Mrs. Gruner. What a storm!"

Jennie smiled at her, "It sure is. What are you doing? Coming over to keep the ole boy company?"

"Yep!" Kathy said as she shook away the rain from her hair.

She told her, "Good for you. I'll see you later, honey." Jennie then ran to her car as the rain continued to pour.

As Andy walked through the swinging door from the prep room he saw Kathy walking from the door to the counter. He couldn't contain the big smile on his face. Kathy grinned at him, "Hey buddy!"

Andy's heart started pounding at the sight of her. Just the person he wanted to see. "Hey, there!"

"Watcha doin'?" She asked.

Andy started to wipe down the top of the glass display case. "Just closin' up."

"Oh!"

Andy could tell she was struggling to say something. He broke the awkward silence. "I got a text from Wes. He said you and Steve broke up."

"Wes is such a gossip," she said, her words rushed. "But yeah, he's right on that one."

Andy watched her closely. "How ya doin'?"

She shrugged, "Kind of bummed actually. Not at all about Steve. I came to learn he was just a big jerk. I just have a lot of things on my mind." She looked at him expectantly.

"Hey, how about hanging out with an old friend tonight to watch an old movie and have some popcorn?" Kathy shyly asked Andy.

He gave her a mischievous smile. "Sounds like a good idea. I'll give Alex a call and see what he's doin'. I'm sure he's free tonight."

Kathy chuckled. "Very funny."

He sighed. "Unfortunately, my mom wants me to bring up some old boxes from the crawlspace of the bakery. It might take a while. How about tomorrow? I can be at your place by 7?"

"That would be great. See you then."

Kathy left Andy and walked outside. The rain was not relenting. There was a violent lightning storm taking place that filled the sky with bright lights. The thunder cracked loudly. She waited for a break in the lightning, and then rushed to her car.

After she left, Andy opened the door to the bakery basement. He always thought it was creepy down there. He definitely did not like to go downstairs unless he had to. It didn't help that there was a vicious thunderstorm outside. He peered down the old wooden stairs as they disappeared into the blackness below. He flipped the switch to turn on the light at the bottom of the stairs, but nothing happened. "Great. Light bulb's dead," he muttered.

Carefully, Andy made his way down the steep staircase. He recalled that, in the middle of the room at the bottom of the stairs, there was an isolated lightbulb on the ceiling with an old pull string. He figured he would get to the room, feel around for the string, and turn the light on. As he was halfway down the stairs, he was startled by a loud clap of thunder from outside. He stopped for a moment, took a deep breath, and continued on. When he reached the bottom of the stairs a wave of cold air seemed to pass right through his body. Andy shivered uncontrollably. As he tried to get his bearings for a second or two, one thought entered his mind: he wanted to get the boxes out of the crawlspace and get out as quickly as possible.

He stumbled around and managed to find the middle of the room. After waving his arms around in the dark, he finally located the string. He pulled it gently, but nothing happened. He pulled a little harder, heard a loud click, and the lightbulb came alive. The result was 40 watts of dim lighting to everything within 15 feet of the lightbulb.

Andy glanced around. In the corner of the basement, 4 feet off the ground, there was a 3-foot by 3-foot opening which was the only point of access into and out of the crawlspace. The lone light source didn't reach the crawlspace. In the darkness, it looked pretty damn creepy.

If he recalled correctly, the boxes his father wanted were located about 5 feet in and 15 feet to the left of the hole. Hesitant to climb in the crawlspace without any light, he walked over to a workbench and started scanning for something to light the way, a lantern, matches, anything. After moving a few of the items on the cluttered workbench he located a beat-up old flashlight. He was surprised that when he turned it on, it actually worked. The light was dim, and he knew the batteries didn't have much life left in them. But, he figured it would work long enough to retrieve the boxes. At this point, Andy would take what he could get.

Andy walked to the opening of the crawlspace and realized it was covered in cobwebs. He used the flashlight to move them out of the way as best he could. He peered into the darkness and shined the flashlight to the left. Sure enough, 5 feet out and 15 feet to the left were two boxes, each about 10 inches high, 3 feet long, and about 2 feet wide. He took another deep breath and confirmed that he had one goal. He wanted to get the boxes, and get out as soon as he could.

He jumped up into the crawlspace and started crawling on his stomach toward the boxes. As he moved closer to the boxes, he laughed inwardly a bit: he confirmed to himself that crawlspace was a fitting and appropriate name for his current surroundings. When he reached the two boxes, he examined the contents.

They were full of an eclectic mix of old items. By the thick layer of dust, he figured that they had not been touched in at least 20 years. There was an old oil can, some black and white pictures, a few musty books, some old bottles, and a rolled tube of stained yellow papers. The roll was tied with a string to keep the pieces of paper from unrolling.

His curiosity piqued, Andy, selected the roll of papers and took off the musty yellow string. He found the paper to be very brittle and frayed at the ends. He carefully unrolled the papers and thought they looked well over 50 years old, maybe older. There were about ten pieces of paper, and each one contained a charcoal sketch of some sort.

He began to study the sketches intently, completely enthralled. He forgot where he was. His father once told him that Andy's great-grandfather was quite an artist, and he figured that these were old drawings of his. There was one drawing of the Ideal Bakery, one of three men that looked like brothers, one of an old man giving the three men something, a drawing of two gravestones, a crudely built stone wall, and a few others. At the bottom-left of each drawing, there was his great-grandfather's signature, Robert Gruner. This confirmed that the drawings were indeed his.

Andy suddenly realized that he had never actually been in the crawlspace before. He took his attention away from the boxes and began to shine his flashlight around the perimeter. The area was vast and empty, except for vertical support columns that were made of stacked stones welded together with cement. Each support column was vertical, about 2-feet by 2-feet wide, 3-feet high from crawlspace floor to the bottom floor of the bakery. They looked old, yet indestructible. There were six of them in total and they were equally spaced apart in the 50-foot by 30-foot crawlspace area.

If the dirt floor of the crawlspace was a clock face, the access hole was at 6 o'clock, and the boxes where at 8 o'clock. When Andy started to shine his light around the perimeter of the area he started at the back corner wall, or the 10 o'clock position. He then slowly moved his flashlight along the back wall from 11 o'clock to 12 o'clock to 1 o'clock to 2 o'clock and to 3 o'clock. As Andy passed 2 o'clock, which was at the exact opposite corner of the crawlspace from where he currently was, he saw something. He wasn't sure what it was, so he scanned that area again with his flashlight but didn't see anything. He moved the flashlight back and forth from 1 o'clock to 3 o'clock several times and he saw it again. He held his flashlight steady at 2 o'clock, and noticed something shining back at him. But he was not sure what it could be. It was a little reflection, like that from a mirror. Andy could not get whatever it was to reflect back to him constantly which meant it had to be very small. He figured it was about 50 feet away. With his dim flashlight, it was about impossible to make out.

The fear of the crawlspace vacated Andy's mind. It was now replaced with unbridled curiosity.

Andy began to crawl toward the reflection he saw with his flashlight. After about 25 feet, he came to an old wooden beam that was perpendicular to his crawl path. It was about 12-feet long and he figured it was 6-inches by 6-inches wide and tall. The beam still had some bark on the ends and the corners. It looked more like a roughly-hewed tree than the type of beam you would get at a lumberyard. He examined the beam and looked above his head. He noticed that the floor above his head was supported with dozens of beams just like the one he was studying. He figured it must have been an extra, and they didn't want to haul it out. He tried to move it with his hands, and it didn't budge. It must have weighed several hundred pounds.

Andy crawled over the beam, when he felt a sharp prick followed by a tugging and rip in his T-shirt on the back of his right shoulder. He reached with his left hand and felt that his T-shirt was ripped. His fingers felt a warm thick liquid. He pulled his hand back, and saw the blood on his fingers through the dim light. He turned his head to the right and looked up and shined his flashlight at the location where his shoulder scraped against the beam. Protruding from the beam was a rusty nail that looked as though it was a hundred years old. It didn't look like any nail he had ever seen before. It looked longer and thicker and resembled a rusty metal peg. Andy turned his head around and looked at the access hole to the crawlspace. With the isolated lightbulb shining in the basement area, the hole resembled a small oasis of light. It was his only exit out of the crawlspace.

Andy turned his head back around, and his curiosity drove him to forget about the blood and resume his mission. As he got closer to the corner of the crawlspace, he saw something that looked interesting, and out of place. The walls of the crawlspace were made out of 3 foot by 2-foot blocks of stone that were melded together with concrete. The walls looked indestructible as if they would easily last another hundred or two hundred years. He figured they had to be sturdy, because they were the foundation for a three-story building. In the corner of the crawlspace, though, it was different. There was a false wall that someone had built in the corner with very old, flat stones. The stones were of varied shapes and sizes. They ranged from 4-inches long and a quarter-inch high to 2-feet long and 3-inches high. Because the stones were not uniform there were many gaps and holes making it possible to see through the porous wall to the other side. The wall was set in diagonally, with each end of the wall 3 feet out from the corner.

Andy got in a perpendicular position to the wall and studied it closely. It was at this point Andy recalled that one of the drawings he examined earlier was of the very wall he was looking at. He deduced that there was a small triangular space between the false wall and the foundation. He estimated each of the three walls of the hidden space to be 3 feet long. He examined the stones carefully with his flashlight and when he shined it on the open gaps he could see through to the other side. He moved the flashlight side-to-side and up and down, trying to locate the reflection he saw from the far corner of the crawlspace. Finally, something reflected back into Andy's eyes. He focused his efforts on a small hole, low and to the left. Through the light of the flashlight, it looked as though some sort of metal box was on the other side. He did his best to get a better look but it was hard to see through the gaps between the stones.

Andy carefully started to remove some of the stones in an effort to extract the box. When he had a hole about the size of a deck of cards, he saw something else on the other side. It wasn't the box; he wasn't sure what it was. Andy shined his light on the object and moved his face closer. Still unable to determine what it was on the other side, he moved his flashlight closer. When it was about 4-inches away, he saw something shiny. The object moved slightly.

All at once, at least eight bats exploded out of the hole and past Andy's face. He felt the fluttering of the wings on his hair, and their squeaking pierced his ears as they scattered past his head. When the bats started to fly out of the hole, Andy buried his face into his arm trying to protect himself. When the fluttering subsided, he realized his heart was pounding, and his breath was labored. He turned his head around and could see the silhouettes of the small mammals flying back and forth against the light of the access hole.

Andy could still hear his own heart beating, but he was determined to get to the box. Cautiously, as he was not sure all of the bats were gone, he got back to work removing the stones.

Suddenly, he was startled by a loud clap of thunder. He turned around to look at his oasis of light on the other side of the access hole. The light flickered once, and then flickered again. Andy heard another loud clap of thunder, turned his head to look at the access hole, and the light went completely out. It was now pitch black with the exception of his dimming flashlight.

Andy shook his head in disbelief, and took a sobering moment to reflect on his situation. It was late at night. He was not only in a basement, he was in the far corner of a creepy crawlspace adjoining the basement. He was covered in dirt, by himself, with a bleeding shoulder, a violent thunder storm outside, in a 100-hundred-year old building with no electricity, but with an abundance of bats! The only comfort he had was a flashlight with weak batteries that could go out any minute.

He took a moment to gain his composure. Finally, his curiosity outweighed the bleakness of his situation. He turned around and continued to remove the stones. When he had a space the size of a child's lunchbox, he shined his flashlight into the hole. He didn't see any bats, which was of slight relief. But what he did see was a beat up black metal box that had a thick layer of dust on the top.

He carefully reached in to extract the box from its crypt. When he lifted the box with one hand he instantly realized it was fairly heavy-about five pounds, he thought. He blew the dust out off of the top of the box and began to study it carefully. It looked very old. It was about 8-inches long, 6-inches wide, and 4-inches tall. He noticed that it opened from the top. The initials "S.B." were etched on the top. And on the side, someone had scratched in the year 1933.

Andy slowly opened the box. He shined his flashlight in small circles to examine the contents. Andy got a puzzled look on his face. As he moved the flashlight around to examine the inside, it revealed several dozen very old coins. One coin in particular had a unique emblem on it that looked similar to a U-shaped harp. The other side of the coin had the number *5* stamped on it. Andy could not explain why, but this bronze-colored coin stood out from the others. He put the box down, selected the coin with the *5* on it, and carefully examined it with his flashlight.

While Andy examined the intricacies of the coin, he distantly noticed that it became more difficult to see the coin. The light from the flashlight grew dimmer ... and dimmer ... and dimmer, and then went completely out.

21

The Appraiser
Sunday, May 8, 2005 – 11:00 am

Although it was a Sunday, the local bank president was able to set up a meeting for Jennie, Ron, and Andy Gruner with the coin appraiser in Toledo. After all, the appraiser was an old college roommate of the bank president in Gibsonburg, and he knew the Gruners were in a desperate situation. He wanted to do anything he could to help his good friends.

The appraiser walked in to the conference room with Ron, Jennie, and Andy sitting across the table.

He smiled at them, "I'm very happy the president of your local bank directed you our way." We are the most respected rare coin firm in the area."

"Thank you for meeting with us on a Sunday. I'm sure this isn't normal practice, but we don't have a normal situation," Ron said.

The appraiser told Ron, "It's no problem at all. I was going to be in today anyway working on another matter. Anyway, I am pleased to tell you that we examined the coins thoroughly. And if I were you, I would put them in a very safe place."

Jennie, Ron, and Andy exchanged glances with one another. They appeared somewhat perplexed.

The appraiser shook his head. "Most of the coins are very rare and would easily get you about $120,000 for all of them if you wanted to sell."

Andy responded. "Seriously?"

The appraiser continued to explain, "However, one of the coins is a 1913 Liberty Head Nickel. The 1913 Liberty Head Nickel is one of the most expensive rare coins in the world! There were only five of them that were minted secretly in the Philadelphia Mint in 1913. An eccentric man named Samuel Brown purchased all five coins in 1913 for $50,000."

Jennie stopped the appraiser to ask, "What happened to the coins?"

The appraiser turned to Jennie. "Rumor has it that 20 years later, in 1933, Samuel Brown found out that he was dying. He traveled around the country and passed them out like regular nickels. He gave them to people that he deemed as *special* or for some reason or another *touched his soul*. When he dispersed each coin, his only words were *I'd hang on to that one if I were you*."

Ron suddenly looked disturbed. Something that the appraiser had said bothered him.

The appraiser continued. "Well, over the years, four of the five coins have been recovered. The fourth coin sold at a Sotheby's auction for $12 million dollars last fall. Everyone assumed the fifth coin was lost forever."

The appraiser smiled warmly at them. He then spoke very softly to explain, "You have the fifth coin. We estimate the value to be between $16 and $20 Million."

Shocked, Jennie started fanning herself. "I think I am feeling a little faint."

Excited, Andy sat up in his chair and looked at Ron.

Surprisingly, Ron looked extremely worried.

Jennie stammered when she spoke. "Our family has a financial situation taking place right now. I understand your firm handles the brokering of the coins."

The appraiser nodded, "That's right Jennie."

"How long would it take you to broker all the coins BUT the 1913 Liberty Head Nickel and get us the money?" she asked.

"Oh, that's an easy one." The appraiser said. "Our firm would purchase them and get you a check in about . . . oh . . . three days."

In a quiet voice, Ron said, "Let's do that. We will take the 1913 nickel and put it in a safe location until we decide what to do with it."

Smiling, the appraiser shook all their hands and told them, "Congratulations. This is a rare find, indeed! I'm very happy for you."

Andy, Jennie, and Ron walked out of the appraiser's office. Ron was clearly bothered.

As they walked out of the building, Andy excitedly told his parents, "It's just like what Coach Rase said. You never give up. Ever! No matter what the circumstances. He also said you should believe. You gotta believe in yourself, and believe in those around you at all times."

"That's what he said, huh!" Ron snapped.

Andy looked confused "Dad, what's wrong? This is great news for us."

22

The Origin Of The Coin

Ron grimaced. "Andy, let me tell you a story my dad told me right before he passed away. A long time ago a man walked into the bakery. This was when your great-grandfather and his two brothers owned the bakery."

Andy looked quizzically at his father. "Yeah, so?"

Ron sighed deeply, "Well, all your great-grandfather and his brothers did was spend a little time with this man. They listened to him."

"Was this man Samuel Brown?" Andy asked. "The initials S.B. were on the box I found."

Ron shook his head. "I don't know. What I do know is that this man gave all three of them a whole box of coins. He pulled out one coin in particular and made a point to say, I'd hang onto to that one if I were you. The man's words made the brother's curious, so they got the coins appraised shortly thereafter. Back then, dad said only one of the coins was worth anything. I don't know the amount, but that one coin was worth a lot of money. Your grandfather, my dad, was only about ten at the time. I think this was in the year 1933, a few years after the stock market crash."

"Ron, you never told me all this." Jennie interrupted

Ron shrugged, "I didn't see the point. To be honest, I never really believed it. Dad had pretty bad dementia at the time."

Andy looked at his dad, surprised by new. "Wow, dad! That's sort of amazing."

Ron continued his story. "Well, these three brothers, who were the best of friends as well, were torn apart once they got this special coin. They never actually cashed the coin in, but the idea of the wealth and what they could do with their share ruined the family. For the first time in their lives, all three brothers were fighting with each other. The stress caused one of the brothers to have a heart attack. The other brother was killed in a car accident-in a car he bought with money he didn't have. He purchased the car on credit, knowing that he would soon be rich when they sold the coin."

Jennie and Andy were attentively listening to each word Ron spoke.

"My dad told me that he saw his father leaving the house one day," Ron continued. "Remember, he was only ten at the time. He asked his father where he was going. This is what he said:

"Son, we had a great family. We had our health, our God, good homes and good families. Once money entered the picture, everything collapsed like a cheap house of cards. Now, my two brothers-my best friends in the world-are gone. I'm gonna take this coin and put it in a place where nobody will ever find it. I'm also gonna pray that fortune never finds anyone in our family again. I'm gonna pray real hard for this."

Ron looked at his son. "Dad passed away two days after he told me this story."

Andy was trying to absorb the information. "What do you think we should do dad? Do you really think . . ."

Ron looked at his son sharply. "Think what Andy?"

Andy was almost afraid to say it. "That the coin is kind of . . . You know? Cursed?"

Ron didn't say anything at first. He then broke the silence. "I don't know if I believe in that type of stuff, son. But, this is what I want you to do. Take this coin, put it in the box, and put it back where you got it. Nobody goes down in the basement of the bakery anyway. It will be safer there than any bank or safe deposit box."

Andy nodded his head to confirm his father's request.

Ron looked intently at his family. "And another thing. Let's all keep this very quiet."

23

A Date With Kathy
Sunday, May 8, 2005 – 8 pm

On an unseasonably warm May evening Andy and Kathy were sitting on a small wicker love seat in Kathy's yard. They watched the sunset over their pond with the old wooden dock that jutted out from underneath a weeping willow tree. Kathy usually sat by herself to watch the sun set over the family pond, the glorious orange light reflecting off the water created some of the prettiest sunsets she'd ever seen.

Andy nudged her, "Can I ask you a question?"

Kathy stared contently at the colorful water. "Sure."

He looked at her. "If you have a situation, and you really have no idea what you should do, what's the best way to decide?"

Kathy looked at Andy. "I don't know. I would say just follow your heart and it will be hard to go wrong."

Andy looked away for a moment. "I just think my heart is confused too."

Kathy looked straight ahead and smiled. "I understand. More than you can imagine."

Kathy and Andy looked into each other's eyes. Andy reached for a glass of water that was on a little table next to Kathy. When he leaned in for the glass he looked in her eyes. It was just for a moment, but long enough to make it awkward. Their lips were just a few inches apart and they came as close as you could get to kissing, without kissing. Andy pulled away and they both looked forward. Despite being friends since the third grade, Andy had no idea what to say. Their friendship was changing.

In somewhat of a surprising move, Kathy snatched the hat Andy wore backwards on his head. She put it on her own head, and jumped up off the love seat. She pretended she was holding a microphone and started talking like a sports broadcaster and treated Andy to her best over-the-top sports broadcaster voice. "Here we are sports fans. Andy Gruner, captain of the Gibsonburg baseball team, is supposedly up to any and all challenges."

Andy smiled.

"What's this?" She continued, her voice playful. "A little ole farm girl challenges Andy to a race to the dock. Will he accept? Can he win? Can he catch the speedy Kathy?"

He laughed. "Very funny!"

Kathy started backing up slowly. "And they're off!"

Andy stood up and started to walk toward Kathy. In response, she backed up faster. With a giggle, she continued, "And no wonder they went 6 and 17! Gruner, runs like a turtle."

When Kathy said *turtle*, Andy took off and ran toward her. When Andy started to run, Kathy turned around, screamed and took off for the dock while Andy chased her.

Andy finally caught Kathy. He picked her up around the waist in front of the dock. He held her up and spun her around, her laughter filling the evening air. By the time he put her down on her feet, his laughter came to match hers. Slowly, Kathy's hand met Andy's. Andy felt a rush of heat go to his cheeks. Together, hand-in-hand, they walked out and sat at the end of the dock to watch the sun slowly sink from the sky.

"This old farm has a lot of nice views, doesn't it?" Kathy said softly.

Andy turned to look at her. "They're amazing."

This time when their eyes met, there wasn't the same awkwardness as before. They became lost in each other's eyes, the emotion and romantic intensity continued to grow. In all the years they had known each other they had never kissed. Now, nothing could stop it.

As the soft orange glow from the sunset splashed upon their faces, Kathy slowly looked down at Andy's mouth and then moved her eyes back up to his eyes. Kathy moved closer and kissed Andy and he kissed her back. It was their very first kiss. No longer were they just the young friends who met on the bus in the third grade. It would be the most memorable kiss either would ever have.

When it ended, Kathy looked up at Andy. After a few moments she whispered, "I've been waiting for that kiss for a long time."

Andy looked into Kathy's eyes His mind could not easily process all that he felt. It was overwhelming. He leaned down, and they kissed again just as the sun was dipping below the horizon.

24

Game #3 – Gibsonburg vs. Fremont St. Joe
Monday, May 16, 2005

It was getting a little easier to find Gibsonburg on Pudge's wall, as the number of teams had been cut by 25 percent. If you searched the board, you would eventually locate Fremont St. Joe (24-1) vs. Gibsonburg (8-17). It would be the third game for both teams and they would play on Monday, May 16, 2005 at 4:30 pm.

Coach Rase was in the middle of a heated conversation with the Gibsonburg principal in the hallway of the school entrance. "But it's the State Tournament!"

Principal Grugg shook his head. "I'm sorry coach. Whoever is not here by 11 am does not play."

Coach Rase looked at his watch and saw that it was 10:40 am.

Frustrated, he continued to plead his case. "But none of the seniors are here. It's senior skip day!"

Principal Grugg shrugged. "Rules are rules coach."

It was May 16, 2005 and Gibsonburg was supposed to play Fremont St. Joe at 4:30 pm. However, it was senior skip day and no seniors were at school. Senior skip day was an unofficial, non-sanctioned, skip day organized by the seniors, and not the school. Most school administrators take the day in stride and don't make too much of a fuss. It was 10:40 am and if the senior players did not get to school by 11 am, they could not play in the St. Joe game.

Coach Rase walked outside in front of the school and frantically began dialing his mobile phone. He tried to contact all seniors directly. He then attempted to contact their parents and at 10:55 am, and with no success, he walked back into the school. He threw his hat on the floor, put his hands on his hips, and stared at the ceiling tiles above him when the principal walked up beside him.

"Coach, does it really matter? With or without your seniors St. Joe will kill us." said Principal Grugg.

Two minutes before 11 am, Andy, Alex, Wes, Wyatt, and Bobby all burst through the door of the school, startling Coach Rase and the principal. They were all out of breath.

Coach Rase excitedly, but cautiously, looked at Principal Grugg and said, "Principal?"

Principal Grugg didn't say anything at first. The excitement left Coach Rase's face. After an uncomfortable few seconds, he sternly chimed in and said, "All right, they can play."

Coach Rase sighed deeply. He then looked at the seniors and said, "Some folks are gonna owe me a few extra sprints after tonight's game, win or lose!"

The boys smiled and laughed, glad to have made it on time. A relieved Coach Rase finally smiled as well and said, "Bus leaves at 2:30 fellas. Don't be late."

A half hour before the team bus was set to leave the school parking lot, Andy was dressed in his baseball uniform and was doing the unthinkable. He was in the crawlspace of the Ideal Bakery. He made certain to put new batteries in his flashlight before he climbed in through the access hole. Unbeknownst to anyone, he carefully extracted the metal box from the wall in the crawlspace and opened it. Paranoid about getting caught, he turned his head around and stared at the access hole into the crawlspace. He didn't expect to see anyone there, but he looked, just the same.

He selected the only item in the box, the 1913 Liberty Head Nickel. He examined it carefully, like a jeweler appraising a diamond, by shining his flashlight directly on the coin that he held between his thumb and forefinger. He looked at the coin like an old friend and said to himself, "Well, I don't think we could play any worse! Maybe you can bring us a little luck."

With that, Andy took the coin and put it into the left rear pocket of his baseball pants.

At 2:30 pm, Jim the bus driver took a left out of the school parking lot and headed north on Route 300. He hit the red traffic light at the four corners of Gibsonburg, and waited for it to turn green. He sometimes wondered why he always seemed to hit the light when it was red. When the light turned green, Jim turned right on Route 600. He was taking Gibsonburg to their third game in the tournament to play Fremont St. Joe. The game was to be played on neutral ground at Old Fort High School.

As the bus rumbled along, Wyatt Kiser was staring out the bus window. Several rows back he could hear two members of *Scrub Nation* talking.

Jeff Feasel was talking to Trent Snowden. "I don't know about you, but I don't think we have a chance today."

"I know, but at least we get to watch Tyler Pinkus. My dad says we will see him pitching in the *bigs* in a few years," Jeff replied.

As Wyatt overheard the comments, he continued to stare out the window in deep thought.

Fremont St. Joe had been playing Gibsonburg in baseball as long as there had been baseball in those parts. In all that time, nobody ever remembered Gibsonburg winning a game. Ever!

This season was no different. And for some reason, Pinkus had it out for Wyatt Kiser. As Wyatt sat on the bus, his mind wandered and he replayed Pinkus hitting him with a high velocity fastball when he was six. When he was nine. When he was twelve. When he was fifteen. And then there was the time just two weeks ago when Pinkus hit him when St. Joe was winning the game by a score of 10 to nothing.

Wyatt had never had a home run in his life and never came close to being a threat to Pinkus. But for some reason, Pinkus really enjoyed throwing at Wyatt. It was just an amusing hobby for Pinkus to throw his fastballs at Wyatt. Maybe it made the one-sided games with Gibsonburg more interesting for him.

The bus jerked to a stop and Wyatt snapped out of his thoughts. He and the rest of the team reluctantly got off the bus to face their number one nemesis, Fremont St. Joe.

When the bus arrived, to the team's surprise, there were a few more fans then they expected. Not a lot, but definitely more than usual. And of course, as always, Henry Tillman was already waiting in the stands when the bus arrived ready for the game to begin.

As Gibsonburg entered the dugout on the third base side of the field, the team spotted her. It was Tyler Pinkus' mother, in all her glory, sitting on her crimson throne behind the fence near the first base on deck circle.

Farther down to the left of her and just past the dugout, they saw him as well. It was Tyler Pinkus warming up in the bullpen. Even though they were pretty far away, you could still hear the hard slap of his fastballs hitting the warm-up catcher's glove. Because of their velocity, they sounded much different than any other pitcher they had ever faced. They were louder. Much louder.

The St. Joe parents certainly did not care for the antics of Tyler Pinkus' mother, but they tolerated her. She was a joke in their minds and her unimaginable behavior was so ridiculous that they just shook their heads and observed. Most of the St. Joe players had been together since they were six years old and the parents of the players had long ago built up a sort of numbness to the shenanigans of Pinkus' mother.

As the two teams warmed up, she spoke to two other mothers seated in lawn chairs to her immediate right. She loudly declared, "I wasn't even gonna come to this game. Gibsonburg stinks! This is just a formality." She said laughing, "But hey, I was bored. So I figured: why the hell not?"

His mother had an obnoxious laugh, akin to that of a fat hyena. She continued to tell the two women seated by her, "My nephew plays for Jackson Center. We will probably have to beat them on our way to the State Championship. I'll feel bad when my baby mows down my own sister's child. Well, maybe not THAT bad!"

She belted out that annoying laugh again and screamed, "Come on, Tyler!"

As Gibsonburg was warming up their arms in the outfield, Bo Smith pulled up by himself in his white truck.

As he parked, Andy and Bobby, who were side by side playing catch, took notice. Andy nodded in Bo Smith's direction and asked Bobby, "Your sister still dating him?"

Bobby laughed and said, "Naw. She dumped him once she found out he liked Justin Timberlake . . . and wearing women's under-wear."

Andy and Bobby both laughed. After thinking about Bobby's comment for another second, Andy bent over and laughed harder. He couldn't get the mental picture of his mind.

When Bo Smith got out of his truck, a tournament coordinator flagged him down. She told him he couldn't park at that location. "I'm sorry, ma'am. I'll move it right away," Bo said, uncharacteristically polite.

The woman thanked Bo and as soon as she left Bo continued on to the stands. "Screw you lady," he muttered

As Gibsonburg continued to win, Jimmy continued to call their games for *720AM*, out of Fostoria.

He leaned into the microphone and recapped the team's efforts.

"The big question today is how can the Golden Bears of Gibson-burg beat Tyler Pinkus and the legendary Fremont St. Joe Eagles? Gibsonburg has been hot lately. They have yet to record an error and their number one pitcher, Alex Black, has been nothing short of sensational."

"However, Fremont St. Joe is Fremont St. Joe. They went to the state final four last year, but lost their first semi-final game to Lancaster Fisher Catholic. They have every starter back from that talented team. They already beat Gibsonburg 10-0 and 16-4 earlier in the year. Pinkus' fastball has been clocked in the mid-90s. If you look around in the stands you will see many scouts here today just to watch Pinkus. Lots of pressure on the big guy!"

Inside the dugout, Coach Rase addressed the team. "Here we are fellas," he said nervously.

As he looked at the team, none of them look too excited.

He turned around and gazed at the field. "I know we have not had much luck against this guy. But remember: It's baseball. Anything can happen. They could have a bad day. We could have a great day. Let's just take this game inning-by-inning. Win one inning at a time, and see what happens. Bring it in, Gruner."

Everyone got in a tight circle around Andy Gruner.

"All right!" shouted Andy. "Go Bears' on three. One. Two. Three. GO BEARS!"

Everyone on the team cheered, and Gibsonburg ran out to go through warm-ups on the field.

As Gibsonburg warmed up, Jimmy set up the game and announced, "This is an interesting match up between two very different teams.

One team has very little in the way of a winning tradition: the other is a legend in the state.

Gibsonburg has a less than stellar 8-17 record. St. Joe sits at 24-1.

When you look at Gibsonburg, they average about 5 feet, 8 inches and 140 pounds. St. Joe has eight players over 6 feet tall.

St. Joe has a remarkable eight players batting over .300. Gibsonburg has one player batting over .300.

During the regular season, St. Joe trounced Gibsonburg 10-0 in one game and 16-4 in the other.

Gibsonburg has never played in a State Championship. Last year, St. Joe made it to the state semi-finals and lost to Lancaster Fisher Catholic. They returned every starter from that great team.

This is your classic country ball vs. city ball.

Just look at the legion of St. Joe Fans. They outnumber Gibsonburg fans four to one. You would think they were playing in the State Championship already."

As the team was warming up, Josh Sanchez was in right field getting ready to catch fly balls next to Derek Hetrick. As they waited for the coach to finish up hitting to the infield, the outfielders played catch with one another. Wes Milleson in centerfield threw a ball way over Josh's head. Sanchez chased after the ball. When he ran about 70 feet he stopped dead in his tracks.

He gazed up slowly and saw a St. Joe player holding the ball that went over his head. Sanchez was 5 feet, 5 inches tall. He looked in awe at the gargantuan St. Joe player that stood a foot in front of him. He was at least 6 feet, 9 inches tall. While Sanchez stared at the St. Joe player, he recalled that the St. Joe first baseman was a basketball player that signed a letter of intent to play basketball for the University of Cincinnati. From a side view, it looked like a first grader staring up at Kobe Bryant.

The St. Joe player had the overthrown ball in his hand. In a deep voice he asked, "You lookin' for this?"

Sanchez was still in awe and could not stop staring at the sheer size of the St. Joe first baseman. The St. Joe player dropped the ball from his hand to Sanchez' open glove but he was too stunned to move or try to catch it. The ball landed on the ground with a thump!

The announcers told the listeners at home. "I'd have to say, Gibsonburg's chances probably aren't too good today."

Right before the game started the Gibsonburg team sat on the bench and got ready to take the field as they were the home team. Andy Gruner pulled the 1913 Liberty Head Nickel out of his back left pocket and held it in his right hand. He looked at the coin curiously until the umpire yelled, "Let's go Gibsonburg! Time to take the field!"

He put the coin away and ran to his position at shortstop. The other players followed closely behind.

The game got underway. In the bottom of the first inning with no score, two outs, and nobody on, Wyatt Kiser stepped up to the plate.

Before Wyatt stepped into the batters box, his thoughts drifted away and his world went silent. He thought about Pinkus beaning him when he was 12. Pinkus beaning him when he was 14. Pinkus beaning him earlier in the year. His flashbacks disappeared quickly when the umpire jolted him out of his daydream by shouting, "Batter up!"

Jimmy continued to make the call on Wyatt's at bat. "Here's the windup and the first pitch to Kiser. It's high and inside! Uh-oh! Watch out! Kiser hits the dirt! I don't see how that ball did not hit him in the head! We have a 1 and 0 count."

On the mound, you could see an amused Pinkus chuckling as he waited for the catcher to throw him the ball.

Wyatt stepped back up to the plate and shot Pinkus an intense look. Jimmy announced the second pitch. "Here's Pinkus getting his sign, going set, winding up, and delivering. Holy cow, it's another high and inside pitch! This pitch causes Kiser to hit the dirt again! I don't understand how Pinkus could be so wild after easily striking out the first two Gibsonburg batters."

On the mound, Pinkus was laughing at the fun he was having with Kiser. His other team members were not amused and the shortstop from St. Joe yelled at him. "Quit screwin' around and get this guy!"

Pinkus turned to the shortstop. "Shut up! I'll get him now!"

Pinkus' mom got out of her Crimson throne and ran to the fence. "Go ahead and hit him if you want to baby. You'll just strike the next three out anyway!"

Wyatt took a deep breath and stepped back into the batter's box.

Jimmy started up again, "Okay. The count is 2 balls and no strikes to Kiser. Pinkus delivers. It looks like a hard fastball belt high and inside. Kiser swings . . ."

Wyatt swung his bat with all of his might. As his bat struck the fastball it was launched like a missile toward the centerfield field fence.

Jimmy jerked forward in his chair. "And this ball is crushed. It's going, going, going, and gone over the centerfield fence."

Wyatt was already rounding first when he saw the ball go over the fence. When it did go over he jumped in the air and pumped his fist.

A radar gun held by one of the scouts watching Pinkus registered the pitch speed at 94 miles per hour.

Tyler Pinkus' mom yelled, "What!"

When she yelled, she accidentally spit out her gum. She quickly picked it off the dirt and put it back into her mouth. She looked around, smiled curtly to her left and right, hoping nobody else saw her.

As Wyatt was running between second and third base, she exploded out of her chair and slammed her body into the backstop fence. She screamed, "You got lucky on that one hick! Try opening your eyes next time!"

Jimmy, the announcer, glanced at his stat book. "From what I am reading in our stat book, this is the first home run of Wyatt Kiser's high school career. And it is off the best pitcher in the state. Just like that the score is one to nothing, with Gibsonburg on top."

Tyler Pinkus was very upset. As Wyatt rounded third base, Pinkus walked off the mound toward him. "You got lucky on that one farm boy," he growled. "Enjoy it, 'cause it'll never happen again."

When Wyatt approached home plate, Pinkus' mother was still at the fence and yelled, "You're a cheat batter. Nobody does that to my baby! Check his bat ump! It can't be legal!" she screamed.

At home plate, the entire Gibsonburg team was waiting for Wyatt. When his foot touched home, they mobbed him and celebrated.

Jimmy smiled. "Pinkus obviously upset with that pitch. Let's see how he reacts."

Tyler Pinkus struck out the next batter, Andy Gruner, to end the inning. He then continued to register strike out after strike out with his 95 mile-per-hour fastballs. He wasn't perfect though. In the third and fourth innings he hit two batters and walked a few more.

One of the batters hit by a pitch was Wes Milleson in the third inning. Wes stole his way to third and then stole home on a passed ball scoring Gibsonburg's second run. The score, after four complete innings, was tied at 2-2.

On the bench the four members of *Scrub Nation* all discussed how this was not a bad time to be a scrub. None of them wanted to bat against Pinkus. He seemed a little wild today.

After St. Joe batted in the top of the fifth inning Jimmy told the people at home, "Pinkus cannot only pitch but he can hit as well. His fifth-inning triple brought in three runs to make the score Gibsonburg 2, St. Joe 5, after five and a half innings of play."

Coach Rase and the rest of Gibsonburg team were dejected.

They didn't have much hope. There wasn't much of a chance to get three runs against St. Joe with the way Pinkus was pitching. He seemed to be getting stronger and more accurate as the game went on.

In the stands, Ron and Jennie Gruner looked at each other in disappointment. "Well, the season has to end sometime," Ron said.

As the team prepared to bat in the bottom of the fifth inning, Andy Gruner pulled the coin out of his back left pocket and studied it in his hand for moment. By his expression, it looked as though he was telling the coin, "Now its time."

He placed it back in his back left pocket and watched his team get ready to face Pinkus.

The announcer never let up. "Here we are sports fans in the bottom of the fifth inning, no outs, nobody on and a score of Gibsonburg 2, Fremont St. Joe 5. Alex Black will be leading the inning off for Gibsonburg.

Black stepped out of the box. "Come on Black, start something here," Coach Rase yelled.

Alex Black nodded confidently to Coach Rase and stepped back into the batters box.

Jimmy called the play. "Here's the first pitch to Black and he fouls it up very high! It goes out of play behind the first base side of the field."

Alex Black's foul ball came down right in the middle of the windshield of Bo Smith's truck, which was parked illegally behind the third base dugout. There was an audible crash as the windshield was completely shattered.

Bo Smith jumped up from his seat. "Shit!" He screamed, and sprinted toward his truck.

From their vantage point in the Gibsonburg dugout Andy and Bobby saw everything. They just looked at each other and chuckled.

Jimmy continued to call Alex's at bat. "Here's the 0-1 pitch by Pinkus . . . and Black hits a deep fly ball to right center. It's going, going, it might be out of here! No, it stays in the ballpark, hits the fence and bounces back. Black is rounding second as the right fielder's throw hits the cut-off man. With no outs, Coach Rase is not taking any chances and he holds his arms up to keep Black at second, but Black must not see him! He is not slowing down at all. There's the throw as Black goes for a triple. Black slides headfirst into third. It's gonna be close."

Coach Rase yelled at him. "Slide! Slide!" right as the throw was going into the third baseman's glove.

Jimmy continued calling the game. "Black slid head first into third. It's too close for us to call. The ump is hesitating a little bit. SAFE! Black is safe at third. Unbelievable! Gibsonburg now has a runner on third with no outs and Wes Milleson coming up to the plate!"

Alex was lying on the ground with his head down. He was just waiting to get chewed out for not holding up at second. He remembered Coach Rase always saying:

"And fellas, one of the cardinal rules of baseball is that you never make your first or third out at third base. If you are on second, you will most likely score on a hit so being on third gets you nothing."

Coach Rase shouted, "TIME OUT!" which the umpire confirmed by holding both arms up in the air.

Alex got up slowly and Coach Rase extended an arm to help him up. Player and Coach looked eye to eye. Alex looked sheepishly at the coach, who remained stone-faced. Finally, the coach broke out into a happy smile. Coach Rase told Alex, "Nice hit buddy! Nice hit." To Alex's surprise, he didn't get chewed out. Coach Rase knew Alex was giving everything he could to beat St. Joe.

Coach Rase patted him on the back and then got ready to watch Wes Milleson bat. This was a turning point in the Coach Rase/Alex

Black relationship.

Alex hit the ball hard and for one of the first times, Pinkus was not sure of himself. His confidence was a little rattled. He thought, "This Wyatt kid gets a home run and another lousy player hits it to the fence. What am I doing wrong? What am I doing wrong?"

Pinkus was not thinking they were still up by three runs. His thoughts were clouded by the two hard hit balls he had given up in the game. He was confused. Other pitchers gave up those types of hits-not me he thought.

Wes Milleson worked hard and finally walked on a very close pitch with a 3-2 count. This brought Wyatt Kiser up to the plate for his third time. After his first inning home run, Wyatt had struck out in his second at bat.

Jimmy called the play. "Here we are in the bottom of the fifth inning, two runners on and no outs. Wyatt Kiser for Gibsonburg is approaching the plate. The score is Gibsonburg 2, Fremont St. Joe 5."

As Wyatt walked up to the plate he had another flashback. He saw himself getting hit by Pinkus when he was 6, 9, and 12. He then saw himself hitting that home run earlier in the game. He felt some sort of change come over his body. He was not sure what it was, but it felt good. He felt strong. Even though he did not understand it at the time, Wyatt was feeling an overpowering dose of confidence. He smiled, and then took his place in the batter's box.

As Wyatt stepped up to the plate, Jimmy began to speak, "Pinkus looks very intense. I wouldn't want to be up to bat here. He doesn't look like he is in any mood to mess around. Kiser steps up to the plate. You know, you have an All-State pitcher, and a batter with no home runs in his career knocking one out of the park. You have to chalk that up to luck. A total fluke play. I don't think Pinkus is going to make another mistake here."

Both teams were out of their seats and in front of their dugouts watching the showdown. Many of the fans were on their feet. Wyatt and Pinkus both looked very intense.

Jimmy called the at bat. "Pinkus gets his sign, checks the runners at first and third, and goes set. He is glaring at Wyatt with an intense stare."

The scene was like a western showdown. But instead of guns, one gunslinger had a baseball and the other had a baseball bat. As pitcher and batter stared each other down, Wyatt did something that was out of character. He winked at Pinkus and smiled as to say "I got you!" Nobody else could see this.

Pinkus turned beet red in the face and got mad. He was visibly upset and was about to unravel. In an uncontrolled manner, he hurried his motion and unleashed his hardest fastball toward Wyatt. He sent it right over the middle of the plate belt high.

Jimmy continued to announce Wyatt's at bat, "Pinkus delivers and it is a good strong fastball. Kiser swings and I can't believe it! This ball is drilled! It is going, going, going, gone! It completely flies over the left field fence by at least 50 feet. We now have a tie ball game at five runs a piece folks!"

A radar gun held by one of the scouts looking at Pinkus clocked his pitch speed at 97 miles per hour.

The Gibsonburg bench erupted in a frenzy! They charged to home plate to meet Wyatt. The Gibsonburg fans went crazy. The St. Joe fans were in a state of disbelief.

Pinkus' mom screamed, "That son of a bitch!" She then sprang from her throne and came completely unglued! She began by throwing her drink at the backstop. She then picked up her precious crimson chair, raised it high and threw it down on the ground. She took her purse, and started to swing it around like she was in a hammer throw competition and let go of it and watched as it sailed into the crowd. She charged the backstop and grabbed it with her hands and began shaking it like some sort of madwoman. She was screaming uncontrollably. She actually tried to climb up the back-stop!

Pinkus was rattled. As Wyatt jogged around the bases, he stomped around the pitchers mound unleashing a plethora of expletives.

As Wyatt took his home run jog around the bases, Jimmy continued, "Unbelievable. Wyatt Kiser. This is only the second home run of his career and it is off of one of the best pitchers in the state. The score is now tied at 5 to 5. Ladies and gentlemen, we have a baseball game."

After Wyatt touched home plate and was congratulated by his teammates, Pinkus' mom shouted at Wyatt from behind the back-stop, "You stink hitter. Nobody does that to my baby. I hate you! You stink too ump!"

The ump jerked around and glared at Pinkus' mom and she glared right back at him. Another St. Joe parent standing by Pinkus' mom said, "The ump is calling a great game lady."

She responded to the fan while she was staring at the umpire, "Yeah maybe, but he still stinks!"

She took her attention away from the umpire and in disgust shifted her attention to the parent and said, "And you stink too!"

The St. Joe parent just shook his head and walked away as he said to himself, "You're a joke, lady."

The umpire motioned to the tournament director to get Pinkus' mother under control. The tournament director approached and told her nicely that she must go sit down. He said, "Ma'am, you are going to have to go back to your seat."

The director then gently touched her on the sleeve.

Pinkus' mom jerked her body away and yelled, "Get your hands off me! You're hurting me! Don't you know who I am. I am Tyler Pinkus' mom!

"I know lady, I know. Everyone knows you, believe me," he replied, exasperated.

She then stomped away, reset her chair and sat down.

Still in disbelief, Jimmy continued announcing. "Pinkus is in a state of shock. That was a great pitch, and Kiser just nailed it. He certainly has Pinkus' number today. Well, let's see what happens now."

Pinkus struck out the next three batters, Gruner, Hetrick, and Eddings on nine straight pitches to retire the side. None of the batters had a chance.

Jimmy summed it up as best he could. "Three strike outs on nine pitches. Those pitches were as powerful as anything Pinkus has thrown all game. I almost felt bad for the batters, as they did not even have a chance. It looked like a major leaguer pitching against kids. The question is, can Gibsonburg get any more runs with Pinkus appearing to peak after giving up that home run to Kiser? After five innings our score is Gibsonburg 5, Fremont St. Joe, 5."

After a scoreless one and a half innings, Jimmy spoke again. "All right, we have the bottom of 7, men on second and third, one out, and a score that is tied 5-5. Pinkus is obviously rattled: he hit one batter, walked another, and then threw a wild pitch that advanced both base runners. We now have Alex Black on third and Wes Milleson on second. Wyatt Kiser is up to bat for Gibsonburg. This should be very interesting."

The St. Joe coach got Pinkus' attention. When Pinkus looked at the coach, he received the sign for an intentional walk.

"No way man! I ain't walking him!" Pinkus yelled back at his coach.

The St. Joe coach gave the sign to Pinkus again, and Pinkus shook his head "No!"

The St. Joe coach erupted! He threw his hat down on the ground and kicked over the five gallon bucket of baseballs. He looked at

Pinkus with a fiery intensity and screamed, "YOU WALK HIM!" He didn't care that everyone knew. It didn't matter as it was not a surprise.

The St. Joe catcher stood up and stepped to the side for a pitch out.

Jimmy confirmed the coach's decision. "This is a smart move by St. Joe. Kiser has two home runs. Loading the bases will make it easier for them to get the next out, and potentially get a double play. Plus, Andy Gruner is up next, and he has three strike outs on the day. They would rather take their chances on Gruner than pitch to Kiser again. Ok. Here is the first pitch to Kiser."

Both benches were on their feet as were the fans. Everyone wanted to see what was going to happen in the fourth meeting between Pinkus and Kiser.

"We are at the bottom of the seventh inning, one out, men at second and third, and the score is tied at five. The winning run for Gibsonburg is on third base," the announcer said.

"Pinkus gets his sign," Jimmy continued. "He goes set. He checks the runner at second, and then the runner at third. He looks very calm. The catcher steps out for the pitch out. Pinkus delivers and look out! It is a hard fastball and Kiser can't get out of the way. It hit him right in the side and Kiser goes down hard. Oh, man. That hurt! That's a 90-plus mile-per-hour fastball right in the ribs. That must feel like getting shot with a bazooka!"

The radar gun held by the scouts clocked the pitch that hit Wyatt at 98 miles per hour.

Everyone in the stands held their breath to see if Wyatt was okay.

The St. Joe coach threw his hat down in disgust. He wanted Pinkus to walk Kiser. Coach Rase went ballistic. He demanded that the home plate umpire throw Pinkus out of the game for throwing at Kiser intentionally.

Pinkus turned around and walked back to the mound smiling and proud of himself. As he walked, the home plate umpire followed him. "Hey pitch! That's a warning. One more time and you are out of here."

Pinkus flipped around and pleaded with the umpire. "It was an accident! Plus, he was all over the plate, blue!"

The home plate umpire yelled back at him. "One more word and you're gone!"

The fans were all talking, the benches were on the edge of their seats, the St. Joe coach and the umpire were all over Pinkus, and Coach Rase was still making his case to the umpires to throw Pinkus out of the game. The scouts that came to watch Pinkus had seen enough. They got up to leave. The game suddenly became very chaotic.

While the entire game was in an uproar, the on-deck batter, Andy Gruner, ran up to check on Wyatt who was on one knee, beside home plate. He was holding his ribs and was in a great amount of pain.

Andy bent over and said, "You all right?"

Wyatt cringed and held his side. "I'll be okay."

Wyatt gave a painful smile, looked up at Andy and calmly said, "Hey, we ever beat these guys?"

Amused at Wyatt's attempt to make humor in such a tough situation, Andy smiled at him and said, "Nope. Don't think we ever had."

Still on one knee, in great pain, Wyatt said, "This would be a pretty good game to win, huh?"

Andy nodded. "It sure would. The only trouble is I've never even hit a foul ball off of Pinkus."

Encouraging as he could be, Wyatt told him, "Just make contact man, it'll go!

The umpire then shouted, "C'mon! Let's go!"

Andy looked at the umpire, and held up his index finger. One more minute.

Andy stood up from Wyatt and looked at the scoreboard. It was the bottom of the seventh inning, with one out, and a score of Gibsonburg 5, St. Joe 5.

Andy took his eyes off of the scoreboard and then looked at Tyler Pinkus. His confidence on the mound had returned as he awaited striking out Andy for the fourth time in the game.

Then he bent down to Wyatt, smiled confidently, and repeated Wyatt's advice, "Just make contact, huh?"

Wyatt forced a smile. "Just make contact."

Andy and Wyatt then smiled at one another. Andy's grin widened as to say, "Let's get Pinkus."

The umpire shouted again. "I said let's go! PLAY BALL!"

Wyatt got up slowly and hobbled down the baseline. As he made his way to first base, Pinkus' mom yelled out loud enough for him to hear. "You should have thrown at his head!"

Jimmy the announcer continued, "I don't know how Kiser can even live, yet alone run after that one."

When Kiser got to first base, the 6 foot, 9 inch tall first baseman for St. Joe looked at him and said, "You okay, man?"

Wyatt winced. "Yup. No big deal."

The first baseman gave him a sympathetic look. "That was a dick move by Pinkus. He's a doucher."

Taking a small lead, Wyatt mildly smiled at the first baseman as he got into position to hold Wyatt on first base.

Jimmy continued. "Kiser will be feeling that one tomorrow. That was just a low-class act by Pinkus. Just ridiculous! He won't impress too many scouts with that attitude. That does display the toughness of Kiser, though. He showed some grit the way he handled that situation."

Andy stepped out of the batter's box and looked down to Coach

Rase at third base. Coach Rase yelled at him. "Come on Andy, bases are loaded! Hit 'em around!"

Andy nodded confidently to his coach and stepped back into the batters box. There was not a single person in their seats. The St. Joe team was at the front of their bench, as was the entire Gibsonburg team-even the members of *Scrub Nation*. All parents, including Ron and Jennie Gruner watched with great anticipation. Henry was biting his nails. Kathy Colaner had her hand over her mouth and could barely stand to watch.

Pinkus' mother was a nervous wreck. Sitting in her throne, she pulled a bag full of strawberries out from under her seat. She pulled one out, held it in her hand, and told the woman sitting next to her, "I gotta eat when I'm nervous. I gotta eat. I'm so nervous. I can't take it."

Two little girls in the stands took notice of Pinkus' mom with the strawberry. The one girl shrugged as she told her friend, "At least she's eating something healthy."

At that point, Pinkus' mom produced a can of Cheese Wiz from her St. Joe-inspired purse. She then covered the entire strawberry in Cheese Wiz and devoured it all in one bite. The two little girls watched in disgusted amazement.

"Gross!" One little girl exclaimed.

Jimmy summarized the situation, "Well, it doesn't get any better than this! Bottom of the seventh inning, one out, bases loaded, tie score, and the winner advances to game four. Andy Gruner is up to bat for Gibsonburg. Alex Black on third base represents the go ahead run. If Gruner can get Black to score, Gibsonburg wins the game. Gruner has three strike-outs for the day, and I would guess that Pinkus will go right after him. Gibsonburg has to avoid a double play situation at all costs."

Fans, parents, players, umpires, and the announcer were all standing up as the tension of the situation continued to mount.

"Gruner is at the plate with one out and bases loaded," the announcer continued. "Pinkus gets his sign. He goes set and checks the runners. Gruner, who has struck out three times today, waits on the pitch. Pinkus goes into his motion and delivers. It is a hard fastball on the inside corner. Gruner swings and how about this! He hits a deep fly ball to left field."

It looked like the ball would be caught. Coach Rase told Alex Black who was on third base.

"Eyes on me. When the left fielder catches the ball, I'll tell you to go. Whatever you do, don't leave too soon or you'll be called out!"

Alex anxiously waited. His eyes remained fixated on Coach Rase. Rase spoke slowly at first. "Ready. Ready. Ready. Caught!"

He then immediately started screaming, "Go! Go! Go! Go! Go! Go!"

Alex Black tagged up and was shot like a pistol from third base. The Gibsonburg bench on the third base side of the field was jumping up and down cheering. The St. Joe Coach watched on nervously and was about to explode with anticipation. The crowd was going crazy. Kathy had her hands on each side of her face. Henry stood up as straight as he could to see over the people in front of him. Jennie Gruner was gripping Ron's arm.

"Get that bum out at the plate!" yelled Tyler Pinkus' mom.

Jimmy called the play for the folks at home. "The St. Joe left fielder makes the catch for out number two. Black tags up at third. The left fielder hurriedly throws a laser all the way home to the St. Joe catcher. The catcher is waiting for the throw between home plate and the charging Alex Black. The ball hits the catcher's glove two steps ahead of Black. Black collides into the St. Joe catcher like a freight train crashing through a wooden barrier knocking him back 12 feet. The umpire calls Black out at home! But I don't believe it! The catcher gets slammed to the ground and the ball flies out of his glove! The umpire switches his call: "SAFE! SAFE! SAFE at home!"

The reactions around the ballpark ran the gamut of emotions.

The Gibsonburg bench erupted and mobbed Alex at home plate.

Coach Rase jumped several feet in air, screamed "YES!" and charged toward the mob at home plate.

Tyler Pinkus slammed his glove down on the pitcher's mound in disgust. His coach threw his hat against the dugout wall.

The Gibsonburg fans were in delirium as the St. Joe fans were in stunned disbelief.

Kathy was jumping up and down and hugging the other students sitting around her.

Henry, never one for emotion, smiled broadly and started to make his way to his car. Jennie and Ron hugged while Tyler Pinkus' mom had her hands in her face. She was sobbing and inconsolable.

Andy Gruner looked at the scoreboard. It displayed FINAL SCORE: Gibsonburg 6, St. Joe 5.

Jimmy finished the broadcast. "There you have it. An unbeliev-able finish today! Probably one of the biggest upsets in Ohio High School baseball. Little Gibsonburg with their 8 and 17 record takes down the storied Fremont St. Joe team and Tyler Pinkus, a team that played in the state semi-finals last year. The question is: How far can destiny's darling go?"

Tyler Pinkus' mom walked toward the parking lot after the game. As she walked through the parking lot, she came upon the Gibsonburg bus. She stopped, turned around, and stomped back to the bus. She stared at the name GIBSONBURG on the bus for sever-al seconds, her anger mounting each and every second. Finally, she spit on the name GIBSONBURG as hard as she could and screamed, "CHEATS!"

She then marched off into the darkness.

When the team filed on the bus after the St. Joe victory they were jubilant and still celebrating. Coach Rase gave them time and allowed them to savor the moment. After a few minutes, he addressed the team. "Fellas, I have to be real honest with you. At the beginning of the season I asked each of you to never give up. I also asked each of you to believe. When we had our first tournament game, I had already given up. I didn't believe."

He took his time and looked at the members of the team. "But after today . . ."

Coach Rase paused for a moment and shouted, "But after today, I'm back in business! As long as I have been a head coach . . ."

Wes Milleson interrupted and said, "Coach, this is your very first head coaching job."

"I know Wes. Keep quiet," he replied. Everyone on the bus laughed.

Coach Rase continued, "This is the best win I have ever had. I would guess it is the best win all of you have ever had. Great job everyone!"

The bus erupted into a crazy celebration.

As Jim drove the team back to Gibsonburg on the bus, Andy carved a third notch onto his wooden bat handle. He proceeded to pull the coin out of his pocket and examined it carefully. He held it between his thumb and forefinger and rubbed the front of the coin with his thumb. He smiled at the coin and placed it into his back left pocket.

Back at OHSAA headquarters, Pudge physically moved Gibsonburg in position to play Van Buren on May 20th. It would be the fourth game for both teams.

The bus arrived in Gibsonburg at 10 pm. Andy drove by himself to the Ideal Bakery. It was closed, as he knew it would be. He secretly put the coin back in its hiding place, making sure no one saw him. He then drove home for some well-deserved rest.

25

The Day After St. Joe
Tuesday, May 17, 2005

News spread quickly about Gibsonburg beating St. Joe. It seemed to put everyone in the town in a good mood.

There was a lot of activity and chatter inside the Ideal Bakery. It was a focal point of Gibsonburg, and the crowd was larger than normal. Everyone was talking about the big win.

Gary Kathrens and Tim Mallett were sitting at their favorite table reading the newspaper. Tim was reading the article on the victory. He said to Gary, "Big win against St. Joe, eh?

Gary responded while he continued to study his newspaper, "I called it all the way."

Tim dropped his newspaper, looked at Gary, and shook his head at his hypocritical, fair-weathered fan of a friend.

26

Game #4 – Gibsonburg vs. Van Buren
Friday, May 20, 2005

Pudge got to know Gibsonburg fairly well as they continued to win. The conference wall at OHSAA headquarters showed that Gibsonburg (9-17) would play Van Buren (21-5) at Tiffin University on Friday, May 20, 2005. It would be the fourth game for both teams.

The bus for the Van Buren game would leave in 30 minutes. Andy was dressed in his baseball uniform, and just like he did for the St. Joe game, he carefully extracted the metal box from the wall in the crawlspace and opened it. He took the coin and put it into the back left rear pocket of his baseball pants. He clambered out and drove to the school in time to catch the bus.

As the team got on the bus Coach Rase noticed there was a different bus driver, Trina. The old bus driver, Jim, was sitting in the seat right behind Trina.

Coach Rase looked at Trina, and then at Jim. "What's goin' on, Jim?"

Jim looked at him. "I have pneumonia, coach. I'm taking antibiotics that cause drowsiness. I can't drive the bus on the antibiotics but I kind of think I am good luck so I am riding along so's I don't mess anything up."

Coach Rase smiled and patted Jim on the shoulder. "We'll take all the luck we can get."

The new bus driver, Trina, took a left out of the school parking lot and headed north on Route 300. She hit the red traffic light at the four corners of Gibsonburg, and waited for it to turn green. When the light turned green, Trina turned right on Route 600. She was taking Gibsonburg to their fourth game in the tournament to play Van Buren. This game was on neutral ground at Tiffin University.

When the bus arrived, there were a fair number of Gibsonburg fans waiting on the team. There were many more than normal, in fact. As usual, Henry Tillman was at the game well ahead of the first pitch. He was never late.

Jimmy kicked off his calling of the game. "Well sports fans, today we have Gibsonburg fresh off their great win Monday against Fremont St. Joe. They are playing today for the District Championship. Gibsonburg has a 9 and 17 record and they are playing 21 and 5 Van Buren. Van Buren boasts their All-District pitcher, Marty Baird, who has already signed on to play for Division I Bowling Green State University. Like Tyler Pinkus, Marty Baird has beaten up on Gibsonburg quite a bit. Earlier in the year, they beat Gibsonburg 11 to 3."

Gibsonburg ended up beating Van Buren in a very unconventional manner. Gibsonburg had Bobby Graff on second and Cody Fisher on third with one out. When Van Buren's pitcher struck out Thom Brinker for out number two, the Van Buren catcher ran to the dugout and the rest of the team followed. They thought it was the third out!

Cody Fisher and Bobby Graff were very smart players. They knew it was only the second out. Once they saw the Van Buren team jogging off of the field they both took off and made it to home before Van Buren realized their mistake!

Gibsonburg was definitely on a roll. Alex Black pitched another strong game and, unlike Van Buren, they did not have any errors. To everyone's surprise, they had won four games in a row.

Afterwards, as Trina drove the team back to Gibsonburg, Andy Gruner carved a fourth notch onto his wooden bat handle. "First Tyler Pinkus, now Marty Baird. I wonder who's next?" Andy said to himself.

He proceeded to pull the 1913 coin out of his pocket and rubbed it between his two hands. He held it between his thumb and forefinger, looked at it quizzically and studied the craftsmanship of the coin. He gripped it with a tight fist and placed it into his back left pocket.

Back at OHSAA headquarters, Pudge moved Gibsonburg in position to play Kalida on Friday May 27, 2005. It would be the fifth game for both teams.

After the bus arrived in Gibsonburg it was about 11 pm. Again, Andy drove to the closed Ideal Bakery and put the coin in its hiding place.

27

Wyatt And The Bully
Saturday Afternoon, May 21, 2005

Wyatt was reflecting on the Van Buren game on the Saturday afternoon after the win. He had just unloaded a flat wagon full of hay and was driving an old green tractor down a narrow country road. This road had a deep drainage ditch that ran parallel to it. He was headed to the hay field to get another load. He was holding a baseball in his hand and was applying different grips.

Out of nowhere, a small black coupe screamed past him and the tractor hauling the flat wagon. It stopped in front of the path of the tractor partially blocking the road. Wyatt stopped and shut off the engine. Three boys got out of the black coupe.

The first boy he saw was the bully he and Alex encountered after the basketball game against Elmwood. He had two older boys with him that Wyatt didn't recognize. The bully shouted out, "Hey, farm boy. Remember me?"

Wyatt had both his hands on the oversized wheel of the tractor. He put his head down onto the steering wheel as to say, "Are you kidding me!"

After a few seconds he pulled his head up and said, "Move your car."

The bully, Kurt, said, "Why don't you come down here and make me?"

Not scared at all, Wyatt calmly stated, "Hey, I don't want to fight."

Kurt told Wyatt, "You aren't so tough without your friend around. I got my two cousins here with me to make sure things are fair."

Each of the two cousins were about 5 feet, 10 inches tall. One of the bully's cousins was very muscular with short blond hair. His nickname was, Tank. Wyatt wondered if that cousin was a boxer or something like that. The other cousin was smaller, more slender but still muscular. His name was, Rat. He wore a black baseball hat backwards on his head, and his arms were covered in tattoos. They both wore T-shirts that had the sleeves cut off.

Kurt continued, "When we're done with you, maybe we'll just pull a little train on your hot little sister. What's her name anyway? *Courtney?*" The three boys roared with laughter.

While they were laughing, Wyatt slammed the baseball down on the fender of the tractor and jumped down. In an instant, he was standing nose-to-nose with Kurt. The look in Wyatt's eyes was similar to the rare look that Alex noticed at the lockers with Kurt after the Elmwood game. Kurt recognized that same look and got a little frightened, but did everything he could to mask his fear.

Five inches away from Kurt, a calm but angry Wyatt said, "I can't believe you just said that."

For the first time in the encounter, Kurt could not mask his feelings, and his fear began to show. Wyatt saw the fear in his eyes as it began to creep in.

If a casual observer looked at Wyatt and Kurt standing side-by-side they would say Kurt looked taller, heavier and was a little more muscular than Wyatt. They would also tell you that Wyatt looked tougher and scrappier. This was a look he achieved from working hard on a farm his entire life. If anyone had to bet, they would bet on Wyatt without a doubt.

The larger of the two cousins, Tank, said, "Go ahead, bitch slap him. We got your back."

There were three of them, and Wyatt was by himself-but he didn't care. He looked right into Kurt's eyes without flinching. With fists clenched, Wyatt was ready to do whatever he had to do. He was waiting for Kurt to make the first move. Like a tightly wound spring, Wyatt was ready to pounce with all his fury as the look in his eyes intensified.

As his two cousins stood 20 feet behind him, Kurt started stuttering a little and said, "Listen, I . . . I . . . I . . ."

Recognizing his hesitation, Wyatt calmly told him, "Come on, bring it. Let's see what happens."

Kurt looked back at his cousins nervously. He looked back at Wyatt and as tough as he could, told him, "It's your lucky day. I'll let you off with a warning. Get back on your fag tractor and get out of here before I change my mind."

Wyatt laughed and began to walk back to the tractor. Kurt walked back toward his cousins and said, "Let's get outta' here."

The bigger cousin, Tank, shook his head, tapped the smaller cousin, Rat, on his chest, and charged toward Wyatt's back. Wyatt heard the footsteps, but did not have enough time to turn around. From behind, Tank grabbed Wyatt by the head, slammed his head on the side of the tractor engine, and threw him to the ground where Wyatt rolled toward the deep drainage ditch that ran parallel to the country road. Tank then approached Wyatt and kicked him in the ribs at least six times while he was down. In great pain, Wyatt got on all fours in the small grassy area between the ditch and the narrow road. He looked straight down at the ground and attempted to reorient himself. He spit and it was completely red with blood. When Tank slammed his head against the tractor, Wyatt's bottom teeth cut a gash into his lower lip.

As soon as Wyatt was upright, Tank charged him at full speed. Wyatt noticed he was coming hard so he took advantage of Tank's momentum. He got low and when Tank got close enough, Wyatt grabbed his legs and flipped him over his right shoulder. He landed on the steep downslope of the ditch and rolled 20 feet into the 2 feet of water at the bottom.

Exhausted and hurt, Wyatt made his way back to the tractor and leaned on the fender. The smaller cousin, Rat, noticed that Wyatt was winded and hurt. He looked at Tank trying to climb out of the ditch. He shook his head and cried out, "Now you're gonna get it!" He then charged full speed at Wyatt.

Wyatt saw him running out of the corner of his eye. With quick reflexes, he grabbed the baseball that he put on the fender, locked in a four-seam grip with his right hand, and threw it as hard as he could at the charging cousin. The baseball hit Rat squarely in the balls, and he collapsed like a house of cards, screaming in pain.

After the ball hit Rat, it rolled back and rested near the rear tire of the tractor. As Rat was in a fetal position on the ground in pain, Tank was crawling out of the ditch, completely wet, and furious.

With all his might, he charged the still-recovering Wyatt and picked him up at his thighs. He used his momentum to carry Wyatt ten feet forward, and slammed him on the bed of the flatbed trailer. Tank's head was buried in Wyatt's stomach, and his arms were around Wyatt's legs. Wyatt wrapped his strong left arm around Tank's mid section so he could not disengage. He then unleashed ten hard punches to the left side of Tank's body with his right hand. Each blow felt like a small, hard sledgehammer to Tank's ribs.

Wyatt let go, kicked Tank backwards and watched him stumble back several feet, in significant pain, from Wyatt's blows. Wyatt noticed that Tank was unstable so he charged him. Tank threw a feeble roundhouse at Wyatt's head and missed. After Wyatt ducked he stood erect and hit him in the face with a series of punches.

Tank fell to the ground and slowly got on all fours in the same grassy area where Wyatt was on all fours earlier. Tank turned his head to the left and was looking up at Wyatt. Sensing that he was getting ready to get up and charge him again Wyatt quickly walked up, and hit Tank on the left side of his face with his right hand driving his head to the ground. It didn't look like he would be getting up for a while.

Tired, bloody, hurt, and exhausted, Wyatt walked about twenty feet toward the bully that started everything, Kurt. Kurt had done nothing but watch as Wyatt fought the two cousins. Tank was knocked out in the grass. Rat was still writhing in pain in the middle of the road.

Wyatt glared at Kurt and could tell he was rattled. Wyatt was unsure if all the fighting was finished. Kurt looked past Wyatt and over his right shoulder. Kurt got a surprised look on his face as he watched Tank stumble to his feet behind Wyatt. He was wobbly. Wyatt noticed the change in the Kurt's expression and slowly turned around. Wyatt and Tank looked at each other like two warriors who had been through a long battle. Wyatt looked down and saw the baseball that had bounced back from his throw earlier. Slowly, he reach down and picked it up and locked in a four-seam grip with his right hand. Tank was staring at Wyatt. He was tired and hurt, but relentless. When Tank took a half a step toward Wyatt, Wyatt reared back and threw the baseball as hard as he could at Tank. The ball struck him right in the middle of his forehead knocking him backward and causing him to roll back down into the ditch and the water for the second time. The baseball bounced directly back to Wyatt. He reached down and picked it up and again locked in a four-seam grip like a gunslinger cocks his Colt 45.

Exhausted, Wyatt turned around and faced Kurt. Kurt wanted no part of Wyatt, especially since he was holding a baseball.

Kurt was not sure about what was going to happen next.

Wyatt smiled and Kurt looked confused and unsure. Wyatt then gently flipped the baseball to him and he caught it with both hands.

Wyatt turned around and slowly staggered back to the tractor, got on, and started it up. He drove around the left side of the black coupe between the car and the drainage ditch. As Kurt watched Wyatt drive past, he had a look on his face that said, "I'm sorry about all of this, Wyatt."

As Wyatt drove down the road with the three boys behind him, his bruised face produced a smile and he continued on to the field to pick up another load of hay. There was much work left to do and a good amount of light left in the day to get it done.

28

The Riding Lesson
Late Saturday Afternoon, May 21, 2005

It was late Saturday afternoon the day after the Van Buren victory. Kathy and Andy had been dating for a few weeks and they couldn't be happier.

She had the reins of her horse in her right hand as she and Andy strolled by a scenic fence row on her property. There was a small picnic basket hanging from the saddle of the horse.

As they walked together they both glanced over the fence at a foal playfully challenging its mother. "Hey, after three lessons, you're finally starting to catch on." Kathy said.

"It's hard to admit, but this is kind of fun, actually. I like it. The first two lessons were a little awkward but I think I am getting the hang of it." Andy responded.

Kathy was happy with the notion that they had yet another common interest. Her train of thought was interrupted when Andy asked, "Now where are we going?"

Kathy chuckled. "You ask too many questions."

"C'mon! Tell me."

Kathy smiled. "I'm gonna show you my favorite place on the whole farm."

"And where's that?"

"What? Another question?" She said in mock annoyance.

Andy laughed. "All right. All right. I'll stop."

They walked a little farther, and then Kathy stopped.

Andy looked at her. "Are we here?"

"Almost," she said as she took a red handkerchief out of her saddlebag. She quickly set to the task of blindfolding him.

"What's this for?" He asked, puzzled.

"I don't want you to see my favorite spot as we walk up. I want to do my own personal unveiling," she explained.

He laughed, then playfully replied. "You are too funny."

She carefully led him through a thick group of evergreen trees. Eventually, they came to a clearing that overlooked a beautiful lake. There was a firepit and a gorgeous view.

"Now stand right here for a minute," she said. "Trust me: it's worth the wait."

Kathy prepared for the unveiling. She placed a colorful soft quilt on the ground next to the nearby firepit. She pulled out some cheese, crackers, grapes and strawberries from the picnic basket and placed them on the quilt. Finally, she lit the dry kindling and wood in the firepit, which she prepared earlier in the day. With the sun beginning to set, and the fire starting to crackle, Kathy quietly walked behind Andy. She softly placed her arms around him and said, "Are you ready?"

Andy nodded his head, yes. Kathy untied the blindfold. She stood next to Andy, and proudly said, "Ta da!"

Andy struggled to pull his gaze from the wonder in front of him. But he was eager to meet Kathy's eyes. He shifted his view over to her. "Wow! This is amazing. Thank you."

As they looked into each other's eyes, they could see the reflection of the sunset coming off the lake in the distance. They kissed softly.

With Kathy's head on Andy's shoulder and his arm around

her, they sat on the blanket enjoying the warmth of the fire. The retreating sun splashed its remaining soft orange light upon their faces.

Kathy and Andy did not say much more. They didn't need to. They just enjoyed the setting and each other's company. They were both content, happy, and didn't want the evening to end.

29

Game #5 – Kalida – Friday, May 27, 2005 and Game #6 – Edgerton – Saturday, May 28, 2005

Pudge was breaking his unwritten rule: He had started to follow Gibsonburg on his big board. He usually just kept track of the wins and losses of the Ohio teams without particular interest. In game number 5, Gibsonburg beat Kalida 4-0. Next up was Edgerton.

The conference wall at OHSAA headquarters showed that Gibsonburg (11-17) would play Edgerton (21-4) at Eastwood High School on Saturday, May 28th at 4:30 pm. It would be the sixth game for both teams. The winner would be one of four teams to advance to the state semi-finals at Huntington Park in Columbus, Ohio.

Eastwood High School was only eight miles from Gibsonburg, which meant many fans would be in attendance.

The bus for the Edgerton game was set to leave in ten minutes. Running late, Andy crawled as fast as he could to retrieve the metal box from the wall in the crawlspace. He grabbed the coin, put it into the left rear pocket of his baseball pants, and scurried out to catch the team bus.

Trina, with Jim behind her, took a left out of the school parking lot and headed north on Route 300. She hit the red traffic light at the four corners of Gibsonburg, and waited for it to turn green.

When the light turned green, Trina turned left on Route 600 and headed to Eastwood High School for game number six of the post-season.

When the bus arrived, there was a sea of fans wearing orange and black awaiting them. This was a big event for Gibsonburg. If they could somehow manufacture a win, they would be one of four teams to play in the State Championships in Columbus, Ohio. School spirit was high and there were many students wearing face and body paint. Parents, locals, friends, and relatives were all at Eastwood High School to root for Gibsonburg. As usual, Henry Tillman was at the game early, waiting to watch the biggest game in the history of Gibsonburg Boys High School Baseball.

Jimmy was the announcer again. "Well sports fans, today we have Gibsonburg fresh off their great 4-0 win last night against Kalida. In the Kalida game catcher, Thom Brinker was a one man wrecking crew. He was five for five at the plate and drove in all four of Gibsonburg's runs!

I have another interesting fact about Kalida. Ten years ago, Coach Rase played high school baseball for Jim Wharton at Crestview High School. His high school team played Kalida in the regional semi-final and lost! At the time, the Kalida team was coached by Ohio legend, Coach McBride. Last night, Gibsonburg played Kalida and beat Coach McBride in the state semi-final. This was the same coach that beat Coach Rase ten years ago!

Live from Eastwood High School, today, Gibsonburg is playing Edgerton for the Regional Championship. They have an 11-17 record versus Edgerton with a 21-4 record. Edgerton will be tired today. Last night, it took them 18 innings to beat Ottawa Hills. In the process, they used up all of their pitching staff. And the stakes are high! The winner of today's game will advance to the State Championships at Huntington Park in Columbus, Ohio."

Gibsonburg handled the tired Edgerton ball team rather easily. Because they had to play 18-innings the night before against Ottawa Hills, they were exhausted, and out of pitchers. In the game against Gibsonburg they had to use pitchers that had never pitched before!

When the game was over, Jimmy wrapped it up. "Gibsonburg trounced pitcher-depleted Edgerton by a score of 8 to 2. Gibsonburg will be one of four teams heading to the State Championship tournament at Huntington Park in Columbus, Ohio."

When Gibsonburg beat Edgerton, there was a mass celebration after the game. The students wearing orange and black body paint, parents, relatives, and the legion of others dressed in school colors were laughing, talking and making plans to drive South to the State Championships in Columbus, Ohio.

Keeping with his normal protocol, Coach Rase wanted the team to remain focused. So, he required them to go directly to the bus and not talk with anyone. This was no easy task, as there was a massive celebration going on after the game. The team had to weave through the thick crowd of orange and black well-wishers. The crowd was laughing and cheering loudly. Here and there, you would hear conversations about travel plans and how they were all going to get down to Columbus to watch Gibsonburg play in the final four.

When the bus was loaded with all of the players, Coach Rase addressed the jubilant team. "All right. All right! Listen up. This was a huge win today. I still can't believe it, we are going to state."

Everyone on the bus cheered.

Coach Rase continued his speech. "Now, STATE is the real deal. You don't go there without talent."

He paused, smiled, and continued, "Or a little luck!"

The team started laughing and hollering as the coach explained.

"Only four teams make it to state. And we are one of the four. You're a good team. Everyone on this team *lived* our team motto.

You believed in yourselves and you never gave up!"

As Coach Rase took on more of a serious tone, the players sat up in their seats and listened carefully.

"On June 3rd, we will play Jackson Center in Huntington Park in the state semi-finals," he said. "Their stud left handed pitcher, Kevin Mann, will be the third pitcher we will face with a Division I scholarship. Now, tomorrow is graduation for you seniors. I want you to know that I am proud of you. As a responsible adult, I should be telling all of you to settle down and start thinking about your trip to Columbus."

Coach Rase paused. The team looked at him with mounting anticipation. With a twinkle in his eye, the coach blurted, "But, I tell you what: Screw it! Enjoy this win! It's incredible! We are goin' to state!"

The bus erupted into a full-blown celebration with much laughing, horsing around, and cheering.

Soon, everyone on the bus started to chant, "State! State! State! State! State! State! State!"

Coach Rase suddenly recalled that he was supposed to be at the bachelor party in Chicago on May 28th. The phone conversation seemed like so long ago. Things were different now. His team had just won the regional championship.

He sat down, pulled out his mobile phone and called his friend, Keith, in Chicago. When he answered, the background noise was deafening. He could tell they were at a bar. Coach Rase assumed the bachelor party was in full swing.

Coach Rase explained, "Hey, sorry I couldn't make it. How was the rooftop view of the Cubs game? From all the noise, it sounds like you guys are having a great time."

On the other line, his friend, Keith, replied, "The noise isn't for the bachelor party dude! It's for you! We just heard the great news and all drank a shot of tequila in your honor. Congratulations!

We'll all be at the big game next Friday!"

Very humbly, Coach Rase smiled. "Thanks, man. You guys stay out of trouble." He hung up the phone with a content look on his face and enjoyed the country scenery as the bus made its way back to Gibsonburg.

As Trina drove the team back to Gibsonburg, Andy carved a sixth notch onto his wooden bat handle.

With a big smile, he proceeded to pull the coin out of his pocket. He felt a sudden wave of shock. The coin was gone! It was NOT in his back left pocket! He checked his other pockets. He looked behind him on the seat. He looked on the floor. Frantic, he stuck his fingers in the crease where the back of the seat met the part of the seat that you sat on. He took off his hat and looked all around. He was distraught and did not know what to do!

Alex was sitting directly behind Andy. He noticed that Andy was searching for something so he leaned forward and asked, "What's wrong buddy?"

Andy masked his frantic emotions, forced a smile, and said, "What's wrong? Nothin'! We are going to state!"

Andy gave Alex a high five, turned around, and the forced smile quickly left his face and he turned very white and got a horrified look on his face. He whispered to himself, "I can't believe I lost the frickin' coin."

Andy stared blankly out the window into space. Amidst all of the clamoring around him, he was in a cold and quiet place of distress. He could feel his skin turn white and he started to perspire. He lost an 18 million dollar coin! He whispered to himself, "What did I do?"

Back at OHSAA headquarters, Pudge moved Gibsonburg in position to play Jackson Center on Friday, June 3, 2005 in the state semi-final. The winner of this game would play the winner of the other semi-final game in the Ohio State Championship game.

30

The Coin Is Lost
Sunday Morning, May 29, 2005

It was Sunday morning after the Edgerton game and Ron looked very upset. He and Andy were sitting on the loading platform behind the bakery. Neither of them were talking as Ron was attempting to absorb what Andy had just told him. He was at a total loss for words; he didn't know even where to start. What could he say?

Ron's emotions got the better of him as he laid into his son. "Andy! I don't know what to tell you! You know you shouldn't have taken the coin! Even if you did ask, there is no way in the world we would have let you take it! This is beyond words! I just can't believe it!"

Andy knew there were no words he could say to fix the situation. "Dad, I feel so bad."

Ron looked very upset. He just looked around and shook his head, searching for the right thing to say. He put his hands on his hips, looked down at the ground and didn't say anything for a long while. Ron was quiet for an uncomfortable period of time. It looked like he was going to start and say something, and then stopped.

Andy sensed there was something else going on. "What dad? What is it?"

Ron gave the type of chuckle you hear when there is great irony. He looked directly at Andy, spoke softly and said, "Part of me. Part of me thinks about what my great-grandfather did. Maybe he was right."

"What do you mean?" Andy was puzzled.

Ron calmed himself down a little bit. "What I mean is look at us. We have a good life. The last year has been very stressful, but things worked out. The other coins took care of the debt and allowed us to put a good chunk of cash away. I guess we should be happy with that."

Sincerely, Andy told his dad, "I'll retrace my steps dad and go back to the field. I'll look everywhere until I find it."

Ron was quiet for some time after Andy spoke. He finally smiled warmly and placed a reaffirming arm around Andy's shoulder. "You know what, Andy? Go ahead and do that if it makes you feel better. It's gonna be like finding a needle in a haystack, though. If you find it, all right. If not, that's all right too. Look what money did to our family before. Maybe it would have destroyed our family as well."

Andy looked at his dad and seemed to grasp what he was saying.

Ron patted his arm. "C'mon, your graduation ceremony is in three hours. Let's clean up and get ready."

31

Gibsonburg High School Graduation
Sunday Afternoon, May 29, 2005

It was Sunday, May 29, 2005 at 2:00 pm. Gibsonburg was graduating their 2005 senior class in the high school gymnasium.

After the walk-in, and a few speeches by the administration, the Superintendent made his way to the podium to introduce the 2005 Class Valedictorian.

"I would now like to introduce your valedictorian, Bobby Graff. Bobby just learned that he has been accepted to Princeton and will be attending in the fall. Bobby also plays second base on our boy's baseball team that won the regional final game yesterday. This team is one of the elite four teams going to State. They will be playing in the State Semi-Final game next Friday against Jackson Center. If they win, they will play in the State Championship on Saturday. Ladies and gentlemen. I present to you, Mr. Bobby Graff."

Bobby Graff humbly walked up to the podium amid a healthy smattering of applause.

"My speech to you today is entitled *Little Things That Make A Difference*. I never thought I would be in front of all of you today. Not because of the grades, or the honors or any of that. I never thought I would be in front of you for another reason. I would like to share with you a personal story that nobody else knows about.

Not my parents. Not my friends. Not my teachers. Not anyone."

When Bobby made his opening comments, there was a hint of whispering in the audience.

Bobby continued, "As most of you know, I am new to Gibsonburg. I moved here from Indiana and started classes in the fall. Let me tell you, moving to a new school for your senior year is not easy. You have no friends. You have new teachers. You have no social life. All the girls were taken, or at least seemed to be taken. None of the cliques liked to open their doors to new kids. Basically, life was miserable. When I walked through the halls I heard whispers like, "there's the new kid." My locker would get stacked so the books would fall out when you opened it. There were a few kids really giving me a hard time and I got into more than one fight. One kid heated up a welding clamp and hooked it to the inside of my arm in shop class. By the way. Wyatt Kiser later kicked this guy's ass for me. Thanks Wyatt!"

The audience chuckled. Wyatt confirmed the statement with a smile and a proud head nod.

Bobby continued, "I . . . have never felt so alone in my life. As the year progressed, things got worse. I found school to be a real struggle. I had to work extra hard. My loneliness seemed to get worse and worse. I was very depressed. I got to the point where I couldn't take it any more when something . . . something very special happened. I was walking home from school one Friday in early March. My arms were full of books, papers, notebooks, and all kinds of things. Then, this kid, who you all know as Andy Gruner, pulls up and asks me if I want a ride."

Andy smiled directly at Bobby.

Bobby looked at Andy, smiled back and said, "It took him a long time, but he finally convinced me to get in his truck and he gave me a ride home. We talked and I laughed for the first time in a long while. He convinced me to join the baseball team which, as you all know, has been a blast. Until today, I don't think Andy really understood what he did on that day in early March. That very small gesture on Andy's part really changed my life."

Ron and Jennie Gruner looked at each other, full of pride in their son.

Bobby started to get a little choked up. "You see everyone. What Andy didn't know . . ."

Bobby paused, then continued, "and what my parents didn't know . . ." he paused.

He was struggling to get the words out. Bobby paused for a long time and his eyes began to tear up. "Is that I planned on killing myself that night in March."

Most people in the audience gasped at Bobby's announcement.

Bobby continued his speech by saying. "I cleaned out my locker and was taking all my stuff home so my mom would not have to go through the embarrassment of cleaning it out the next day."

Andy looked completely shocked and began to tear up. Ron and Jennie Gruner looked at each other in shock. Alex, Wes, and Wyatt made eye contact with each other as they couldn't believe what Bobby was saying. Kathy smiled gently and looked at Andy with a great deal of pride.

There was much chatter in the audience. It took everyone by surprise and some of the students and parents were holding hands.

Bobby went on to tell the audience, "If Andy would not have been so convincing to get me in that car on that March afternoon, I would probably not be here with you today."

Smiling, Bobby made the last point of his valedictorian speech. With quiet confidence said, "So, let me get to the point. If you have ever felt that the little things you do will not make a difference, then I would ask you to think of my talk today. Andy Gruner did one little thing. That *little thing* made a *big difference* in my life. I only ask that each one of you here today, give yourself the opportunity to make a difference in someone else's life. Don't underestimate the power of doing little things to help other people."

Bobby concluded by looking directly at Andy. "Thank you, Andy Gruner! And thank you all for listening. I'm Bobby Graff. "

Everyone in the audience stood up and gave Bobby a standing ovation. When he walked down the stairs to head back to his seat, Andy met him.

"Thank you," Bobby whispered.

32

Getting Ready For State
Tuesday Morning, May 31, 2005

It was Tuesday, May 31, 2005 and school was out for the seniors. Although it rained hard in the morning, the weather looked like it would be in the 70s and sunny for the rest of the week.

Coach Rase scheduled practices for Monday through Thursday from 2 pm to 4:30 pm. The team would leave for Columbus on Thursday afternoon, right after practice, to get ready to play Jackson Center on Friday.

Outside of practice, Coach Rase spent all his time studying everything he could about their next opponent, Jackson Center.

In addition to the regular scheduled practices, each team member, on their own, worked out an additional two hours or more a day getting ready for their next game. This was the same team that didn't want to practice at all between the last game of the regular season and their first post season game against Bettsville. Their confidence was high and there wasn't a single player on the team who didn't think they could go all the way. They wanted it badly.

On Tuesday morning Andy was working in the prep room of the bakery, but his mind was constantly drawn to Kathy. So, when he saw her walk in the front door, he was thrilled to see her.

Kathy peered in the small porthole window on the swinging

door. She looked into the prep room and saw him folding boxes. She swung open the door with the porthole and said, "Getting ready for state?"

Andy smiled when he saw Kathy and replied, "Yup. We head down to Columbus on Thursday afternoon."

She walked in and stood beside him. "Everyone in town is so proud of the team. You'll have a lot of fans. Everyone is so excited."

He nodded. "I can honestly say we are having a good time."

She smiled back at him and said, "Hey, we still going to your family's barbeque tonight?"

"You bet! Unless of course, you are too busy."

"Well . . . " She teasingly said, like she had plans.

Smirking, he replied, "Very funny!"

She tilted her head and gave him a meaningful look. "I have had a great time seeing you. We have had some fun over the last few weeks, huh?"

Getting sentimental as well, Andy told her, "Yeah. It has been really good. All of a sudden my life seems over, and then it seems like it couldn't get any better. Funny, isn't it?"

She nodded quickly. "Very funny. I know what you mean."

"Okay if I pick you up at six?" he asked.

"Sounds good."

Andy kissed Kathy on the cheek before she left. His eyes were fixed on her as she walked away and out the prep room door. He couldn't stop grinning, even after she was gone. He was happy and content that he was with that very special girl that he had a crush on since the third grade.

33

A Little Mud On The Tires
Early Tuesday Evening, May 31, 2005

After the barbeque, Andy drove down the country road in his red pickup truck, enjoying the evening air. Kathy sat beside him in the front seat, looking as beautiful as ever.

"Great night Andy. That was a fun barbeque with your folks. Where to now?" she asked.

Andy gestured to the back of his pickup and said, "I just need to drop the moving blankets off at Uncle Joe's, and then I'll take you home."

She smiled wistfully. "So soon? I thought we could hang out for a little more."

Andy grinned back at Kathy as he continued to drive.

Andy turned left onto an old dirt road between two farm fields when Kathy said, "Now where are we going?"

Andy gestured towards the road with his chin. "We'll just take a short-cut through Brinker's farm and past their woods."

Looking outside Kathy noticed the wet fields and figured it would be dark in about 30 minutes. In a mildly concerned tone, she said, "It's clear now, but with all that rain this morning, you sure this is a good idea?" she asked, mildly concerned.

He shot her a confident look. "Hey, I know what I'm doing."

Kathy shrugged. She trusted him.

A few short minutes later, the back tires of Andy's truck were buried solid up the axle. He feebly tried to accelerate forward and backwards, but the tires spun without moving the truck an inch. It would be impossible to get out without some sort of heavy equipment.

They were stuck on a farm path that ran by the woods on Thom Brinker's farm. They were at least a mile from any road or house.

Andy got out and looked at the back left tire of the truck and sighed. Kathy stepped out of the truck and walked up to his side. They both looked at the tire for several seconds unsure as to what they should do. Andy walked over to the bed of the truck, pulled the tailgate down and sat.

Like a boy that knows he is in trouble, Andy said, "My dad's gonna kill me. I just finished getting the bakery truck fixed and now I probably just screwed up my truck. I'll call him to come get us."

Andy started to press the call pad on his phone and stopped. He looked up at Kathy and laughed as to say, "This can't be happening."

After looking at his mobile phone Andy said, "Nice, my phone's dead."

Kathy casually walked over and sat right next to Andy on the tailgate of the pickup truck. For a few moments, she didn't say anything.

Kathy smiled and then playfully elbowed Andy in the side and said, "Nice short-cut!"

He laughed as he looked up at the sky. He laid back in the truck bed, put his hands behind his head, looked straight up and nodded. "Check it out."

Using his right arm as a pillow, Kathy snuggled close to him and gazed in wonder up at the sky. While the sun was going down it reflected on the sky and clouds to display a portrait full of dark and rich colors. It was very unique, tranquil, and breathtaking.

While they were lying down in the truck bed, Kathy turned to face Andy. They looked deeply into each other's eyes for a long time. Kathy then moved her head slowly toward Andy and kissed him gently.

They kissed for several minutes. While they were kissing, Kathy took her right arm and slid Andy's T-shirt up as far as she could. They stopped kissing. Andy sat up, removed his T-shirt and laid back down.

They continued to kiss, increasing in intensity. After a few more minutes Kathy slowly started to unbuckle Andy's belt buckle. After she unbuckled his belt buckle, she unfastened the button on his jeans and gently glided down the zipper on his jeans. She put her right hand down his pants and gently rubbed for some time. Andy reached around to Kathy's back with his left hand. Awkwardly, Andy did what he could and after a struggle, he was able to successfully unhook Kathy's bra. After her bra was unfastened Kathy sat up, removed her blouse, and laid back down.

They continued to kiss. As Kathy rubbed Andy, he slowly massaged her breasts for a few minutes. He moved his hand down slowly gently rubbing the back of his fingers on her flat stomach and his hand eventually reached the beltline of her pants. He unfastened the button on her jeans, slid the zipper down, and glided his left hand down between her legs. As Kathy slowly rubbed Andy, Andy gently rubbed Kathy. After another few minutes, Andy started to slide her jeans down as far as they would go.

They stopped kissing for a moment and each pulled their pants and underwear off completely. They used the soft and warm furniture blankets as a comfortable bed, and a cozy blanket. With their clothes removed, they started to kiss some more.

The vibrant and colorful sky gave way to a dark canvas filled with stars.

Under those stars, among the sounds of nature in an intimate country setting, and in a makeshift bed of soft blankets, Andy and Kathy made love to one another. It was the first time for both of them.

34

Huntington Park
Thursday – June 2, 2005

The conference wall at OHSAA headquarters looked empty as there were only four teams left on the 50-foot expanse. On Friday, June 3, 2005 Gibsonburg (12-17) would play Jackson Center (26-3) in the first semi-final game. Lancaster Fisher Catholic (29-0) would play Dalton Wooster (25-4) in the other semi-final game.

The two semi-final winners would play for the Ohio State Boys High School Championship on Saturday at 4:30 pm.

The bus for Columbus left at 5:30 pm, one hour after the team practice. Trina, with Jim behind her, took a left out of the school parking lot and headed north on Route 300. She hit the traffic light at the four corners of Gibsonburg. For the first time she could remember, the light was green and she didn't have to stop for a red light. Trina turned left on Route 600, drove five miles and took another left on Route 23 to head two hours south to Columbus.

Excited and anxious, Coach Rase instructed Trina to go right to Huntington Park so the team could see where they would be playing.

The bus pulled up to Huntington Park at 8:00 pm on Thursday, June 2, 2005.

When Trina opened the door, the players rushed out like little kids getting the go-ahead to hunt for Easter Eggs. Nobody was around and the field looked empty. They all stood in front of the sign that said:

Welcome

To the 2005

Boys High School State Tournament

Coach Rase noticed a groundskeeper working on the field, so he yelled at him through the fence. The groundskeeper walked up and Coach Rase said, "Listen. I'm Coach Rase from Gibsonburg."

The groundskeeper interrupted him. "I know. I heard about you guys. Nice story."

Coach Rase squinted at him. "We are playing tomorrow and I was wondering if there was anyway the kids could come in and walk around the field."

The groundskeeper scratched his head. "Well, I really ain't supposed to. The General Manager is a crotchety ole cuss and he wouldn't be happy if he found out I let ya on the field."

He thought for a moment and looked around to see if there was anyone else around on the crew. He broke into a grin. "Well, who's gonna tell him?"

The groundskeeper chuckled to himself and opened the gate.

The 2005 Gibsonburg Baseball Team walked around Huntington Park in awe. They couldn't imagine what it would be like to play in such an incredible place. Some of the players started roaming around the outfield. Others checked out the bench. Some started to run the bases.

Andy stood at the shortstop position and slowly turned around 360 degrees looking at the entire field. He was very proud.

After 30 minutes, the team indulged their fantasy of playing in the picturesque ballpark. They then thanked the groundskeeper and left for the hotel.

35

Game #7 – Gibsonburg vs. Jackson Center
Friday, June 3, 2005

As the team entered the playing field at Huntington Park from the locker room, they were greeted by hundreds of fans wearing orange and black. As they looked in the stands, they were perplexed. It looked like there were more people than the total number that lived in the whole town of Gibsonburg!

It was a big day for everyone in and around Gibsonburg. If Gibsonburg won, they would be playing for the State Championship. Like the previous games, many students were decked out in face paint and body paint. Parents, locals, friends, and relatives were there in abundance rooting for Gibsonburg. Henry Tillman didn't leave town often for overnight trips. But this was an exception. He wasn't going to miss the biggest game in school history.

The Gibsonburg fans cheered wildly when the team walked out. Unsure as to what to do, the team waved back awkwardly.

Jackson Center had just as many of their own fans, dressed in navy blue and gray. They gave their Jackson Center team a warm welcome as well.

Standing up behind the lower level seats along the third base line *she* stood. All decked out in her usual crimson, gray, and white was someone that nobody had seen in a long time. It was Tyler

Pinkus' mom. What was she doing there? Didn't St. Joe get beat? She stood near a few Jackson Center fans and declared, "My nephew, Kyle, plays for Jackson Center. I hope they light that Gibsonburg team up!"

The field was immaculate as was the stadium. It was located in downtown Columbus, Ohio and was surrounded by several high-rise office buildings. The team was warming up their arms in left field. As usual, Bobby Graff and Andy Gruner stood next to each other as they played catch with two other players. While they tossed the ball back and forth to their throwing partners, Andy asked, "Bobby?"

Bobby replied, "Yeah."

"What happened that was so bad when you were a freshman that made you quit baseball." He asked

Bobby let out a small laugh. "Well, we were playing a team called North Baltimore. We only had eight players and I was at shortstop. I had eight errors in that game. The coach could not yank me or we would have to forfeit. He kept me at shortstop to rub it in, and I guess, to teach me some sort of lesson."

Andy chuckled at Bobby's story and said, "Really?"

"Yup." He said. "And I still remember this old guy—old man Knitz—was standing at the fence and he was drinking an orange soda pop out of a paper cup. This one play, I overthrew the first baseman and the ball hit him right in the hand—and BAM! The soda went everywhere like some sort of orange explosion."

Andy stopped in mid-throw laughing too hard to continue.

"After each game," Bobby continued, "We usually had four people bag equipment. The coach made me bag it all. And I had to make three trips to get everything to the bus parked a quarter mile away."

Their laughter escalated, as to them, the story seemed much funnier than it actually was. The rest of the team looked at them, wondering what could be so funny. They both doubled over. After a minute or so, they attempted to regain their composure and started to play catch again.

As their laughter subsided, Andy told Bobby, "Sounds like it is a good thing we have you at second base! You don't have a long throw to first from there."

Bobby smiled and replied, "Funny! Very funny!"

After Gibsonburg warmed up, Coach Rase called the team over to the dugout. They sat on the bench and observed as Jackson Center went through their warm up.

Coach Rase was silent as he locked eyes with each and every member of the team. Finally, he spoke and said, "Here we go."

He looked at the team again and noticed they looked very anxious. He turned around and looked at the field for a moment, and then faced the team. "Gang, this is just another game. Just. Another. Game. Let's take it one inning at a time and see what happens. And remember, more than anything. We never give up. No matter what. Also, we believe. Believe in yourself. Believe in your teammates. It has gotten us this far, right?"

The team nodded in agreement. "Right coach."

"Now, we don't see many lefties." He continued. "Just hold up and be patient. That ole curve ball of his will come right into your wheelhouse if you just wait on it. Be patient. Okay, bring it in Gruner."

Everyone got in a tight circle around Andy Gruner in front of the dugout. He shouted. "All right. Go Bears' on three. One. Two. Three. GO BEARS!"

The players sprinted out to their positions. For some reason, they felt like they could run faster and jump higher on the Huntington Park field. It was the same feeling little kids get when they put on a new pair of sneakers.

Jimmy, the announcer who called Gibsonburg's six tournament games, would not be calling this one. Although, for his efforts, he won a $500 scholarship award specifically for the job he did calling the St. Joe game.

At Huntington Park, celebrity announcers were brought in to call the semi-final game and the championship games. The announcers for the 2005 games were Tim McMahon and Kent Mercker. McMahon was the play-by-play announcer and Mercker was the color commentator. Tim McMahon was a sportscaster for NBC. Kent Mercker was a retired Major League Baseball Player. He was the fifth draft pick out of high school in 1986 and enjoyed an 18-year career in the majors. He threw a no hitter against the San Diego Padres in 1991 and was a World Series Champion in 1995 when the Braves won it all. Mercker was from Columbus and was happy to be part of the Ohio High School Tournament.

McMahon was the first to speak. "Welcome to the Ohio High School Baseball Tournament at beautiful Huntington Park in Columbus, Ohio. I'm Tim McMahon and with me in the booth today is Kent Mercker. In today's semi-final match-up we have Gibsonburg and their 12 and 17 record playing Jackson Center with a 26 and 3 record. Gibsonburg is certainly the talk of the tournament, aren't they Kent?"

Mercker leaned into the microphone. "That's right, Tim. Cinderella story Gibsonburg, and their 12 and 17 record is the first team ever, to reach state with a losing record. They have a first year coach in Kyle Rase and during the regular season they had a record of 6 wins and 17 losses. They had a stretch where they lost 13 games in a row and where mercy ruled 7 times. And if that wasn't bad enough, they lost the last game of the season by a score of 17 to 0."

McMahon was great at playing up the game. "Wow, Kent! What are they doing here?"

Mercker chuckled. "I don't think Gibsonburg even knows how they got here. What I do know, though, is that they have figured out a way to win."

McMahon continued his banter. "The other team, Jackson Center is a legend in the state. Jackson Center's left handed pitcher, Kevin Mann, has already committed to play for Ohio State."

"He's a good player," Mercker replied. "He will be the third pitcher Gibsonburg has faced with a Division I scholarship. He has a hard fastball in the high-80s to low-90s, a great change-up, and a solid curveball."

"Can Gibsonburg pull off another victory?" McMahon asked the listeners at home. "We will soon see. Now, its time to get this game underway!"

The Gibsonburg/Jackson Center game, developed into a fast-moving pitching dual between Alex Black and left hander Kevin Mann.

McMahon looked at the field intently. "All right. Neither team has scored a run and this game is moving very fast. Both pitchers are throwing extremely well. We are in the fourth inning, two outs, the runner Nicely is on second, and Kevin Mann is up for Jackson Center. Kevin Mann can do much more than pitch, can't he Kent?"

Mercker nodded. "That's right, Tim. He's definitely a dual threat. Black better be careful because Mann has a batting average for the year of .412."

McMahon kept his eye trained on Black. "Alex Black gets his sign. He goes set. He checks the runner at second and delivers. It's a hard fastball to Kevin Mann and Mann drills the ball to the left center gap. Gibsonburg centerfielder, Wes Milleson, gets to the ball first and throws it to the cut-off man Gruner, who then brings it home but it isn't even close. Nicely scores easily."

McMahon sighed. "That was a hard hit double by Mann which makes the score Jackson Center, 1. Gibsonburg, 0."

The pace of the game quickened as Black and Mann continued to strike out the sides and get the hitters to pop up or dribble grounders for easy outs. Players for both teams were standing at the front rail of the dugouts watching the game closely.

McMahon addressed the listeners at home. "While Gibsonburg is getting ready to hit I might point out that after six and half innings, Kevin Mann has only faced 22 batters. He is really on his game today."

Mercker was quick to reply. "Kevin Mann definitely looks like a high-caliber pitcher. Alex Black on the other hand has a very unorthodox delivery. He doesn't throw very hard but does a nice job of keeping the hitters off balance. He is very different than Kevin Mann but today, he is equally effective giving up only two hits."

McMahon raised an eyebrow. "Okay. Here we are in the bottom of the seventh inning. We have an interesting situation here. Two outs, with Milleson on second and Kiser on first for Gibsonburg. Alex Black is up to bat and he has a 3-1 count. Jackson Center leads by one run. Jackson Center is one out from getting to the State Championship game."

Mercker's voice was filled with excitement. "There is not a person in their seat. Gibsonburg has not been able to hit Kevin Mann all day. With a 3-1 count on Black and two outs, I would say that Jackson Center must like their odds right now."

McMahon called the play. "Mann gets his sign. He checks the runners on first and second. It is a showdown between Alex Black at the plate and Kevin Mann on the mound."

As Mann continued to check the runners, Tyler Pinkus' mom left the tunnel on the third base side of the field, turned left, and headed to her seat in the stands. In her arms she had one tray that overflowed with hot dogs, large drinks, a large tub of popcorn, and peanuts.

Fans for both teams were on their feet. When she got to her seat, she looked at the Jackson Center fan to her left. "Gibsonburg stinks." She said, her voice filled with contempt. "They are nothing but a bunch of cheats. My nephew's team, Jackson Center, is going to the championship game for sure." She spotted her nephew on the field. "GO JACKSON CENTER!" she bellowed, then belted out her obnoxious hyena laugh.

The fan Tyler Pinkus' mom was talking to was clearly annoyed. Pinkus' mom looked at the batter. "Who's up?" Oh, never mind. It's that crappy pitcher of theirs, Black."

She shifted her attention to the field and screamed. "He can't pitch or hit his way out of a paper bag. Strike 'em out Mann, he's got no stick!"

McMahon called the at bat. "Here's the windup and the pitch. It's belt high and inside. Black connects and pulls a hard foul line drive into the left field stands."

When Alex Black connected on the foul line drive to left field, she spoke again to the fan beside her. "Mann will strike Black out for sure. I've known Alex Black since he was little and he's no good."

Right after she said the word "good," the foul line drive struck her in the top third of her head with full force and the food went flying all over like an explosion and knocked her right to the ground.

Groggy, she tried to sit up and moaned, "He did that on purpose! I'm filing a police report!"

Several people rushed in to help her, but she screamed at them. "Get away from me. I don't need any help. I've got a hard head."

Tyler Pinkus' mom sat on the ground dazed and confused with all of the food from her tray surrounding her. She snatched up a lone hot dog on the ground, without a bun. She looked at the hot dog for a second, and chomped a bite out of it like a snapping turtle. She then mumbled to herself, "I hate Gibsonburg!"

McMahon peered at the stands behind third base. "There's a lot of commotion on the third base side of field. I hope everyone is okay."

Mercker looked over as well. "Yeah I hope that hit an empty

seat. It was a hard hit foul ball."

McMahon turned his attention back to the play. "Okay, here we are. Bottom of seven, two outs, Kiser is on first and Milleson is on second with Black up to bat on a 3-2 count. The score is Jackson Center, 1. Gibsonburg, 0. What's gonna happen now, Kent?"

"With two outs and a full count, the runners will be running on the pitch! Alex Black needs to somehow, someway, get this ball in play to give his team any chance at tying the game." Mercker's excitement was contagious.

McMahon called the final play. "Mann gets his sign. He checks the runners on first and second. Here's the windup and the pitch. The runners are moving on the pitch. It's a high fastball and Black hits a mile high pop up right above his head. I don't understand what is going on here. Black throws his bat down in disgust and starts walking back to his dugout. Jackson Center looks confused. Everyone is looking at Black. The base runners are sprinting around the bases. The third baseman runs into the confusing situation and the ball drops a few inches in front of home plate and rolls toward the pitcher's mound! It's a fair ball! It's a fair ball! From a dead stop, Alex Black now takes off for first. The third baseman picks up the baseball. He looks to second, he looks to third. The third baseman has an easy out at first base. Black is running his heart out. The third baseman throws the ball to first base. Uh-oh! I don't believe it! The throw is high! The throw is high! It goes way over his head! The first baseman cannot get to it! Milleson scores. Kiser scores! This game is over! Gibsonburg wins! Gibsonburg wins! Final score. Gibsonburg, 2. Jackson Center, 1."

The Gibsonburg bench erupted in joy and rushed to home plate. Coach Rase sprinted to join the team as Jackson Center stared in disbelief. Kathy and the other fans were jumping all around. Henry shook his head and smiled happily. Jennie Gruner hugged her husband.

The giant scoreboard at Huntington Park displayed FINAL: Gibsonburg 2, Jackson Center 1.

McMahon finished off the broadcast. "There you have it! A remarkable finish! Little Gibsonburg with their regular season record of 6 and 17 takes down Jackson Center and their star pitcher, Kevin Mann. Unbelievable!"

Mercker nodded. "Gibsonburg will be playing in the State Championship tomorrow against the winner of the next semi-final game between Lancaster Fisher Catholic and Dalton Wooster."

Tyler Pinkus' mom was sitting on a curb outside of Huntington Park holding a cup of ice on her head. Her clothes were dirty, she had mustard and ketchup stains on her body, her hair looked like a rat's nest, and although she was sober, she appeared drunk and disoriented.

A person on the street walked by and looked at her with pity. They stopped and placed a coin in her cup thinking she was a homeless person. She looked at the person, looked in the cup, and began to cry. He had only given her a nickel!

The players were on the bus cheering, screaming, and hollering like never before. Coach Rase looked around and addressed the team, "Hey Gibsonburg. Anyone wanna' play in the State Championship?"

Coach Rase singled out Alex Black. "Alex Black. I don't know whether to chew you out for throwing your bat and not running or give ya a hug."

There was an uproar of laughter and the team cheered again.

Coach Rase continued. "That crazy play got us in the State Championship. Men, I am so proud of you! So proud! Let's get something to eat, get a good night's sleep, and get ready to play in the State Championship tomorrow."

Coach Jackson looked at Coach Reiter, "Hey, is this a dream or is it really happening?"

Everyone laughed again.

Coach Rase finished his speech. "Great job today everyone! Great job!"

It was pandemonium on the bus. It would be the first time Gibsonburg had ever played in the State Championship.

As Trina drove the team back to the hotel, Andy Gruner carved a seventh notch onto his wooden bat handle.

Coach Rase looked a little nervous as he stared out the window as the bus passed the office buildings in downtown Columbus en route to the hotel.

36

How Did We Get Here?
Friday Evening – June 3, 2005

Coach Rase and Coach Jackson left the hotel after having dinner with the team and doing a bed check. They walked outside and found a little pool hall around the corner from the hotel. They grabbed seats at the corner of the bar and ordered up two Mountain Dews. Coach Rase did not seem himself. He seemed nervous.

As they sat at the bar, Coach Rase stared straight ahead. He was deep in thought. He tilted his baseball cap up on his forehead, turned toward Coach Jackson and asked a rhetorical question, "Coach? What are we doing here? Really? How in the heck does a team like us, beat three Division I pitchers, and get to play in the State Championship?"

Coach Jackson smiled broadly. He could tell Coach Rase was questioning whether they really belonged in the State Championship game. He told his boss and good friend, "You know. When you think about it, some sort of crazy fluke has helped us win every game. Wyatt has never had a home run in his life, and he hits two home runs against the best pitcher in the state. C'mon!"

Coach Rase's attention heightened as he listened to Coach Jackson.

Coach Jackson continued, "Then we caught weird lucky breaks

with Van Buren and Kalida."

Coach Rase nodded.

"We just cruised by Edgerton because they used up all of their pitchers up in that 18-inning game the night before," he reminded Coach Rase.

Coach Rase's confidence was returning. "I know. I know."

Coach Jackson was amused. "And then today, there's no way we should have won. If Black wouldn't have confused everyone by throwing his bat down, that ball would have been caught for sure. I mean, Jackson Center was one easy catch away from beating us."

Coach Rase was lost in thought.

Coach Jackson nudged him. "Rase! What's up, man?"

Rase didn't look at him. "These kids just don't give up. They really believe we can do it."

Coach Rase then shifted his attention to Coach Jackson. He looked him dead in the eyes, all business. "You think we can get one more tomorrow?"

Coach Jackson laughed. "Absolutely! I mean, just look at all the first-year coaches, like you, that have won state with a 6 and 17 regular season record."

Coach Jackson slapped Coach Rase on the shoulder. Coach Jackson said, "Hey, go get some sleep. Big day tomorrow. I'm outta here."

Coach Rase nodded. "Thanks Coach. See you in the morning. I'll be along shortly."

37

A Good Nights Sleep
Friday Evening, June 3, 2005

It was a big day. Gibsonburg had knocked off Jackson Center in the State Semi-final. Earlier in the evening they learned that tomorrow they would be playing undefeated Lancaster Fisher Catholic, a team that lost in the State Championship game the prior year.

It was 1 am and Coach Rase was looking through papers at his hotel room desk. They were scouting reports on Lancaster Fisher Catholic.

Alex Black was lying in his bed. With his right hand he continually tossed a baseball toward the ceiling and softly caught it in his hand when it came back down.

Wyatt Kiser was wide awake. He lay on his side looking out his hotel window at the lights of downtown Columbus.

Wes Milleson was rocking out. With his headphones on, he enthusiastically played the air guitar while he jumped around on his bed.

Andy Gruner was awake as well. He stared at the ceiling while he cracked the knuckles in his hands. It had been a whirlwind month for Andy. With all the thoughts running through his mind it was impossible for him to get any good sleep.

Josh Sanchez. Josh Sanchez was sound asleep. He had his oversized *Shrek* doll by his side and his Bigfoot slippers on his feet. He wasn't waking up any time soon.

38

Game #8 – STATE CHAMPIONSHIP:
Gibsonburg vs. Lancaster Fisher Catholic
Saturday, June 4, 2005

The conference wall at OHSAA headquarters was barren. There were two names remaining on the wall and they were Lancaster Fisher Catholic (30-0) and Gibsonburg (13-17). They would play at 4 pm on Saturday, June 4, 2005 at Huntington Park.

The winner would be named the 2005 State Champ.

With the unlit cigar nub in his mouth and John Deere hat pushed up on his forehead, Pudge stepped back from the wall and looked at the two teams. Pudge was the tournament administrator, and that's all he did. He kept a record of the winners and the losers but had never been to a championship game. When he looked at the wall, he smiled. He then locked up and went to attend his first ever Championship Game. He wanted to see the Gibsonburg team in person. He looked at his watch and noticed the game would start in two hours.

The bus for Huntington Park left the hotel at 2 pm. Trina, with Jim behind her, traveled silently through the streets of downtown Columbus.

Without thinking, Andy Gruner started to reach into his back left pocket for the coin when he remembered that it was lost. He stopped himself, smiled and looked out the bus window at the city landscape. He would be playing in the State Championship game in two hours.

Anxiously, Coach Rase examined the program they sold at Huntington Park which featured the four teams competing for the State Championship. In the back of the program, it provided details and statistics for the past 100 years. It listed the teams that won, the final scores, and records.

Coach Rase was looking for one specific piece of information. He wanted to see, if any team in the past 100 years, was ever "mercy" ruled in the State Championship Game. Mercy ruled means they stopped the game after five innings because the team was getting beat by more than ten runs.

The bus pulled up to Huntington Park at 2:15 pm on Saturday, June 4, 2005.

As they walked onto the playing field at Huntington Park they were greeted by a sea of orange and black. The crowd was even bigger than the day before. The fans gave Gibsonburg a thundering ovation and cheered wildly.

It was a big day for everyone in and around Gibsonburg. If Gibsonburg won, they would be named the 2005 State Champion. This would be a feat so far out of reach that nobody in Gibsonburg ever came close to even considering the possibility.

Like the previous games, many students were wearing face paint and body paint. Parents, locals, friends, and relatives were there in abundance rooting for Gibsonburg. Henry Tillman sat down in his seat and anxiously waited for the game to begin.

Although Gibsonburg had many fans, Lancaster Fisher Catholic was well represented too. After all, they had been there before. Last year, in 2004, they had played in the State Championship Game and lost. They had six State Championships under their belt from the past 20 years. They considered baseball to be their main high school sport.

McMahon began his pre-game banter. "Welcome to the Ohio High School Baseball Championship Game. I'm Tim McMahon and with me in the booth is Kent Mercker. In today's championship we have Gibsonburg and their 13 and 17 record versus Lancaster Fisher Catholic with a perfect record of 30 and 0. Kent this is a real David and Goliath story isn't it?"

Mercker jumped in. "It sure is Tim. But I don't think David looked *this* small. I am amazed at the size of the Gibsonburg team. Looking at them on the field and then examining their stat sheet their players average 5 feet, 8 inches, and 140 pounds. They look like little kids warming up next to Fisher Catholic."

Half of the Gibsonburg team was taking batting practice while the other half was catching fly balls in the outfield. Coach Rase walked up to scrub, Jeff Feasel. "Hey Jeff, could you go tell Josh Sanchez to get in there and take BP?"

With enthusiasm, Feasel responded, "Sure coach!"

Feasel then ran off to give Sanchez the message while Coach Rase and Coach Jackson went over the batting order for the game.

About three minutes later, Jeff Feasel ran up to Coach Rase and out of breath he said, "Coach I talked to Sanchez."

Preoccupied, Coach Rase looked at him. "Yeah?"

Feasel hesitated. "Sanchez said that he probably wasn't going to bat. He said that he hoped he didn't even get in. He is just too nervous. Can't he just sit back and enjoy the game?"

When Coach Rase and Coach Jackson heard what Feasel had to say, they didn't get mad at all. They both were amused and chuckled as it broke a little of the pregame tension. Coach Rase smiled. "Go tell Sanchez no problem. That's fine."

McMahon continued his pre-game commentary, "Gibsonburg is the talk of the tournament. In the regular season they had a 6 and 17 record and came in last place in their division. They were mercy ruled seven times and went through a stretch where they lost 13 games in a row. They lost their last game of the regular season by a score of seventeen to zero. When you look at the stats, they only have one player batting over .300. Lancaster Fisher Catholic has six players batting over .300."

Mercker took over the commentary and said, "Here's an interesting fact. During the regular season Gibsonburg only won six games. So far, they have won seven games in a row which means they have won more games post season than they did during their 23 game regular season."

McMahon leaned in with a question. "Does Gibsonburg have a chance? It seems as though they continue to find a way to win each game. They have players hitting home runs that have never had a home run before. They have quirky plays that seem to get them runs when they need to win."

Mercker was excited. "If Gibsonburg does win today, they could make history as the only baseball team, in any state, to win a state championship with a losing record!"

McMahon finished up. "Fisher Catholic and Gibsonburg, ready to get underway."

It was very quiet in the dugout. This was foreign territory for everyone on the Gibsonburg team. Coach Rase was getting ready to speak when he noticed something. The players were watching Lancaster Fisher Catholic warm-up from their seats on the bench and were staring in awe. Fisher Catholic looked like a minor league team!

Coach Rase turned around to watch the flawless execution of the Fisher Catholic infield warm-up. Although he was in awe himself, Coach Rase ordered his team to stand. "Get off the bench! Everyone on the rail! All eyes on me!"

Coach Rase walked and stood with his back to the bench so he was looking out onto the field and the team was at the railing looking at him in the dugout. He didn't want them to see any more of Fisher Catholic's pro-style warm-up.

Coach Rase locked eyes with each team member. He didn't say anything. They looked nervous and very anxious.

He finally spoke and said, "Not much to say men."

He lowered his voice. "It is just another game."

He whispered again. "It is just another game.

Again. He whispered, "It. Is. Just. Another Game."

"We have won seven in a row. I think winning suits us and is contagious. As a team . . . as a real team we have accomplished more than anyone could have ever imagined. Let's just take it inning by inning and stick to what has gotten us this far."

Coach Rase studied his team like he was studying Advanced Calculus.

He then finished his pre-game speech, "And remember, more than anything. We never give up. No matter what! Believe! Believe in yourself. Believe in your teammates. It's been working so far so let's keep doin' it. Gibsonburg has never won a State Championship. Let's bring one home today!"

Coach Rase suddenly smiled and pointed at the field. "Let's go get these guys. Bring 'em in Gruner!"

Everyone got in a tight circle around Andy Gruner. Andy shouted. "All right. Go Bears' on three. One. Two. Three. GO BEARS!"

The Gibsonburg Golden Bears sprinted to their positions at Huntington Park and began playing in the 2005 State Championship game.

The Gibsonburg fans cheered and shouted as the team ran onto the field.

OHSAA rules gave the team with the worst record the home field advantage so they would have more of a fighting chance. Although Gibsonburg had many fans at the game and they surely wanted Gibsonburg to win, not too many people thought they had a prayer against fabled Fisher Catholic.

McMahon began his call of the game. "What a great day for baseball. Gibsonburg, and their 13 and 17 record is the first team ever, to reach the championship game with a losing record. Their opponent, Lancaster Fisher Catholic has a very storied baseball past in the state of Ohio. Lancaster's pitcher, Andy Welch, has already committed to play for Kent State. He will be the fourth pitcher Gibsonburg has faced with a Division I scholarship! Tell us a little about Welch, Kent."

Mercker followed. "He's a smart pitcher. He reminds me of a young Greg Maddux. He throws in the low 90s, but also has an excellent change-up, slider, and curve. He's methodical. He studies the hitters on the teams he will be facing and figures out what they cannot hit and builds a plan to get each hitter out. He definitely has the three C's of pitching: Command of the strike zone, control, and change of speed."

Andy Welch and Alex Black were both warming up in the bull-pen.

McMahon continued. "The question is can David beat Goliath in today's match-up? We will know in about two hours. It's time to get this game underway, Gibsonburg and Fisher Catholic."

Ron and Jennie Gruner were standing up in great anticipation. Henry intently watched the team prepare for the first pitch. Kathy stood in front of her seat, too nervous to speak with anyone around her.

McMahon continued. "We remain in the fourth inning and the score is Gibsonburg 3, Fisher Catholic 2. Gibsonburg has manufac-tured a run in each inning and Fisher Catholic scored two runs in the top of the third. We have two outs with bases loaded for Fisher Catholic. All-State pitcher Andy Welch steps up to the plate. Black seems to be struggling a bit. This is certainly not a good situation for Gibsonburg but it is a great opportunity for Fisher Catholic."

Mercker eyed Welch. "Welch is a .370 hitter and he hit a big double in his first at bat. Let's see how Black does under this kind of pressure."

McMahon leaned forward as he watched the play. "Black gets his sign. He checks the runners at first, second, and third. Black delivers and Welch hits the ball hard down the right field line. The umpire calls fair! The ball goes all the way to the corner in right field. Hetrick is having difficulty as the ball is bouncing between the corner walls. All three Fisher Catholic runners will score and Andy Welch is rounding third and sprinting for home. He is going for an inside the park home run! Brinker gets the throw from the cut-off man and they have Welch out by a mile. Welch tries to stop but falls down! He gets up and runs back to third with Brinker chasing after him! It's a pickle! Welch is caught between third and home. Brinker throws to Eddings at third base. Welch dives headfirst to third base knocking down Eddings who was in front of the bag. Did Eddings hold on? He did! Welch is out at third! Welch is out at third! That's out number three but Welch is credited with a triple anyway and gets three RBIs. The score after four and half innings is Gibsonburg, 3, Fisher Catholic, 5. What an inning!"

Mercker jumped in. "That was a terrific opposite field hit by Welch. Kent State will have a great player on their hands when he joins them next year."

Mercker chuckled and continued talking. "He might have to work on his base running a little bit, though!"

McMahon continued his call of the game, "It has been a pitching duel since the fourth inning. Nobody has threatened to score a run until now."

Mercker shook his head, amazed at their tenacity. "But this Gibsonburg team doesn't give up easily. We can see that by looking at their last seven wins."

McMahon nodded. "That's right, Kent. They are trying to

challenge Fisher Catholic right now. We are at the bottom of the seventh inning, one out, with Milleson on third and Kiser on first for Gibsonburg. We have a score of Gibsonburg, 3, Lancaster Fisher Catholic, 5. Welch is on the mound for Fisher Catholic and he has been throwing extremely well."

Mercker picked up the banter. "Gibsonburg has the tying run at first base with one out. If they can find a way to get the man on first to score we will have a tie ball game."

McMahon called the at bat. "Gruner steps up to the plate for Gibsonburg. Welch gets his sign. He checks the runners on first and third. He brings it home on a 2-2 count. The runner at third is going. Gruner brings his bat down to bunt on a 2 and 2 count! Holy Cow, it's a suicide squeeze! Gruner bunts it perfectly down the third base line. The third baseman charges the ball and has no play at home with the speedy Milleson. He throws to get Gruner at first base. It's his only play! This is gonna be close. The umpire calls SAFE! Milleson scored, Gruner is safe at first and Kiser advanced all the way to third base. That was a gutsy call by the coach. What a gutsy call!"

Mercker's eyes widened. "You bet it was. You never want to call a bunt with two strikes because if the batter misses, he is out! It surprised me and everyone else here. That suicide squeeze was executed perfectly and Gibsonburg totally caught Fisher Catholic off guard. The tying run is now on third with the winning run on first base."

McMahon looked at his partner. "Kent, what is Gibsonburg thinking right now?"

Mercker was on the edge of his seat. "If I'm Gibsonburg, I'm thinking of one thing and one thing only. I want to tie the game by somehow getting my runner on third base home."

McMahon called the next at bat. "Our score is Gibsonburg 4, Fisher Catholic 5. The tying run, Kiser, is on third and the winning run, Gruner, is on first. Derek Hetrick is at the plate. The infield is playing in to get the ball home in case of a bunt. Welch checks the runners, delivers, and Hetrick hits a deep fly ball to the left center wall. Kiser scores easily from third while the Fisher Catholic centerfielder grabs the ball after it bounces off of the fence and throws to the cut-off man. The coach will most likely hold Gruner at third, but NO! Gruner doesn't even slow down and is trying to score. The catcher is waiting on the ball in front of home plate. The cut-off man brings the ball home. The throw is perfect and Gruner will be out by four steps. The catcher catches the ball and braces for a collision."

Everyone stood. Both benches were on the rail. Coach Rase held his breath.

Mercker threw in, "This is gonna be ugly!"

McMahon called the play at the plate. "Here comes Gruner. They are going to collide. But what's this? Unbelievable! Incredible! Gruner leaps over the catcher and puts his hand on home plate untouched by the catcher. What incredible athleticism by Gruner! Gibsonburg wins the State Championship! Gibsonburg wins the State Championship!"

Mercker shook his head. "I thought I have seen everything!" He said, incredulously.

McMahon was stunned but somehow managed to finish calling the game. "In a remarkable finish, Gibsonburg knocks of their eighth win a row to become the 2005 State Champ! What an amazing game!"

Andy Gruner took off his helmet and threw it into the stands. "We did it!" He screamed.

Everyone on the Gibsonburg bench charged home plate. They surrounded Andy Gruner and jumped up and down jubilantly, like one giant and happy boisterous clump. Coach Rase quickly joined the mob and the other coaches were right behind him. The Fisher

Catholic players and fans watched the celebration in a state of disbelief.

Henry Tillman stood up, took a deep breath, and with great emotion pumped his arm in the air and screamed, "YES!" Ron and Jennie Gruner stood with their arms around each other and proudly watched the celebration on the field.

Kathy smiled as she watched the team mob Andy at home plate. As the group started to move to the dugout, Andy Gruner walked to the backstop and he looked up to find Kathy. When they made eye contact, he found her beaming with pride and flashing a big smile. Andy pointed at her, smiled, pumped his fist, and ran off to join the rest of the team.

Andy stopped to look at the giant scoreboard at Huntington Park. It displayed: FINAL: Fisher Catholic 5. Gibsonburg 6.

Back at the Ideal Bakery in Gibsonburg Tim and Gary were listening to the entre game on the radio with a crowd of other locals that for some reason or another couldn't make it to the game. When Gibsonburg scored the final run, everyone started cheering and if you drove by on Route 600 and looked through the big plate glass window, you would have thought that somebody had won the lottery and they were having a celebration party inside.

Tim and Gary listened to the game while they sat at their usual table. Tim was smiling and laughing when he said to a somewhat stoic Gary who was reading the Saturday paper, "Can you believe it? We won the State Championship! With a regular season record of 6-17 we won the State Championship! This is the biggest thing to happen in Gibsonburg! Ever!"

Gary dropped the paper down below his face and very matter of factly said, "I called it way back in the spring."

Tim smirked as to say, "Yeah, right."

Tim Mallett got up out of his chair and picked up the one-pint cylinder sugar dispenser with the hole on the top that sat on their table. He walked up behind him and proceeded to take Gary's hat off. He held the cylinder two feet above his head, and dumped the entire contents on top of Gary's head while Gary looked straight ahead.

McMahon gave his final announcement to the listeners at home. "An incredible finish by Gibsonburg! Unbelievable! They beat Lancaster Fisher Catholic 6 to 5 to win the Ohio State High School Boys Baseball Championship."

Mercker completed the call of the State Championship game. "It is now official. Gibsonburg becomes the only team, in any state, not just Ohio, to win a State Championship with a losing record. Their final record for the 2005 season. 14 and 17!"

The boosters had put together a tailgate in the parking lot where fans, friends, relatives and players all met and retold the highlights of the eight game winning streak. The players hugged their parents and you couldn't find a person without a smile or without an outfit of orange and black. After much celebration and laughter, the party started to slow down. It was 8 pm and was starting to get dark so the team finally loaded onto the bus for the two-hour ride back to Gibsonburg.

On the bus, the players were still in celebration mode. They were laughing, jumping on top of one another, and on top of the world.

Coach Rase got on and looked at his Gibsonburg Golden Bears with a sense of pride that could never be rivaled. He let the team have another celebratory moment and when they started to quiet down on their own, he spoke and said, "I am so proud of everyone on this team."

He stood quietly and slowly made eye contact with each player. "We did not just win State. We won State with a regular season record of 6 and 17."

The team started shouting, cheering and high fiving each other.

Coach Rase did not rush them to quiet down. He just smiled broadly at them. When it quieted down a bit, he continued. "From what the stats people from OHSAA tell me, no team in the history of high school baseball has ever won the State Title with a losing record, let alone a record like ours.

It was sheer pandemonium on the bus, but he kept going. Coach Rase got more of a serious look on his face and told the team, "You did something today that, in my opinion, no high school team will ever do again. Many years from now, the significance of what you did on June 4, 2005, will ring as loudly as it does today. Congratulations men!"

The team started to cheer some more and got crazy. They were the 2005 State Champions.

As Trina started to drive the team back to Gibsonburg, Andy Gruner looked out the bus window at the setting sun and smiled. He took out his wooden bat and ceremoniously carved an eighth and final notch onto the bat handle. When he was finished he examined the eight notches and slowly rubbed them with his fingers almost to verify that the State Championship was real and not some sort of dream.

39

The Ride Home
Early Saturday Evening
June 4, 2005

When you go to the State Tournament in Columbus you arrive late Thursday evening. Everyone is excited so nobody gets much sleep on Thursday night. On Friday morning, after breakfast, you typically go to a neutral field and practice hitting and fielding for two hours. You then go to Huntington Park, go through a limited warm-up and play the game.

If you win, you will play in the State Championship the following day so adrenaline hits the bodies of each player hard. After talking with the newspapers and radio stations, you attend a team meal, then travel back to the hotel. Since you will be playing in the State Championship the next day, if you get one hour of good sleep you are lucky.

You get up Saturday morning, eat breakfast, and then go to the neutral field to practice for two hours. After practice, you go to Huntington Park, go through another limited warm-up and play the game.

If you win, you celebrate like nobody has celebrated before. The newspapers and television stations talk to you and everyone wants to hear your story. The fans from your hometown put on a tailgate in the parking lot where you eat, talk, laugh and savor the moment.

Finally, when it gets close to dark, it is time for the long bus ride home. When everything is said and done, you basically get no sleep for 48 hours, your body is exhausted from the ups and downs of the games, and usually on that long ride home, your body crashes and you go into a deep sleep. It is not your standard type of sleep. It is a different realm altogether. One that not many people ever experience.

Coach Rase was happy, proud, and tired. On the ride home, he started to get sleepy himself and before he closed his eyes, he turned around for one last look at his team.

Alex Black was laying on a seat by himself on his side using his glove as a pillow.

Wes Milleson and Wyatt Kiser were in the same seat. Wes had his head on the window and Wyatt's head was tilted to the side. Both of them were sound asleep.

Andy Gruner. Andy was cradling his notched bat like a child cradles his security blanket and his body was against the side of the bus. He slept soundly with a hint of a smile on his face.

As Coach Rase looked around, he noticed that just about everyone on the team was completely zonked out.

But then, Coach Rase got a puzzled look on his face that transformed into a grin from ear to ear. Sitting five rows back, in a seat all by himself, while the rest of the team slept, was Josh Sanchez. He was wide awake and not sleepy at all. There on his lap was the State Championship trophy, which was three feet tall. Sanchez did not play one inning all year. Josh Sanchez smiled broadly as he stared at the player on the top of the trophy like he won it all by himself.

40

The Day After The State Championship
Sunday Mid-Morning, June 5, 2005

It was Sunday morning and Kathy and Andy were in front of the Ideal Bakery. They were reminiscing about the game that took place the day before and Andy still could not believe they were State Champs.

Kathy looked at Andy. "What a crazy end to our senior year."

Andy smiled. "Really."

"What the team did for our whole town was incredible. You should be very proud," she said.

Andy thought for a moment. "This is probably the happiest I have ever been."

Kathy smiled back at him. "Me too."

As they were talking, Alex, Wyatt, and Wes walked toward them on the sidewalk. They were laughing and joking around as was everyone else in Gibsonburg. The entire town was in a good mood!

Kathy nodded her head to the approaching boys, smiled, and said, "Looks like trouble."

"Wassup!" Wes said.

"Not much," Andy replied. "Just getting ready for work. I'm just happy our family still has a bakery I can still work at!"

Alex nodded. "Yeah, I heard the good news about the bakery.

That's awesome, man."

While the kids were talking, they heard the throaty, steady roar of a car engine. Henry Tillman, the town mechanic, pulled up in front of them with a dark green 1968 Pontiac Firebird in mint condition. Henry stepped out of the car, looked at the group, nodded, and said, "Andy. Kathy. Fellas."

"Hey, Henry," said Andy.

Henry looked at Andy. "You know. What you did for this town was really special. You proved to everyone that good things can really happen, if you believe. Andy, as the captain of the team, I have something special for you. I want to thank you for everything you and the rest of the boys did."

Henry flipped the keys to Andy and started to walk away.

Andy was shocked. "No way Henry, I can't accept this."

Henry looked back. "You don't have a choice. Don't worry though, my family is loaded, they own the limestone plant. I just work on cars as a hobby. Be careful, it'll go up to 140 so you need to take it easy. And watch the brakes. On these old cars they can get a little spongy."

Henry then flashed a smile and walked off. He knew how important the red Chevelle was to the Gruner family and he thought they would be excited to get the Firebird.

Andy looked at the keys, then the car. The others in the group looked at the Firebird in awe.

Wes was staring at the car and said, "Shit!"

They were all smiles.

Andy blinked. "Shall we take it for a spin? I have 30 minutes before I start work."

The three other boys started cheering and all raced to get inside the car. Andy looked at Kathy and said, "Kathy, you comin'?"

"No, you guys go ahead." She smiled.

The boys all rushed into the car, fired it up and took off.

The '68 forest green Pontiac Firebird screamed down the country road as the throaty engine begged for more in the cool morning air.

Andy Gruner glanced at the speedometer as it approached 50 miles per hour and then turned his attention back to the road. Beside him, Alex Black sat in the passenger seat, hitting the dashboard with both fists as he hollered with excitement. In the back seat, Wes Milleson hit Andy on the shoulder and pleaded for more speed while Wyatt Kiser, the quiet one in the group, sat with both hands gripping the passenger seat, his eyes focused intently on the road ahead.

Andy smiled at Wes before turning his eyes back on the road. The Firebird approached a baseball field that blended into the country landscape perfectly with its vibrant green grass and contrasting cookie dough colored infield. Acres of lush green open viewing area surrounded the field, nestling it perfectly within the beautiful Ohio farm fields. Their crops, planted only a few weeks ago, had begun peeking out of the soil.

As the Firebird barreled down the country road past the baseball field the boys were oblivious to the old man walking in the outfield, between left field and the shortstop position. He was carrying a two-gallon jug of grass-friendly, but weed-deadly spray. The old man carefully examined the left field grass and, with great precision, applied the poison on the few remaining weeds. This was the masterpiece that he had meticulously cared for all spring.

As the old man examined the grass for weeds, he spotted something hidden deep in the grass but was not sure what it was. He bent down and picked it up. He examined the item. It was an old looking coin. It wasn't an ordinary looking coin either. It was, different. It was about the size of a quarter, bronze colored and although it looked very old, it was in excellent shape.

As the old man examined the coin, the silence of the morning air was pierced by the thunder of the Firebird screaming down the country road that ran parallel to the third baseline of the baseball field. The noise approached quickly and grabbed the groundskeeper's attention. With his back to the passing Firebird, he slowly turned his head to his left to see the Firebird come into, and out of sight, in a matter of seconds. As the sound of the engine faded away, he casually turned his attention back to the unique coin he discovered.

As the Firebird continued to rumble down the road, Wes leaned over the driver's seat from his back seat position, pointed right at Andy and excitedly yelled "Come on Andy, let's see what she'll do."

Alex, beating the dashboard screamed out. "Henry says she'll do 140, let's blow some carbon out and get 'er up to at least 120."

Andy stepped on the gas, and the car began to accelerate. The speedometer steadily climbed to 70, then 80, then 90 miles per hour.

"Come on man. Keep goin!" Shouted Wes.

Andy looked at Wyatt and Wes through the rear view mirror, then shot Alex a look as the speedometer needle slowly climbed from 90 to 110. His palms were beginning to sweat.

As the needle hit 110 miles per hour, Andy's ears rung when Wes let loose a piercing "Yeeeeeehaw!" while his body sweat saturated the back of his shirt between his shoulder blades. Another quick glance in the mirror and he suddenly saw Wyatt's taut jawline. One mistake and they'd all be killed.

Wyatt's voice was terse, emphatic, and suddenly louder—far louder than the screaming engine. "Maybe take it a little easy there, Hos. This rattly old car may fall apart if you push 'er over the limit."

"You got it man, get 'er up to 120!" Wes screamed.

"Oh shit." Alex pointed straight ahead to confirm what Andy

already saw in his focused view of the road, "You got a stop sign up ahead."

The Firebird was now traveling at 175 feet per second and was 1,750 feet from the stop sign. The Firebird would be at the stop sign in 10 seconds. As the adrenaline rushed through the boy's bodies, they didn't realize that there was not a stop sign on the perpendicular road they were approaching. An old farmhouse obstructed their view to the right and nobody in the Firebird could see that two vehicles were quickly approaching the intersection from the right. The two vehicles, a red Pontiac Grand Am, followed 45 feet behind by a beige GMC Yukon, were on pace to hit the intersection in 10 seconds as well.

Andy swallowed hard. The Firebird was only ten seconds away from the stop sign.

Wyatt switched to parent mode. "Better slow this thing down buddy."

Oblivious, Wes sat back and said, "What a rush, though, Andy-man."

As Andy pushed down on the brake, the pedal easily went all the way to the floor without slowing the car down at all.

"No brakes!" Andy screamed.

Wes's eyes widened. "What?"

"Oh fuck!" Alex yelled, bracing himself.

In a haze, Andy saw Wyatt in the rear view mirror staring straight ahead at the intersection and gripping the seat in front of him tighter, and bracing for impact. Andy quickly glanced down at the speedometer to see the needle at 100 miles per hour. Four seconds until they crossed the intersection. He frantically pumped the brake pedal, as he looked straight ahead and tightened his grip on the steering wheel. "Hang on, boys!"

The seconds felt like hours and Andy wondered if this was what free falling felt like . . .

As the Firebird passed the farmhouse to the right, only 20 feet from the intersection, Andy saw a glimpse of the approaching vehicles. Where did they come from? The horrifying intake of breath, gasping lungs, and the sound of whimpering around him told him in a split second that everyone else in the Firebird could see the other vehicles barreling towards them too.

Andy watched as the red Grand Am hit the intersection first. The front left bumper of the Firebird shot past the back left bumper of the red Grand Am, missing it by inches.

At that exact time, Andy jerked his head to the right and was horrified to find the GMC Yukon upon him and about to crash into the side of the Firebird.

There was no escape.

Andy fixated on the fast approaching GMC logo on the Yukon's grill. Suddenly, everything slowed down. For what seemed like an eternity, his life flashed before his eyes. A soothing calm surprisingly took over his body. The visions seemed to last forever, and were filled with a warm glow. There was no sound. Just a peaceful quiet, as the past 18 years of his life played out in slow motion. Time stood still as the fear fell away and left him with a sense that he was safe, secure, and free.

Andy came out of his hypnotic state to hear the other boys screaming and the Yukon just a few feet from slamming into the right side of the Firebird. They all braced for impact when the Yukon swept by the rear bumper of the Firebird by mere inches. The Firebird went through the two vehicles like a football flies through a goalpost.

Still traveling at 90 miles per hour, but slowing down rapidly, the Firebird continued to roll down the country road.

Wes shouted, "HOLY SHIT!"

"JESUS CHRIST!" Yelled Wyatt.

With both of his hands on the dashboard, Alex Black put his

head down into his arms in relief.

Cradling the steering wheel, Andy just put his head down. His back was soaked with sweat.

Wes and Wyatt looked at each other. Alex and Andy finally pulled their heads up and exchanged expressions of relief.

The Firebird finally rolled to a stop a half a mile down the road. All was quiet, except the sound of the engine rumbling.

Andy, Alex, Wes, and Wyatt didn't say a word. They were speechless and they still looked very rattled and scared. Andy's hands were shaking as he removed them from the steering wheel.

Alex finally broke the silence. "Man Andy, we sure seem to get the lucky breaks don't we?"

After recognizing what Alex said, Andy looked at Alex. After looking at Alex, he glanced in the rear view mirror at Wes, then Wyatt. Wyatt and Wes looked back at Andy.

Then Alex's comment hit all of them. The past two months were nothing but a series of lucky breaks! Andy missed getting killed by the train. Andy found the coin. Andy got into a relationship with Kathy. Andy's car just missed getting hit by Bo's foul ball. And, in a crazy fashion, their 6 and 17 team won the State Championship not because of talent. They won eight games in a row because they got the most unimaginable lucky breaks in each and every game.

Andy started laughing, and then they all start laughing. They then took the laughing into high gear and couldn't stop.

After several minutes the laughing died down and while Wes chuckled, he said, "I can't believe we just about got killed."

Andy sighed. "Hey, I have to be at work in 10 minutes."

Alex informed Andy. "If you pump the brakes on this beast, they will probably come back."

Andy started to pump the brakes with his foot and sure enough it built up pressure and they came back. Andy told his friends, "I think that worked. You guys ready to roll."

Alex nodded. "Yeah. Just take it slow. That was enough excitement for one day."

As they started out, they went ten feet and Andy checked the brakes. They went 20 feet and checked the brakes. Andy did this three or four more times and the other boys started to yell at him to get going as it was clear the brakes were now working properly.

The Firebird never reached a top speed that exceeded 20 miles per hour on the drive back to the bakery.

41

The Final Chapter
Late Sunday Morning, June 5, 2005

The display sign in the window of the Ideal Bakery read "Special. Cup of Coffee and Donut - 25 cents."

The old man that found the coin while he was tending to the baseball field walked up to the Ideal Bakery. He examined the sign, shook his head in approval, and entered.

As the old man walked in Andy was finishing up with another customer. The old man approached Andy at the register and smiled. "I'll take the special, son."

Andy recognized the man, but did not know his name or where he was from. The old man knew Andy though, as news of the baseball team had been on television and in the papers.

Andy looked at him. "That'll be 25 cents, please."

While the old man was digging in his jeans pocket for a quarter, Andy retrieved a cup of coffee and a donut.

As he placed the order on the counter, the old man pulled out a handful of coins. "Nice job on the championship game there, fella."

Just then, Kathy entered the bakery, walked up and stood at the display counter about 12 feet from Andy and the old man. She was conscious of not wanting to interrupt a business transaction and said with a smile, "Hey shortstop!"

Kathy's words drew the old man's attention. While he glanced at Kathy and smiled he blindly grabbed a coin out of the collection of coins in his right hand that he thought was a quarter. Inadvertently, he selected the 1913 Liberty Head Nickel, which was about the same size as a quarter.

Andy directed his attention back at the old man and said, "Thank you, sir. We don't know how we did it, but it was a fun ride."

Gesturing toward Kathy's direction, the old man said, "Hey, that little filly is pretty cute."

He continued with, "Can I give you some advice, son?"

The old man leaned toward Andy a little. They were both looking directly at each other. As he placed the 1913 coin in Andy's palm, he softly said, "*I'd hang on to that one if I were you.*"

Andy smiled proudly as the old man was talking about Kathy, and then glanced in Kathy's direction.

Andy didn't look down or pay any attention to what he thought was an ordinary quarter going into his palm. Andy put the coin into the open cash drawer and closed it without looking down.

After he closed the cash drawer, Andy suddenly got a shocked look on his face. The old man said, "*I'd hang on to that one if I were you.*"

Those were the same words Samuel Brown used when he gave the 1913 Liberty Head Nickel to Andy's great-grandfather and his three brothers in 1933.

Thank You

There are many people that I must thank for their assistance in turning this book into reality.

I must thank Coach Kyle Rase and every other member of the 2005 Gibsonburg Boys Baseball Team: Assistant Coach Mark Reiter, Assistant Coach Brian Jackson, Assistant Coach Tom Lawrence, Alex Black, Thom Brinker, Cody Fisher, Andy Gruner, Derek Eddings, Derek Hetrick, Wes Milleson, Wyatt Kiser, Josh Sanchez, Yale Linhoff, Steve Smith, Robby Vela and Scott Stevenson.

Amjed Qamar, Aaron Huffman, and Emily Zapp for assisting me in the consultation, editing, and proofing of the book. They helped me eliminate all the instances of "I ain't got no!"

Brian McManamon for taking this book and going above and beyond the call of duty to get the electronic versions of the book ready as well as handling all the artwork for the book covers.

I would also like to especially thank Todd Balduf for his assistance as a baseball consultant on the book.

Writing a book and producing a movie in the span of twelve months takes some time. My family stood by me the entire time and without their encouragement and support it never would have happened. Thanks to my wonderful wife, Amy, and my three children, Craig, Mark and Kara Jo.

There were countless others that were so beneficial in helping me turn a dream into a reality. I sure hope I don't miss anyone but here it goes: Kyle Price, Ryan Keller, Elliott Stanek, Dom Rossi, Kelly Murphy, Lauren Worthington, Jessica Robison, Kyle Flatter, Emily

Kisela, Chloe Kisela, Liz Williams, Jen Williams, Louis Bonfante, Lili Reinhart, Jonnie Wagner, Kyle Jackson, Ryan Kunk, Greg Murray, Chris Myers, Jim Snyder, Brad Wagner, Diesel Shidaker, Nick Schneider, Michael Maloof, Big Mike Maloof, Troy Balduf, Cameron Kirby, Rob Stock, Alex Hunnell, Ben Graff, Kyle Augsburger, Kyle Madsen, Hunter Mahaffey, Tom Balduf, Sharon Balduf, Nicole Sprouse, Glen Noggle, Ardelle Noggle, Julie Mercker, Mike Lockwood, Joey Parizek, Jillian Graff, Kathy Graff, Freddy Graff, Austin Barnard, Michael Adolph, Addison Stern, Jonathan Kimble, Casey Smith, Tom Sanders, Brian Recker, Amber Dupree, Eryn Montgomery, Becca Amato, Jim Renard, Ryan Dunn, Elise Mahaffey, Keith Garrard, Cassie Jones, Ginger Kathrens, Jessica Browne, Amy Reinhart, Tess Reinhart, Austyn Vovos, Betsy, Weber, Emily Mach, Baylee White, Andrew Boone, Cody Price, Lindsey Triplett, Alyssa Rossi, Dave Keller, Steve Black, Dave Bakalik, Kelly Bryarly, Jay Robison, Kent Mercker, Tim McMahon, Craig Kyles, Doug Myer, Scott Moore, Lauren Mayfield, Liz Szymanski, Kenzie Burness, Jeff Stewart, Sandy Stewart, Steven Stewart, Kendra Stewart, Kent Drake, Cory King, Brian King, Karen Mahaffey, Larry Lentz, Justin Edgell, Chad Russell, Kevin Cunningham, Dallas Hannigan, JJ Koterba, Tim Lockwood, Dave Bowen, Dave Springer, Karen Hough, Bryce Ungerott, Brian Hogue, Marcia Hogue, Denny Smith, Bonnie Kathrens, Gary Kathrens, and last but not least Chris Cochrane.

We must also offer a special thanks to: The awesome Ideal Bakery, The town of Gibsonburg, Gibsonburg High School, The town of Plain City, The City of Dublin, Jeff and Sandy Stewart, Jon and Jan Ketchum, Jerry Rausch and his family, Kyle Widder Photography, the employees of Xcelerate Media, Dave Miller, Mil-Max Farms, Big Mike's Catering, North Union High School, Teays Valley High School, Dublin Jerome High School, Red Oak Advertising, Roush Sporting Goods, Bishop Watterson High School, Crestview Athletic Boosters, the Reynolds Family, and Grover Rutter Mergers and Acquisitions.

CPSIA information can be obtained at www.ICGtesting.com
Printed in the USA
LVOW040829140812

294163LV00001B/7/P